GET IN, GET OUT

Published by Mitanni Publishing LLC
PO Box 13099, Harrisburg, PA 17110, U.S.A.

ISBN 978-0-9846301-4-1

Cover design by Saleem Little

REVIEWS

Praise for Get In, Get Out

"Get In, Get Out is a riveting, action-filled, reflective voyage into manhood not seen since the release of Claude Brown's Manchild In The Promiseland. Salim invites you deep into the conscience of his characters as they contemplate every decision in a cold and unforgiving world."

-Ice Cold Drinks
The True Ingredients in Chocolate

"A Classic...Get In, Get Out sets a standard in street fiction and solidifies its author as a staple in urban literature for years to come. Salim's astute characterization and gripping narration of not only the inner-city struggle but human plight in general lifts he and his gem of a book into echelons of literature not seen in this genre since Sista Souljah's The Coldest Winter Ever."

-Akode Pheonix
Satisfying Nostalgia

"The title says it all......only some weren't quick enough. This was by far one of the best books I've read this year, and the first by Saleem Little. Waiting on the second book. This author is on fire with words."

-Ms. Mikki

"The story was well thought out and engaging... Definitely a good read and comes highly

recommended... Kudos to Saleem Little for a job well done..."

-Anjie

"Embracing. Speaks to those who understand the streets and intrigues those who know of it through music and hearsay. Great read! Keep grinding Mr. Little!"

-Mr. Debonair

"An excellent read, very touching story. I recommend this book to everyone, it is excellent. Story of family having a hard life but always trying to do better."

-Pierre Bondin

"Very good!!! Couldn't put it down. Intense, surprising, engaging. Hope there is a follow up in the works because I would definitely buy it. Great read. Thank you."

-G.D.T.

"Remarkable! I really enjoyed reading this book could not put it down. I felt like I was right there with the characters. Remarkably read... Will be getting part two. I hope they make these into a movie, definitely movie material."

-Regina V Stancell

FOREWARD

Rough, raw, and riveting, Saleem Little's first novel is a gritty portrayal of survival in an urban setting, where working the *game* (or dealing drugs) becomes the only way to escape stifling, racist-driven poverty. To most Americans, the game exists in a fantasy world, a violent world either glamorized by hip hop music or demonized by data and government statistics. Saleem Little illuminates it as a realm inhabited by real families and real children, a world where harsh choices determine outcomes for life or death.

Marquise Jackson inherits the responsibility of caring for his mother and brother when his father is killed in a hail of bullets. As Mar navigates the world of drug dealers, street sharks, and other players in the game, he discovers that his intelligence and caution make him an excellent competitor. He is so successful that he lifts his mother, his brother, and his beautiful fiancé, Lexi, out of street-level poverty into a world of success that results in education, charity, and social responsibility.

Although the rewards are great, this tournament of wits is a dangerous sport, and the stakes are high. Saleem Little creates a surprise ending that twists and turns as Marquise and Lexi discover the fatal price for playing the game. Get

In, Get Out is a high-speed train that carries the reader on a non-stop journey filled with sex, drugs, and violence. In that sense, it is dynamic and action-packed. The story, however, becomes more compelling when the reader discovers Marquise Jackson's deep desire to live a *normal* life: a life where his children can grow up safely, where his little brother can go to college, where his mother can open her own shop and earn a living, where his family can gather for a Thanksgiving dinner like any other family in America.

Saleem Little creates a world where the language of the street reveals an undeniable aspect of American culture, a reality that many Americans try to ignore. The irrefutable fact that a tremendous proportion of young African American men are incarcerated proves Little's point that playing the *GAME* is sometimes the only option to escape street-level poverty.

-Suza Lambert 2011
(Suza Lambert Bowser Productions, LLC)

DEDICATION

In memory of Kareem Williams
(11/24/1980-5/15/2005)

"Therefore, to cope with the purging of morals from his system, James created a motto that helped him deal with the loss of certain morals… 'Ain't no wrong in tryna do right for mine."

-James

1

James Jackson's introduction to crime was pure fortuity. His father, Arthur G. Jackson was a hard-working construction worker and devout black activist. Arthur had no idea he was leading his son directly into the life he had tried so diligently to steer him away from when he sent James out to find work that chilly winter afternoon.

Arthur was a tall man with an almond complexion and a strong build owed to many years of strenuous manual labor from all the construction jobs he had worked in his lifetime. Not only was his body old and weary, but his ideas were as well. Arthur, being the grandson of two Mississippi sharecroppers, believed a strong work ethic had to be instilled in children at a young age or they would grow up to be spoiled and worthless.

The infectious spirit of the Second Great Migration had inspired James' family. It was a migration that had begun in 1940 and seen nearly two million African Americans relocate from their southern towns to northern cities or

California where a new range of defense industry jobs were popping up. Following the flock, James's family had made their way from their hometown of Harrisburg to the industrialized metropolis of New York City in 1953. James' father knew that if they didn't move from the city of Harrisburg, they would never have a chance of escaping the grinding poverty they were experiencing there.

Though Harrisburg was the capital of Pennsylvania, opportunities and resources were as scarce as they were in the rest of America's rudimentary cities at the time. There just weren't enough jobs for an industrious man like Arthur. So, Arthur, along with the cotton that was headed for Harlem and thousands of other ambitious indigents, packed up his family and they made their trip to the Big City of Dreams with stars in their eyes and the same ardor and anticipation as a group of Muslims making their hajj to Mecca.

Stuffed in tight constraints with other black families from the Carolinas, Georgia, and many other southern cities and states - next to Irish, Italian, and Asian immigrants - Arthur had a hard time finding good jobs. Then, on the rare occasions when he did find good work, he had an even harder time keeping it. He and his wife quickly realized New York City was no Promised Land, and that where there were more jobs, there was more competition. Arthur felt he had no choice but to send James out in search of work no matter how young he was.

When James was twelve, he meandered off into a local pool hall in the Crown Heights section of Brooklyn, New York. He was hoping to find the after-school job his father had sent him out in search of. More than a job and the cool of that frigid afternoon in 1956 led James into the warm Gentlemen's club however.

The two-story pool hall, which also served as a storefront, was right down the street from where James lived with his parents. He always knew there was more to that pool hall than met the eye. There were always luxurious cars parked out front. The vehicles lining the sidewalk in front of the pool hall ranged from Cadillacs and Lincolns to Maserati Zagato coupes. The visitor's - mainly pimps, prostitutes, gamblers, hustlers and crooked police officers - were always dressed to kill. James knew this was his opportunity to get down with the in crowd.

James' eyes - fascinated with the finer things being donned by the pool halls' patrons - squinted regularly at the bright extravagance of all the tailored clothing and glittering flawless jewelry. He gawked at the sparkling diamond rings, thick gold bracelets, yellow and white gold bangles, diamond and pearl earring and necklace sets, and wafer-thin platinum watches. With eyes full of wonder and amazement, James studied the charismatic characters that flaunted these affluent amenities. The debonair women who moved as graceful as animated poetry were all Billy Holidays, Lena Hornes', and Dorothy Dandridges' minus the stardom. Most impressive to James were the suave gangsters draped in suits so sharp they had to be worn carefully to prevent being cut. Occasionally the glint of bright cuff links being prepped caught his impressionable eyes. Of course, they were purposely prepped every so often so that the array of colors they reflected could be seen. Fine gator, croc, ostrich, and snakeskin shoes added to the list of opulent luxuries that fascinated James' young, venal mind. This attraction to the pool hall began the day he and his family moved from Harrisburg to Crown Heights three years ago.

When James first started working for the owner of the pool hall - a very large and intimidating man who stood 6 foot 3, weighed close to 350 pounds, and was fittingly referred to as "Biggs" - Arthur and Cecilia were both delighted. James seemed to be happy to be working and making his own money and they could not help but to join in on his happiness. It was, after all, what Arthur had wanted for his son. He had wanted James to gain some early work experience and realize early on that nothing in life came free.

James was willingly giving his father half of every dollar he made to help with the groceries and rent. Everything appeared to be going just fine until Arthur and Cecilia discovered exactly what type of activities went on in that pool hall. Everyone in the neighborhood knew who Biggs was - James' parents included - but Arthur and Cecilia had always figured the pool hall was an honest law-abiding establishment. They had always been the type to mind their own business so they never really looked into what went into Biggs' billiard room. However, once they realized that the place was infested with drugs, prostitution and gambling they made a concerted effort to pull James away from Biggs. They ordered him to quit his job but by then it was too late. James had already seen and experienced too much; he had tasted the fruits of the life. There was no way he would give that job up.

James had been exposed to just how easy it was to make some quick cash by cutting a few corners and rubbing elbows with the right people - connected people. He didn't want to struggle his entire life, barely getting by like his father had done, and he damn sure wasn't about to sit around praying to God to give him what he could get or take himself like his mother. Beatings and punishments were a small price to pay. James told himself it was no different than Biggs paying off dirty cops.

Biggs was a notorious policy king in his blighted Brooklyn neighborhood. His wealth, power, and lure were slowly beginning to demand the same level of reverence as Madam St. Claire, Bumpy Johnson, and the 40 Thieves in Harlem. To the impoverished and hopeless souls that crowded the Crown Heights section of Brooklyn, numbers were their last hope of being rich. Biggs knew the people's plight and he capitalized on their last-ditch efforts to escape hopelessness. He was a prominent figure in New York's underworld and his ruthlessness and wealth had gained him the respect of not only his people, but also the Italian and Irish mobsters that crossed his path. As a gambling-house proprietor, he made his fortune controlling the city's policy racket and numerous other gambling enterprises.

Biggs had very little formal education, though his street IQ was unmatched, and he learned gambling and the numbers racket after taking a job as a porter in a gambling house in Harlem when he was young. Biggs hated to gamble, he hated to lose. However, he paid close attention to the logistics of setting up a gambling house and soon started his own in Harlem before selling that establishment and moving to Brooklyn. Biggs paid off cops, made contributions to political campaigns and if need be, murdered to make sure his criminal enterprise stayed afloat.

His favorite establishment was the pool hall where James worked but his cash cow was the "Prestige Gentlemen's Club", a club that catered strictly to wealthy white men. He referred to his patrons as American Royalty and catered to all their expensive tastes and desires. The people loved and supported Biggs because he did donate benevolently to race advancement causes in the black community. He sat in on neighborhood meetings, and was never known to turn away a person in need. Biggs was like a king in his neighborhood and now to James' greatest delight he was Biggs' runner.

James also did other odd end jobs and errands around the pool hall. He stacked the shelves in the store with groceries, he played lookout when the fences came through to buy swag or sell their own stolen merchandise. James would pour drinks for the gamblers who got together in the renovated basement to shoot craps, play poker, or shoot pool. Whatever Biggs needed James to do he did it. Moreover, he did every job with speed and precision, knowing that his hard work would impress Biggs and he would be rewarded graciously for it.

Soon the pool hall became a fixation for James. It became such a compulsion that he began to disregard his family altogether. Every two- or three-days Truancy Officers were bringing him home from skipping school. To him, school was useless and taught nothing beneficial - nothing that could be applied in the real world. Biggs, on the other hand, was teaching him the ins and outs of the game. Biggs was teaching him how to survive. In James' eyes, learning different kinds of swag and hustle would take him farther in life than learning about some overrated cat named Columbus, who was celebrated for discovering a land where people already lived. James was in the game and nothing existed outside of that game.

One day as James sat on the floor in his bedroom counting change and a few small bills, calculating what his commission would be, and arranging number slips, Cecilia walked in to see her son just as he attempted to slide what she recognized as a small revolver under his bed and out of view. James had on an expensive outfit that she would have sworn belonged to Biggs had it not been so small and draped across her son's skinny frame. Cecilia looked with disgrace at the image her son now portrayed. He looked like a gangster and she could no longer take it.

"Now that's enough James," Cecilia barked after shaking her head in disgust at James' mob costume and the gambling paraphernalia that littered his bedroom.

"You startin' to look and act just like them God damn hoodlums you always following after down at that devil's nest you call a pool hall. It's a hangout for lowlifes, and I'm tired of you imitating them damn gangsters, you hear me?"

Cecilia continued to spew her venom, pausing only to ask Jesus Christ to forgive her for taking the Lord's name in vain. While she rambled on and on about the potential perils of the game and the trap that a life of crime was, a smug smile formed on James' face as complacence and satisfaction twinkled in his eyes. Unbeknownst to Cecilia, she had only flattered James. He had been trying to emulate Biggs and his crew since the day he met them, so he was happy that someone had drawn up a similarity between he and Biggs. To James, there was nothing better in the world than to be like Biggs and his crew - men of respect. For his mother to finally notice and speak on a resemblance was more a compliment than a reprimand.

"Gangstas do what they want mom." James said proudly and defiantly.

"And they don't take nuttin from nobody! They don't let nobody push em around, and they have fun. They don't work for crumbs and scraps they whole life like pops been doin…"

Cecilia cut in.

"Your father works hard to see that we have a roof over our heads and food on the table, and you're gonna respect…"

James just rolled his eyes and curtly cut back in.

"...and they don't sit around prayin to dead white guys in the sky to give them what they want. Gangstas take what they want! They get respect. Why would I wanna be anything else?"

James was fifteen when he made that statement - by the time he was sixteen his father had put him out. James was becoming the scum Arthur's organization was trying to rid the neighborhood of. Arthur felt he had no choice but to disown his son.

James continued to be Biggs right-hand man for the next few years. He kept his eyes wide and his mouth shut. He had no problem being a sponge. Those years under Biggs taught him a lot. Biggs paid James nicely but the money started rolling in as soon as the sixties did.

Heroin was the drug of choice and everybody from Compton to Queens was scratching and nodding their lives away. Biggs introduced James to two Dominicans who were well on their way to being two of the biggest Heroin dealers in Brooklyn.

Fernando and Hector - friends since childhood - both started as smugglers for a wealthy drug lord from the Dominican Republic. When seeing how much money they could make in America, they killed the man they were working for. They managed to get away with over two hundred thousand dollars and left for America, blending into the rapidly growing Hispanic barrios in Washington Heights. After years of scraping and avoiding Immigration and Naturalization Service Agents, they clawed their way to respectable positions in the drug trade. Together, they now owned two bodegas and one supermarket - both of which were fronts for laundering money - and tons of real estate all throughout the Tri-State and Panama. Upon moving to Brooklyn in the sixties, they met Biggs. Biggs, never known to handle drugs of any sorts, arranged for James to meet the men since he knew his protégé was going to deal in heroin regardless of how many times he suggested against it. After a few months of feeling James out, Fernando and Hector took a liking to James and decided to give him a nice amount of consignment.

James began getting kilos of raw cocaine and heroin that fluctuated between sixty and seventy percent pure. Fernando would give him a pack of dope, and a bag of quinine. He was already schooled on how to mix the dope so success had practically been laid out for him. All he had to do was stick to the plan and be loyal. Fernando took care of the rest.

Fernando constantly stressed integrity, morals, and principals. "Nothing's worse than a man that can't face himself in the mirror without feeling shame." He once told James. "Or can't rest because his guilty conscience won't let him sleep. Fernando only asked that James execute business with class and never cross him. In the beginning, that's exactly how business was handled, straight up and down. He hustled relentlessly, accepting the setbacks and inevitable pitfalls that came with the life he chose and soon was very wealthy.

The years that followed were lived fast by James and as he began to inch closer to an early grave and a bed in hell, the most high sent him an angel that took his hand and pulled him out of his living casket. James met a beautiful woman named Josephine and swore no man had been this blessed since the lonely heart of Adam was melted by Eve's appearance in Eden. James married Josephine and she soon birthed two of his children - Marquise and Sean Jackson. Now that he had a family, he was ready to settle down. He had attempted this many times before but this time it was for good. James was ready to turn his back on the life

2

"Diamond in the back, sun roof top, diggin the scene wit a gangsta lean, ooh oooh, ooooooh." The Voice of William Divine and his anthem for contentment - Be thankful for what you got - floated melodically into the streets of Brooklyn out of the lowered windows of James' Shiny new '87 560SL Mercedes Benz. The gleaming automobile turned the corner gracefully and glided smoothly onto Macon Street in Bedford-Stuyvesant, the place he now called home.

There wasn't too much more a man like James could have asked for. He had survived to see the ripe age of forty-two in a life where most are lucky to see their twenty-first birthday. Considering the dangerous, cutthroat life he had lived thus far, this was a blessing from someone, or something. Who or whatever that was, it had graciously had mercy on this stonehearted hustler who instead of warm blood had ice water flowing through his veins. James felt he had no choice but be the ruthless hustler he was. The way he saw it, the only people who got what they wanted in this life were the ones who took it. The whispers of morality were always muffled by the screams of necessity. Therefore, to cope with the purging of morals from his system James created a motto that helped him deal with the loss of certain morals… "Aint no wrong in tryna do right for mine."

For James today was special though. He had scored very big, and he had a surprise for his family that he hoped would bring them much joy. It was a surprise that he felt was long overdue.

James parked his Mercedes in front of his three-story brownstone and walked quickly to the front door, smashing the reddish-orange fire of his cigarette on the cement railing as he made his way up the steps. In his haste, he burned the tip of his finger and began mumbling curse words at himself. Still, this was not enough to stop him from moving swiftly. James' rush to get in the house was not only to share the good news with his family, but also because he did not have time to waste. The longer he stayed in Brooklyn, the more he put his family's lives in danger. There was no question that by now he had a price on his head.

The immediate danger he and his family were facing still could not overpower the joy he was feeling. It had been a long time since he was able to give them some news that would make them happy. James knew how Josephine would respond to the surprise - it was something she had always wanted - his real concern was how his oldest son would take it. He knew Sean would be ecstatic. He was still young and every new occurrence in life was a thrilling adventure. It was Marquise's reaction to the news that worried James.

James could not help but to notice that the older Mar got, the more he started to resemble him. At times, the resemblance was so strong that it scared James. The resemblance transcended physical features. The last thing James wanted was for either of his boys to adopt his lifestyle. James had already escaped death's clutches numerous times so he knew the flip side of the game - the side that's not romanticized.

James quickly came back to the present and away from his thoughts of Marquise. He could not afford to let his mind drift right now it could cost he and his family their lives. James was so anxious to get in the door to tell Josephine about the new house he had just bought in Akron, Ohio that he fumbled around with the keys in the keyhole for at least fifteen seconds before finally getting the door opened. The heavy bag on his shoulders, filled with James' version of a liquidated 401K, had only helped to slow him down. Once inside the house, the first thing his eyes landed on was the stretched out, five foot five-inch frame of his lovely, caramel- skinned wife. She was lying on the sofa watching TV and James wondered how it was that a woman could possibly become more and more beautiful with each passing day. As he allowed himself to be dazzled by his wife's maturated beauty, she looked up at him, but only faintly acknowledged his presence before her glare returned to the glowing screen of their large television set.

Josephine's skin had a luminous glow to it that resembled copper in the sun. Her eyes were two amber flames and her lips - a beautiful espousal of tan and light pink - were seductively pouted. He smiled because even in anger those lips never lost their seductiveness - no matter how large the stream of foul language that flowed from them. Josephine and James had met back in 1966 at a house party in Benson Hurst. All the boys wanted her because she was pure and sweet and all the girls wanted him for the opposite - he was wild and paid. A bad boy that's easy on the eyes turned out to be Josephine's guilty crush.

Back then, Josephine was a real star and in twenty years, nothing had changed but her maturity level. She had given birth to two children and still her body was dazzling. Her breasts were still perky and full, her waist was still fit, and of course, that pretty, brown round was still just that... pretty, brown, and perfectly round.

"Hey gorgeous." James said as he hung his leather trench coat on the rack. He sat the green duffle bag he was carrying on the floor beside the door. Josephine said hi, but could not unglue her face from whatever was on the TV screen.

"Her and them damn soaps." James said after looking at the TV and realizing what was preventing him from receiving his wife's complete attention.

"So I'm losin my wife to another man… Victor Newman huh? Well at least it's a rich tycoon. I couldn't stand you leavin me for some bum."

James' joke made Josephine smile but didn't get him her undivided attention. Irritated, James walked over to Josephine and stood between her and the TV. As she struggled to look around him and he did his best to block her, James put on his best Smokey Robinson and Rick James impersonation.

"I love you…and I bet you didn't know that girl, you didn't know that…I need you…right now baby, right now baby…and I really want you to know that…Ebony Eyes."

Josephine stared up at James shaking her head. Smiling, she thought that this was one of the reasons she was still in love with James. He had a sweet side, a family side that she knew he would not be able to display in the streets because it could get him killed. That didn't matter to her though. That just meant that this side of her husband was exclusive to her and her boys. She was fine with that. As he continued to sing one of their favorite songs, she decided not to stroke his ego. Instead, she just played along with his little game and prolonged giving him her attention; never admitting that he now had it.

"You are entirely too silly. Now move, you know my stories is on." Josephine enforced her words with a playful shove. James decided on a more direct approach to getting Josephine's attention. He walked back over to the door and grabbed the duffle bag from beside the coat rack. He walked back over to Josephine and dropped it on the coffee table right in front of her. This got her attention.

"What's that?" She asked curiously. Victor, Sharon, Jack Abbot and every other character on The Young and the Restless were completely oblivious to her at this point. James reached down and began unzipping the bag slowly.

"C'mon, c'mon." Josephine rushed him impatiently.

"Alright, let me stop before you have a heart attack or something."

James opened the bag completely and once the contents of the bag began to spill out, James said,

"Baby, it's finally over. I'm leavin this shit alone for good. I just bought us a nice house in Akron. I'm moving you and the kids out of Brooklyn today."

"Today…Akron?" Josephine questioned. After fully grasping what James was saying, she asked,

"You're done… for good?"

James had long been ready to get out of the game. He just had to find the right outlet. One that would be lucrative enough to leave him set for life. He knew he had to leave with enough money to be able to support his family from here on out. He needed a heist that would support them for the rest of their lives. The only thing he could come up with that would get him the type of cash he was thinking about was to double cross Fernando and Hector.

James walks nervously up a set of decrepit steps that lead to the entrance of one of Fernando and Hector's tenement buildings in Crown Heights. For years, he has been nothing but loyal to his connects and now, as his heart beats from a slight fear, he is ready to cross them. He's human so guilt hangs heavy on his conscience as he prepares to steal from two men who have become more than partners, they have become his friends. However, the guilt weighing on his conscience is not enough to stop him from doing what he feels he has to do. James takes a deep breath, hears it loudly in his own ears, and knocks three solid times on the door in front of him. He waits two seconds before he hears someone on the other side of the metal door that was put in to secure this particular apartment. It's the apartment Fernando and Hector frequent.

"Who is it?" a heavily Hispanic accented voice calls out from behind the door.

"It's me." James says, trying hard not to be too loud.

"I don't know no ME's." The person on the other side of the door says sarcastically.

"It's James baby. I need to speak to Fernando."

The door opens and the short and stout man standing in the doorway leads James inside after checking the bag of money James is holding in his hand. James peers around the apartment harder than he's ever done. After taking a shot of rum offered by Fernando, James gets right to business.

"Listen, yall know I don't like askin for favors but I fucked up a lil' paper and I need some work."

James looks around the room, waiting for a response. It hits him that no one is in the room but he, Fernando, and the goon that answered the door. There is very little protection here besides the gun on the goon, a person James now recognizes as Fernando's driver. James silently admires how relaxed Fernando is in this rough neighborhood and tenement though he's worth millions in dope money. He struts with the same ease and indifference to threats or danger that Biggs used to when he ran the neighborhood. The man's fidelity, confidence, and courage momentarily intimidate James but he continues. He too has ice in his veins.

"You know I'm good for it daddy. I got something set up already. Got some people comin from Jersey that want ten off top. And the other few you front me, you know my work, you'll have ya money by the end of next week."

Fernando finally speaks up.

"Exactly how many we talkin James?"

"Twenty-five." But look, like I said…"

Fernando cuts James off in mid-sentence.

"I heard exactly what you said James. You already got some buyers set up. I consider you a friend, a longtime friend. I really don't need the long drawn-out explanations. As I see it, my friend ran into some problems and I'm in the position to help him out. I mean, you act like I never gave you consignment before."

Only if James knew it was going to be this easy, he wouldn't have spent this morning rehearsing the story he had concocted or calling his people to set up the plan B robbery.

"I just want you to know it aint gon' be none of that underhand dope fiend shit…"

"Don't produce doubts that don't exist. Now, twenty-five aint a problem. As a matter-of-fact, I think I can trust you with thirty. Same price, eighteen a piece, so you owe me uhhh… five hundred forty thou'. How much you got on you right now?"

Fernando glances at the bag in James' hand. James was excited but doesn't wear it. He doesn't want to give any signs that he was here to burn Fernando and Hector.

"Oh, I got two hundred-seventy on me now. I'ma pay for half of em up front." James says handing Fernando the large gym bag he's holding. Fernando flips through a few of the rubber band wrapped stacks. Once satisfied, he passes the money to his bodyguard to be counted.

"Good, good. Juan'll meet you back here exactly an hour after you walk out of that door."

"Solid." James says. As he turns to leave, Fernando stops him.

"Don't ever change. You've always been reliable, always. Now I already knew about that bad coke you bought uptown. I know it fucked your money up a little bit. Just get it back the right way."

James assures him that he'll get his money and won't have to worry about any underhand business.

"I can't believe you even thinking' like that daddy. I wouldn't dare cross yall man. Not only because I like yall, but I respect yall, seriously. And how long I known yall? Twenty-five years? Yall been looking out for me since I was sixteen, not only that, I would have to be a stupid motherfucka to even think about crossin' yall."

James patronizing their strength is more wool over Fernando's eyes. James knows that if he makes Fernando feel he fears him, Fernando will drop his guard further. Thinking he didn't have to worry about James because of some fear is a miscalculation. He underestimates just how shrewd James is. James strolls to the door and before walking out says,

"Did I ever come at yall sideways or at any other angle?"

Fernando studies James' face. "No James you haven't. All I'm saying is don't start now."

With that, James makes his way out of Fernando and Hector's highly secured building knowing that in exactly sixty minutes he'll be fifteen kilos richer. He also knows that he'll have to move his family immediately. He quickly calls one of his friends, a real estate broker who tells him about the house in Akron, Ohio. Without even seeing it, James says he wants it. At two hundred and forty thousand, it can't be too bad he reasons. He can always tuck his family away in a hotel until the purchase of the house goes through. The broker begins making the proper calls and filing the proper paperwork while James heads back to Crown Heights to retrieve the bricks of blow from Juan. After that, he heads out to Harlem to meet up with a friend of his named Infinite who buys fifteen of the ki's off him for nineteen thousand apiece. Next, he heads to Manhattan to meet one of his Lieutenants; a cousin of his from Harrisburg, PA who ran with a crew known as "The Uptown Bang Gang." He had been in route and should've been entering New York City via the Holland tunnel any minute now. His cousin buys the other fifteen for the same price. James then circles the neighborhood collecting all monies owed to him and heads home with a duffle bag full of cash. Now that he has the money, it's time to relocate.

"Where in the world did all this money come from James?" Josephine asked as the money continued to tumble out of the bag and onto the table. She knew that money like this had to have come at a great risk. The greater the risk, the greater the reward.

"Baby I hope you aint do nothin stupid." Josephine said sounding concerned. Plenty of times, James had put himself as well as his family in danger. This was the reason they were no longer living on Long Island. Josephine loved James unconditionally however. She understood that happiness was an acceptance of imperfections, not perfection itself. She just hoped this money hadn't come at too great a cost.

James could see that Josephine was shocked by the amount of money on the table. He found it funny considering her closet was filled with Mink, Lynx, Chinchilla, and fox furs and her jewelry box was filled with iridescent emerald, oval, and princess cut diamond earrings, necklaces and bracelets. She wasn't new to money at all; she just wasn't used to seeing this much at one time. She looked worried so James assured her that everything was all right.

"Don't you worry about a thing baby. The money's all ours. We don't owe nobody nothing." James kissed Josephine's forehead and ran his fingers through her hair.

"By tomorrow we'll be livin in a new house the way we should've been livin a long time ago. You know I'd die before I see something happen to you or the boys."

Josephine needed that security. She just prayed that James could keep his promise of their safety. There was something she wanted to say but James began kissing her full lips as he laid her back on the sofa. His free hand supported her back as she leaned back. Gently, he began to massage her breast until her nipples became erect. Josephine let out a breathy moan and kissed James back passionately. James could feel her response to his touch through her satin panties. He pulled them down in one swift motion and her warm, wet flesh was pulsing against the palm of his hand. Josephine grew more and more excited and melted in James' clutches.

James was tugging at his belt when he heard the locks on the door unlock. He stuffed Josephine's panties in his pocket and as Josephine got situated, James began tucking the money away. It was hard to wipe away the guilty looks on their faces as Sean and Marquise walked through the door. Mar looked upset and Sean - who had obviously been crying - had a crooked line of mud running from his eyes. His tears had made mud of the dust on his face then left their caked trail once drying.

James covered the money as quickly as possible and tossed it behind the couch in an attempt to hide it from his sons. He wasn't quick enough. Mar had already spotted it though he pretended he had not. Mar had been doing that for years now - pretending he didn't know what his father was into. He knew however, and not second-hand stories. Mar had witnessed James killing a man with his own eyes. He could always recall the event clearly, because the graphic scene was still so vivid in his mind - even after two years.

In his dark room at his family's home on Long Island, Mar's heart is beating fast and hard as he jumps up from his slumber. Startled by a loud noise in the alley directly below his window, he gets up and walks toward the window to see what all the commotion is. As he looks down, he can see someone, someone he cannot recognize because of the pitch darkness, someone that has stumbled into the aluminum trashcans in the alley.

When the Man stands up, Mar notices another shadowy figure. As this man positions himself directly under the cascade of coral light streaming from the streetlight, Mar realizes that the second man is his father. Now he is truly awake. James is waiting to receive something, probably a payment Mar concludes. The amount must be large he reasons as the ocherous streetlight reflects a bright silver glint off the shiny metal object in James' right hand.

The other shadow-like figure James is gesturing to continues to shake his head nervously. Once Mar creeps his window open enough, he can hear the man pleading with his father to spare his life.

"One more week." He's crying; the desperation in his voice tugging at the cords of Mar's forgiving heart. James however is cold and unforgiving. He grows angrier and angrier but he says nothing. After the man makes one more pleas for more time to get the money, James glances around to make sure no one is watching. He has no idea his oldest son is watching everything.

After making sure the coast is clear, James strikes at the other shadow like a puma, plunging the knife into his gut repeatedly. Mar counts fourteen stabs before James finally lets the man's limp body fall to the pavement and runs off into the shadows of the night. Mar cannot believe what he has just witnessed. Sure, he's heard stories about murder before, even heard that his father had done it, but to actually witness it was another thing. Something Mar had no way of preparing his mind for.

It's hard for Mar to get to sleep this night. A bolt of fear shoots through his body as he hears James walk in the house. He lays there staring at the roof until dawn finally arises and washes away the shadows of a horrific night. Mar's confused and wonders what would make his father snap like that. This is the first time Mar actually fears his father.

Josephine's voice interrupted Mar's reverie and helped him shake off the ghost that had crept back into his mind as he remembered why he had begun to pretend he didn't know the particulars of James' occupation. Here again was a large amount of money so of course Mar wondered if his Father had killed for it. It was the same thought that was pestering Josephine.

"Why are you crying Sean?" Josephine asked, glancing back and forth at her two sons. She had directed the question at Sean but could actually care less who answered it, so long as it was answered. Mar could see that Sean wasn't going to answer so he decided to speak up.

"Some lil boys from his school jumped him."

"Well did you fight back?" James shot at Sean. He didn't want to raise a coward who couldn't defend himself.

"Can't you see the boy's hurtin? That aint important right now James." Josephine said. Once again, she was playing the role of comforter.

"Like hell it aint important." James snapped.

"That boy need to learn how to defend his self. Shit is real out here Josephine. This shit is a jungle and you either predator or prey. He gon mess around and be somebody's food out here."

James was irate. Josephine knew the truth but waved James off. "You okay baby?" She asked Sean. She knew James hated when
she babied Sean up but she felt that right now that was what her youngest son needed.
Sean nodded his head and walked over to his mom, burying his face in her lap while she patted his back. James gave her a disgusted look and she defiantly rolled her eyes at him. Next James looked over at Mar angrily. Mar raised his eyebrows, puzzled, and asked,

"What? I did all I could do. I got em up off him and made him fight. He just be acting like a punk sometimes."
Josephine quickly intervened.

"Mar, don't call your brother no punk. He young and he got feelins." She said, once again defending Sean, who was happy that his mom always went to bat for him.

"Yeah, real soft feelins." James replied.

"Let the boy go Josephine." He said, making a face that let her know he was no longer negotiating. He hated watching her pacify his son. James was smart enough to know that Josephine was just fulfilling her maternal obligations, but enough was enough.

"Let's go!" James said leading Mar towards the basement.

"You too Sean!" He demanded once he realized Sean had not moved from his mother's side. Sean looked up at Josephine hoping she would bail him out but she didn't. She knew not to overstep her boundaries. Interfering with James' disciplining of the boys violated the respect they had for each other's positions.

"Go on with your dad now." She said pointing towards the basement door.

James and Mar made their way to the basement. Sean followed reluctantly. They walked past the weight bench and dumbbell set and headed straight for the punching bag. James threw them both a pair of gloves and made them hit the bag until they could hit it no more.

Sean was only nine and already had a nice little form. If James could just get his heart to match his hands, he would be alright. He was a crybaby and James knew that came from him spending so much time under his mom's protective wing.

Marquise was the born pugilist. If anyone was going to box professionally in the family, it was going to be him. He was extraordinarily sharp for fourteen. He had exceptional hand speed and his footwork was just as sharp. James thought he most closely resembled Pernell Whitaker. He had a nice slip game and his defense in general was tremendous. The only major difference between Marquise and Pernell "Sweetpea" Whitaker was punching power. Mar's jabs had already developed more pop than

James could handle with bare hands and his body shots rocked James' torso through the power bag.

Every session he was improving. Being as though hitting the bag was supposed to be a punishment, Mar tried to disguise how much he really enjoyed it but James already knew.

James could tell the first time Mar had hit a bag that boxing was his calling. His prediction was corroborated every subsequent time Mar hit a bag afterwards. His eyes would light up as if he could already envision himself fighting under the lights at the MGM Grand Casino in Vegas. Mar always told his friends he was going to be a professional boxer one day - that his dream was to be a legend like Muhammad Ali. To be that great was Mar's dream since he was able to comprehend life. In Mar's eyes Muhammad Ali's legacy transcended boxing. He was an American Icon. Not only had he knocked out Sonny Liston in 1965 to become a boxing champion, but he had knocked out the American government two years later to become a people's champion.

"Put some power behind them punches Sean. Act like this bag is one of them lil boys that whooped cha ass today." James said, noticing that his youngest son was starting to fatigue. He wasn't about to let either of them stop until he got at least one-hundred punches out of both of them.

When they finished, James told them to sit on the weight bench so he could talk to them.

They sat down and James kneeled down in front of them. Both boys looked up at him with eyes full of admiration. James hadn't left Mar and Sean stranded in the gutter like most of their friends' fathers had. Mar's less fortunate friends always reminded him of this.

"You lucky to have a dad like that." They all would say. However, without their reminders, he already knew and appreciated this. His dad was respected in the neighborhood. Most of their fathers were nothing more than sperm donors and fleeting memories. No matter what his dad did for a living, Mar loved him and aspired to be just like him.

"Dad, whose Benz is that out front?" Mar asked. An image of the black Mercedes he had seen parked in front of their house had come to mind.

"Oh, you like that huh?" James said proudly.

"Yeah, a five-sixty SL, it's definitely fresh." Mar said.

"Fresh, and the only one on the streets. That baby don't come out till next year. It's a eighty-seven."

"Did you trade in the Caddy?" Mar asked.

"Hell no. That's a eighty-five Cadillac Deville, she aint goin nowhere. It's parked up the street."

Mar and Sean were both smiling at the prospect of riding around in a car that no one else would have for at least another year. James felt that was a good time to break the news to them.

"How would yall feel about movin out of Brooklyn?" James asked. The first thought that crossed Mar's mind when James asked them about moving was his friends. How was he supposed to see them? Then what about Lexi? Lexi was his girlfriend and he loved her with a love that was much more mature than his years. Not only did he really like her, but also they had started having sex recently and the way Mar saw it, that was the best thing that could happen to a fourteen-year-old boy.

Mar didn't want to leave Brooklyn now. Life was just starting for him. It was here in Brooklyn where he was becoming a man and building a reputation of his own. He was tired of living off nepotism and the reputation he inherited for being the son of a bona fide gangster. Being the son of a well-known, well-respected thoroughbred like James was cool. It had its benefits. However, Mar was more concerned with the rep he was building as the mastermind of his own crew; as having one of - if not thee - prettiest girls in school; as being an undisputed fighter with an impeccable record. He was becoming one of those rare roses in the concrete gardens Brooklyn. He was a young prospect and the better he got the more the neighborhood got behind him. Mar had already begun to fashion his own legacy. How long would it take to do this all over again in a new town he wondered?

Honestly, Mar dreaded moving now but he was smart. He could see how bad his father wanted his approval on this. Not that it would make James reconsider his decision, but because it would make the move so much easier if everybody in the family agreed.

"Where to?" Mar asked. He knew he had to say something quick or James would notice the discomfort the question had caused him.

"Ohio." James answered. "Akron, Ohio. It's a couple miles outside of Cleveland. Now look, I know it's gon be a lil hard at first. But trust me, you'll get used to it. Eventually you might even like it. I figured we needed a change of scenery. And besides, it's for the better."

It seemed as if James was talking directly to Mar. Mar appreciated that. It made him feel like his opinion mattered and it showed him that his father respected the man he was becoming. Just for him to see that his opinion was valued made Mar decide to consent without giving James a hard time.

"It's coo wit me pops." Mar said smiling at James.

"What I tell you about dat pops shit? You make me sound like some old man…'pops'. Is that what you tryna say, I'm old?" James stood up in front of Mar.

"You are!" Mar replied. His devious smile quickly disappeared as he ducked James' oncoming flurry of harmless jabs. Mar did this with the greatest of ease.

"See, I told you, you gettin old." Mar said after James stopped throwing punches.

"I slipped everything you threw my way. You slowin down old man, you slowin down." Mar said sarcastically. He was shaking his head as if he was disappointed. Before James could respond, Mar threw a quick jab of his own that James successfully dodged as well.

"Not too slow." James said, reminding Mar that he was still the man of the house.

"And what about you lil man?" James asked, switching his attention to Sean.

"How you feel about movin?"

Sean looked confused but unlike Mar, he didn't really have ties to friends that would miss him for more than a week before he would be completely forgotten. He was still young. After a few second of contemplating James' question Sean spoke up.

"Can we get a dog?" He asked full of excitement. Mar couldn't help but to laugh at his brother's naïve response.

"You can get anything you want lil' man. Just don't let me see you come home cryin like that again. You a man…you hear me?"

Sean nodded and James quickly scooped him up off his feet and held him high above his head. He was bench-pressing Sean, who was in turn calling for Josephine's help while Mar jabbed at James' gut in an attempt to get him to let his baby brother down.

These were the moments James lived for - being with his wife and kids. Playing with his sons meant a lot to him. They were his distraction from the destruction. It seemed the only place he could find honesty, peace and tranquility was in the presence of his loving family. There was no hustle and therefore no deceit. Home was his safe haven.

The feeling was mutual of course. Sean and Mar loved being in the presence of James. He was their foundation; the rock they stood on and the shoulder they leaned on when life got too tough. He was their shelter from the storm and the only person besides Josephine that they could truly depend on. James was their life.

When Josephine heard the commotion and Sean calling for her, she jumped up immediately and ran to the basement. The only thing she hated about James' disciplining of the boys was how serious he was. At times, she felt he was just too tough on them. She really didn't mind how he was training them to defend themselves. She knew they would have to be able to hold their own. She knew the cutthroat ways of the streets and the competitive nature of the world in general. She just wished James would take into consideration that Sean was only nine.

Josephine really didn't know what to expect when she got to the stairs that led to the basement. What she did know was that her baby was calling for help. When she got to the bottom of the staircase all she saw was wide smiles however.

"Mom, we movin." Sean said on his way down and out of James'
clutches.

"We gettin a dog too." He finished.

"I know baby." Josephine replied looking at James. Her smiling eyes were full of gratitude. She looked back at Sean.

"And I can see you can't wait, huh?"

"Nope." Sean said with a huge grin on his face.

"Can't wait."

Mar was deep in thought by then. He was trying to figure out how he would explain to Lexi, Chauncy, Nafee, and Brandon that they wouldn't be able to see each other again. He didn't want to leave his friends but he had no real choice in the matter, regardless of how James made it appear. For now, Mar decided to just comply and pretend he was fond of the idea. He did it just to keep the peace, but the reality was he would have to part with his friends now and it was breaking his heart.

3

The next morning, the gloomy weather outside of Mar's window perfectly complimented his dismal mood. Thick, gray clouds cast a dark, ominous shadow over most of the city while the breeze carried a scent that promised rainfall in the near future. For some, the storm clouds were nothing compared to the haunting black cloud that always seemed to hover above Bed-Stuy.

Mar was preparing for school when he heard a knock on his bedroom door. He turned towards it. Chauncy didn't even give Mar time to see who it was, he walked right in and flopped on Mar's bed making himself at home.

Chauncy was Mar's best friend - his ace as Mar referred to him. He was a year older than Mar but the two were almost identical.. They could have easily passed for brothers.

The two had become best friends three years ago. Chauncy was being jumped by a handful of boys at their school and Mar felt the need to help although he didn't even know who Chauncy was at the time. They ended up fighting back to back and though they both wound up a little beat up, they had stuck together. Now, every time you saw one, you saw the other.

"Yo, wait till you see what I got for us." Chauncy said with a mischievous smirk on his face.

"What chu got?" Mar asked curiously.

"Don't worry bout it, you'll see when we get outside. Just hurry up so we can breeze."

Mar finished tying his sneakers, grabbed his book-bag and he and Chauncy quickly left the house. They were a block away when Mar asked again,

"So what chu got?"

Chauncy reached in his pocket and pulled out a joint. He looked at Mar, proud to be the one supplying the get-high for the day.

"Some of that good ganja, you tryna get lifted?"

"You know I am." Mar said grabbing the joint out of Chauncy's hand. Smoking weed wasn't something that was new to Mar. He had been doing it since he was twelve. Occasionally James would sneak and let Mar smoke with him but most of the time he did it with Chauncy.

"You got a light?" Mar asked, looking over at Chauncy after checking his pockets and coming up empty.

"Don't I always?" Chauncy replied, pulling out a book of matches. "Let's just wait till we get to my crib." He added, wanting to avoid any run-ins with truant officers or housing police.

"Ight." Mar said. He put the joint away and they headed over to Brownsville where Chauncy stayed.

The rain that the sky had been threatening to drop all morning finally began to fall. Lucky for Mar and Chauncy it came down in a small drizzle at first. They knew the heavy downpour would be coming in a matter of minutes. They ran the rest of the way to Chauncy's building in Brownsville projects. Like the rest of the project buildings in Brownsville - Seth Low, Langston Hughes, Van Dyck, Marcus Garvey Village, Riverdale Towers, Howard, Prospect Plaza and Dixie Court - the Brownsville housing complex was dilapidated and in desperate need of renovation; better yet, demolition. The bricks were chipped where would-be killers had shot and missed their targets. Crackheads paraded through the projects in clothes they had been wearing for weeks - selling everything from TV's to their own decaying bodies.

Mar never really liked going inside of Chauncy's apartment, but of course, he never told him. The small tenement was too depressing. It was like walking into a mortuary where death greeted you at the door in the form of a small, frail skeleton who life's breath had failed to escape at the moment of mortality. The diminutive woman had obviously visited hell. Her clothes reeked of fire, brimstone, and the scent of death. Coming here always reminded Mar of just how good he had it.

There was one aging couch in the living room that ranked with the smell of urine. Chauncy was fifteen and the piss stain was from an accident he had when he was four years old. Mar kept telling Chauncy to get rid of it, and of course Chauncy always said he would but never did.

To improvise for the lack of furniture, Chauncy and Mar sat on milk crates they had taken from the bodega up the street. There was no TV in the place, no radio, and no forms of entertainment whatsoever. Sometimes Mar wondered how Chauncy managed to survive all of these years under these harsh living conditions. Disease carrying roaches and rabies -infested mice; blazing hot summers, freezing cold winters, and a lack of food; it definitely explained why his skin was so thick. Many people would have crumbled under similar circumstances.

Chauncy had been failed by society, his strung-out mother, his now-deceased father, the child welfare system as well as his juvenile justice system. All of the adults in his life who should have protected, encouraged, shielded, and nurtured him had abandoned him through, negligence, indifference, and lack of concern.

At eight years old, Chauncy was taken from his mother because of her addiction and inability to provide care for him. He was placed in foster care - a place he had a hard time adjusting to. When he was nine years old, he was charged with a misdemeanor assault on a staff member after an outburst in his foster care placement. Anger and depression were big parts of Chauncy's makeup and as his behavior got worse, he was moved to a therapeutic foster care where those issues were supposed to be addressed and slowly rectified. However, his psyche was never thoroughly analyzed and his treatment was never adjusted or enforced. Instead of providing the therapy that was needed, they simply called the police and had him arrested for his assault on the staff member - an assault that caused no serious injuries at all. Chauncy was charged and convicted and his criminal record has been growing ever since. Though he was nowhere near eighteen yet, the child welfare system released him back to his dope addict mother with no support or resources at all. Every step Chauncy now took was a step towards the prison cell that had been reserved for him since he exited the polluted womb of his mother and was carried into his depressing, self-destructive neighborhood.

As if the apartment's condition was not enough, Chauncy's mom, Nadine, was a full-blown drug addict. Base, powder, crack, horse; it didn't matter, she used it all. Nadine indignantly exchanged sex for drugs in the apartment and if Chauncy wasn't hearing it through the wall he was stumbling across the act by mistake. Chauncy's love left completely the morning he walked into the bathroom to see his mom sitting on the toilet with a man's penis in her mouth. Her only reaction was to slam the door then scorn Chauncy as if he had done something wrong. She had no shame at all. Whatever little she did have, left the same day her dignity did. Though Chauncy always tried to hide his feelings, Mar could see the pain Nadine's addiction was causing him.

They finally made it to Chauncy's room, which wasn't too much better than the rest of the apartment. It too was fairly bare, and messy. Chauncy and Mar sat down on their crates and Mar wasted no time lighting the tip of the joint; inhaling the potent smoke deeply.

"I'm movin soon." Mar said, imitating his father's smooth nasal release of the weeds blue and gray smoke.

"What? Where to?" Chauncy asked. He was surprised but also frightened by the prospect of losing his best friend.

"Ohio." Mar said before passing the joint to Chauncy. "Why so far?"

"I don't know. My pops was real happy yesterday. He had this big ass bag of money and was like, 'how would yall feel about movin outta Brooklyn?'"

"So what chu say?"

"I told him I was coo wit it. I don't know though, I don't really want to move." Mar said sounding depressed.

"What? is you crazy? Man, I don't want chu to leave either, but yo kid; you know what I would do to get outta here? Outta this hell. B K aint the spot to be growin up in. Every corner dudes is shootin, hustlin, starvin. Either you pumpin or you bumpin out here. I'm young but even I know this shit is a trap. This shit aint life. Word is bond, this is death forreal homie. You betta be lucky ya pops wanna get chu up outta here. Ya dad's the man Mar, straight up and down. Be happy for what he tryna do for yall. I wish I had that, somebody who gave a fuck about my future enough to make some sacrifices like that for me. Shit..."

Chauncy paused, allowing himself a split second to fantasize about how nice it would be to get away from his own tormenting hell.

"Don't be stupid kid; if you got the chance to get outta here take it...I'll write" Chauncy finished, adding a smile and some humor to lighten the load he had just dropped on his comrade.

"You probably right." Mar said, thinking to himself that Chauncy made a lot of sense. He realized Chauncy was venting his own frustrations - expressing his own desire to run away.

"I know I'm right. Anyway, how you think ya old man came up on all that paper." Chauncy's fascination with the street life quickly reemerged.

"Man I don't know. You know I try not to get into his business
like that."

"Yeah I here you." Chauncy said, brushing off Mar's indifference. "He probably robbed somebody or some shit like that. You know ya pops is a wild dude. Word! everybody know Broadway James G'd up. Yo Mar, I don't think you know man; ya old man a O.G. forreal. My uncle told me about him. He said not even that Blue Magic shit was fuckin wit the dope ya old man wasn't getting from them Dominicans. That shit is probably blood money B."

"Yeah, I don't know and I don't care. Pass the smoke." Mar said noticing that the joint was almost gone. He never got excited about what his dad was into. It wasn't a big deal to him. He lived with James. It was always the people that didn't know him personally that sensationalized the things he did.

The only thing Mar was thinking about at this point was the fact that he had to leave his best friend in the world. He felt bad that he had to leave Chauncy in the messed-up predicament he was in. He wished he could bring Chauncy with him.

"Shit, he deserves it more than I do." Mar thought as he stood up to throw his book bag over his shoulder. He was somewhat glad that the session was finally over. He couldn't wait to get out of the apartment - it had a smell that even the weed's aroma couldn't cover.

"I'm goin to Lexi's crib from here, you tryna come?" Mar asked, knowing that Chauncy would.

Chauncy had a crush on Shanika, Lexi's older sister. She was a beauty. A nineteen years old red-bone with the face of a super model and the body of a thoroughbred. Chauncy continuously tried his luck with her and although she thought he was cute and admired his confidence, he was just too young and too broke.

"You a day late and a dollar short baby boy." She would always tell him. Shanika was into older guys. Preferably older hustlers. She was a go-getter and would settle for nothing less.

"Yeah, I'll walk you over there." Chauncy said.

"Shanika gon be there?" He couldn't help but to ask.

"I don't really know, but Lexi said she wasn't goin to school today so I'ma go see her.

Just walk over there wit me, you might get lucky."

On their way out, Nadine, who had been sleeping when they first came in, stopped them at the door. In a drunken slur she said,

"You lil nappy-headed bastard, you smoked my shit didn't you? Where my reefer at?"

"Aint nobody steal shit from you, and if they did, Good! You don't need that shit no way." Chauncy said on his way out of the door. Before he got out Nadine said,

"And why aint you in school? They gon come take yo ass."

"I sure as hell wish they would hurry up, it aint like you care." Chauncy said, slamming the door behind him.

The halls in Chauncy's building smelled like fresh piss and whiskey. The smell stung their noses as they left Chauncy's apartment. It didn't take them long to locate the culprit as they came down the steps and stepped over the dope fiend that was nodding at the bottom of the staircase. Climbing the steps to his apartment - if he even had one in this building - had obviously proven to be too difficult a task for the man so he pissed behind the staircase and passed out on the steps.

Outside, the scent of smog and wet cement was a relief to Mar's nose. As they walked towards Flatbush Mar looked over at his partner, who he could sense was angry and embarrassed.

"Don't worry about it man. When I turn eighteen I'ma come back and we gon get crazy money and we gon buy our own cribs."

Mar was trying to make Chauncy feel better.

"You betta!" Chauncy said seriously.

"I can't take this shit no more Mar. I hate my moms. I hate my my fuckin dad for leavin me here like this, in this fucked up situation..."

Chauncy couldn't even get the rest out. Mar put his arm around Chauncy's shoulder and assured him that they would both be fine.

"You gon be straight C. Trust me...We gon be right."

When they got to Lexi's house Mar noticed that once again something was bothering Chauncy. He knew the look on his face all too well - it was the look of jealousy. Mar followed Chauncy's stare to a red Saab where Shanika had her tongue down the driver's throat. Chauncy wanted to say something. Better yet, he wanted to go over to the car and pull Shanika out of Larnell's car but the cranberry-red Saab pulled off before he could get a word out.

"Man, what he got that I aint got?"

Chauncy asked. His frustration was comical to Mar.

"A car, money and his own house." Mar said sarcastically.

"Oh yeah, and let's not forget…Game!" He said, adding insult to
injury.

"You only fifteen Chauncy, she nineteen years old. What could
you possibly do for her?"

"Damn, I thought you was supposed to be on my side."

"Man, I'm just bein real wit chu. L's a real live G. They say he the one that killed Caesar Black. Anybody crazy enough to go at Caesar gotta be about his work."

"Man fuck Larnell and fuck Lex too, straight up. Wait till I get on, I'm lockin all this shit down. I'ma have all the fresh clothes, the biggest jewels, and the flyest car out. I'ma have the baddest broads, I'ma be Doug'E as a mufucka. Watch, I bet Shanika throw the shot at me then."

Chauncy's head was in the clouds by the time he finished revealing his pipe dreams to Mar. All Mar could say was,

"You right, we gon be bigger than all these cats one day."

"Is yall comin up or what?" A voice called out from above their heads. They looked up simultaneously to see Lexi peering down at them from her third-floor window impatiently.

"The door's open." She said before pulling her head back inside and shutting the window.

"Yo, I'ma go wait for Nafee and Brandon to get outta school, I'll get up wit chu later." Chauncy said.

"Ight, just make sure you come by da crib tonight." Mar said as they gave each other a pound.

"I'll be there." Chauncy replied before spinning coolly and strolling off in search of something to get into - preferably trouble.

to their lovemaking. They were just two teenagers going through the motions. Mar climbed on top of Lexi and in thirty seconds was jerking embarrassingly then sliding his jeans back up.

"What do it feel like?" Lexi asked after sliding her own clothes back on and nestling close to Mar's side.

"What do what feel like?" Mar asked. Lexi's question confused him.

"You know…when you nut." Lexi said. Mar's eyes shot open, he was surprised by the question.

"I don't know, kinda like when you peein I guess…but way, way better." Mar said. He felt stupid talking to Lexi about this.

"I wish you could make me cum." Lexi said boldly.

"My sister said it's the best feelin in the world besides spending a dude's money."

"Ya sister don't know nothing, she a ho." Mar said. The attitude was provoked by the wound his pride had just endured because of Lexi's comment about his inability to make her have an orgasm.

"Don't call my sister no ho!" Lexi was defensive now as well. "She is Lexi."

"No she aint!"

"Man, everybody know she is, anyway, I'm movin." Mar said changing the subject before their petty argument could escalate any further.

Honestly, Mar could care less about Shanika's promiscuity and once Lexi heard exactly what Mar was saying, she realized she didn't either. She looked worried.

"Why?"

"My dad want us to." Mar said.

"He said it's for the better. I think he got into some shit though. He had this big bag of money yesterday."

"Well where yall movin to, Queens or somethin?" Lexi asked. She was hoping Mar wouldn't be moving too far away.

"Nah, we movin to Ohio, some spot called Akron. I don't really wanna go. I'ma miss you."

"I'ma miss you too Quise." Lexi said before pausing briefly.

"You still gon be my boyfriend right?"

"Do you want me to be?" Mar asked.

"Yeah, but how we gon see each other?"

"I don't know...We'll find a way." Mar said. He wanted to say so much more and if he were older, he probably would have. The fact was, he was only fourteen and unable to articulate how deeply he loved and would miss Lexi.

"I promise though, when I get old enough I'ma come back and get chu and we gon get married and have kids and all that." Mar said trying to remain optimistic. He also hoped this would lift Lexi's spirits.

"Two girls and two boys." Lexi said. At that moment, Lexi kissed Mar harder and hugged him tighter than she had ever done before.

"I'ma miss you baby." She said, sounding twice her age. It was as if this event was making them grow up in a matter of minutes.

"I'ma miss you too Lexi."

Mar spent a little more time with Alexis and they gave another try at giving Lexi the orgasm she so desperately wanted. She didn't get it, but to Mar's credit he did last a full five minutes that second time. When they were done playing grown-up, Mar gave Lexi a kiss goodbye and left to pick Sean up from school.

That night Mar was supposed to be going to the gym to train. In the book bag he held flung over his shoulder were a pair of black and white trunks, black Adidas boxing shoes, and a pair of white gloves. It would have been therapeutic to throw a couple punches and break a nice sweat. Instead, he decided to sneak off to the cinema with Nafee, Chauncy, and Brandon to catch a flick.

Sneaking into the Deuce movie theaters on 42nd St. in Manhattan or the Pavilion on Prospect Park West in Brooklyn. Was Mar and his friends' favorite past-time. They all considered themselves young movie connoisseurs. Early on, their favorite movies were anything with Pam Grier in it - Sheba Baby, Coffy, Foxy Brown -

simply because they knew they were promised a shot of her voluptuous breast. The nympho in Spike Lee's She's Gotta Have it also stimulated their adolescent lusts'. This night however was Kung Fu night so they were off to the Deuce.

Kung Fu: The movie had come out that year so that's what Mar and his crew went to see. Afterwards they walked the streets debating the movie and others.

"I aint really like that shit." Chauncy said. "It was coo." Mar countered.

"I mean, I don't know about the white dude, what's his name… David Carradine?" Mar said.

"Yeah, that's dude from the show kung-fu, he kinda slow…" Brandon added. Everybody seemed to agree

"Hey boy…the nigga's whole style is chump." Chauncy joked, quoting Wolf from The Education of Sonny Carson. They all broke into laughter after Chauncy's impersonation.

"I would have rather seen some monks, or the old Chinese cats wit da long mustaches." Mar said.

"We shoulda went to see Real Kung Fu of Shaolin. That got the official Chinese dudes in it, and that just came out too." Brandon chimed in. Brandon was the most outspoken of Mar's friends.

"So yo, wus the best kung fu joint of all time?" He asked, knowing this would spark a nice debate. Something he seemed to live for.

"The Seven Grand Masters!" Nafee quickly called out. There was an echo of moans. No one agreed. It was a great movie but in no way the best of all time.

"Hell no, everybody know The Five Deadly Venoms is the best karate flick of all time." Mar said. His statement didn't receive the same mumbles of disagreement but Chauncy stated an alternative.

"Man, you got Chinese Boxer, The 36th Chamber of Shaolin, The Tai Chi Master joint. It's too many to say one is the best." Chauncy reasoned. Everyone shook their heads in agreement.

"Ight, Best Blaxploitation flick?" Brandon asked, not satisfied with how the last debate ended. An array of movies was called out:

"Buck & the Preacher, Let's Do it Again, Uptown Saturday Night, Cooley High, Cornbread Earl and Me, Cotton Comes to Harlem, Black Caesar, Across 110th Street, Willie Dynamite, The Mack..."

"Anything wit my main man Huggy Bear in it." Brandon said and they all laughed again. Just hearing his friends laugh made Mar feel sad. It reminded him that he wouldn't enjoy this laughter anymore after tomorrow.

"Yo, I gotta tell yall something." Mar said, hating to have to dampen the mood. He had finally mustered up the courage to tell them what he had to. His friends looked at him curiously, and the look on his own face made them expect the worse.

"I'm about to move out of town."

In unison, Brandon, Nafee, and Chauncy shook their heads in disappointment. Even though Chauncy had already heard the bad news, it hurt him to hear it again. There was a barrage of questions and Mar answered them the best he could. After departing with his friends, Mar walked around the city in a daze - staring at the streets he had grown to love and was now being forced to part with.

4

Fernando paced back and forth impatiently with his Italian crafted tumbler in hand. The glass alone was a reflection of his immense wealth. Wealth built on the strength of crime and criminal enterprise. The mug he held was made from hand-blown Murano glass and cost over a hundred dollars. His Belgian loafers sank deep into the eastern accented, plush Persian rug that adorned his posh black marble floor as he paced menacingly in his palatial estate in Panama City, Panama. This was supposed to be his home away from home - the place he retired to when the streets got too messy. His line of profession however, required a massive time and energy investment and it was very rare that he got away from his Crown Heights flat where he spied balefully on his workers and enemies. After selling James fifteen kilos of powder and matching his purchase with consignment, he was sure he was going to have the opportunity to finally enjoy the home he had bought for him and his wife. Life was never that cooperative however.

A drop of tequila spilled down Fernando's silk Gucci robe and amplified his anger even more. Hector, who was sitting on an expensive hand twisted waive chaise lounge, made from stainless steel and velvet fabric, shook his head at his comrade in utter disappointment.

Fernando had just gotten off the phone with one of his lieutenants back in Crown Heights, who reported to him that there were still no signs of James or his family.

"Did you go to his home?" Fernando had asked through tightly clenched teeth.

"Of course I did Fernando; it was the first place I went. He must've moved his family out of there. The place was completely empty." Manuel had told Fernando in his own defense.

"Just Find him!"

He slammed the phone down and sat across from Hector. Through vacant eyes, Fernando gazed out of the stained-glass windows that decorated the living room. The raindrops splashed against the windows in synchronized rhythm; hypnotizing Fernando while giving depth to his thoughts. He was past trying to figure out why James would betray him like this after all they had done for him; he was trying to figure out the best way to murder him and his family.

Fernando took another sip of his tequila and said to Hector.

"This aint like James."

Hector just shook his head again.

"Yes it is." Hector reminded him. Hector couldn't understand for the life of him why Fernando was acting so naïve. He was acting as if he wasn't aware of the slimy games people play in this life.

"It's just like them ungrateful black bastards." He continued.

"We're black too Hector." Fernando reminded his partner.

"We're Dominican." Hector argued.

"It's all black Hector, don't be racist against yourself. We were slaves too. We all came from the same continent as slaves. We just so happen to speak the language of our Spanish captors and they speak the language of their English ones, same people though my friend."

"What the fuck are you…whatever." Hector said irritated by Fernando's mistimed discourse on slavery and genetics.

"You try to help your brothers, you know, show em how to get some real money, the right way, and what do they do? They turn around and stab you in the back with a rusty blade. I don't know why you ever allowed him so close to us in the first place. He should've been dealt with just like everybody else; without an ounce more favor."

Hector seemed to be even angrier than Fernando. He couldn't believe Fernando would trust James with so much work.

There was no disguising Fernando's anger however, and whenever he got this angry, there were only two things that could make him feel better- tequila and sex. Considering the sap of Mexico wasn't doing the trick, he called for his wife. Fernando's wife was a twenty-two-year-old sepia princess named Sophia who looked like a queen from the Nile River Valley. Fernando had snatched Sophia up from the streets of Crown Heights when she was seventeen. The two of them eloped a month after meeting.

Sophia was scared and even a little skeptical when Fernando first asked her to marry him. She was still young and deathly afraid of Fernando. He was known to murder and on top of that he had a harem of women who pleasured his every desire. She felt she would never be able to compete with so many women. It was Sophia's sister who reminded her that he had asked her to marry him - she hadn't chased him like the thousands of parasitic dream chasers he eluded regularly. She also felt it important to remind her younger sister that a life of leisure, indolence, and opulence would be hers as Fernando's wife. Eventually Sophia took heed to her older sister's wisdom.

Fernando looked over at Hector and asked him to excuse him. Hector swallowed the rest of his tequila and left without saying another word. He was too upset with Fernando to speak to him right now. Fernando's trust and faith - gullibility he wanted to label it - had cost them close to three hundred thousand dollars and would now put their soldiers on an unnecessary mission. Hector just left the house shaking his head in disbelief. Once he was gone, Fernando called for Sophia, who came out half-naked as if she already knew what she was being summoned for.

The candles that illuminated the room cast a dim orange glow to her brown skin as she walked into the living room like a stallion. Her thick hips swayed seductively from side to side and she held her head up confidently. Her satin robe blew freely as the draft caught it, revealing her naturally round D cup breast and the finely trimmed line of soft black hair that led to the moist heat between her legs. Sophia was the only person that could calm the beast inside of Fernando and the source of that power lie right between her thick thighs.

When Sophia spoke, her voice was deep and sexy. Like Sade's or Toni Braxtons', her voice had an airy, feminine deepness to it.

"Is this what you want daddy?" She said, sliding her middle finger over her throbbing lips, up her stomach, between her breasts, and finally into her pretty mouth where she sucked on her own juices enticingly. She moaned deeply and Fernando made a beast-like sound. The guttural groan resembled a hungry dog's growl.

"You damn right that's what I want!" He grunted, grabbing Sophia by her shoulders, spinning her around, and pressing her face against the wall. Fernando grabbed her by the back of her neck and with no hesitation or warning thrust himself inside of her. Sophia let out a high pitch scream before a succession of pain-releasing grunts escaped her lips.

Fernando didn't have time to waste playing control and mind games with Sophia tonight. Tonight, he was angry and had only one intention - shoot a load inside of his young wife that he hoped would release a lot of pressure and stress with it.

With her face banging into the wall, Fernando's hands pressing hard on the back of her neck, and her nails almost through the wall and into the next room, Sophia cried out.

"Stop…slow down papi, you hurtin me."

She had the grimace on her face of a woman in labor. "Please…it hurts."

Fernando heard her but was possessed right now. He continued to thrust hard from behind. His thrust grew faster and harder the closer he came to losing control.

"I'll kill him!" Fernando shouted, James' face stopping his orgasm just before climax. No longer concerned with sex, he yanked himself out of Sophia and walked away naked to have another drink and cigar. He was mumbling a bunch of Spanish that Sophia couldn't understand. She was in too much pain to care however. Sophia laid back on the couch with her legs spread wide while she bit her bottom lip and massaged her swollen vulva.

5

When Josephine stepped out of the moving van, her liquid brown eyes glittered with amazement as she stared at the architectural gem she would now be proudly calling home.

"Oh my God James, it's so beautiful." She said hugging James' arm tightly. Her eyes were now very close to tears she was so amassed in joy. The house was definitely a step up from their brownstone in Brooklyn. The first thing she noticed - before taking in all the other details - was the size of the place.

"It's so big." Josephine commented as she continued to survey the house and the five-acres of land that it sat on; land that was all theirs to do with as they chose. The house was two stories high, with five bedrooms and two baths. It was the kind of house she dreamed of as a little girl growing up in that poverty-stricken tenement building in the Mitchell projects in the South Bronx.

In dread, Josephine began to think about that mouse-hole in the wall right next to the 40th precinct on 138th St. and Alexander Ave. The way she remembered it, the household was shaky, never stable, and always lacking adequate income - even violent at times.

Josephine's father was a former auto mechanic who was forced into early retirement and forced to collect disability checks because of a severe injury that cost him the bottom half of his left leg. He had always been such a proud and dignified man, until of course, the injury made him a cripple and his ego was irreparably wounded. It was as if he blamed the world for what had happened to him and now carried this immense chip on his shoulder. He became more and more grouchy and easily agitated. He wound up being just another drunk who abused his wife and neglected his child. If he wasn't home causing a ruckus, he was hanging around near the Patterson projects, in a bodega with his Spanish friends gambling away the family's savings playing dominoes and poker.

Josephine's mom, who suffered from Battered Woman's Syndrome, stayed with Josephine's father because one, she thought she was obligated to since the vows they exchanged said "In sickness and in health" and two, she was blinded by love. She believed his abusiveness stemmed from his injury therefore he could get better. He used to be a really good man. She knew it was the inability to work - which he had loved - that had driven him to the bottle and that it was the bottle that intensified his rage and depression.

Then it was the extreme rage and depression that caused him to hit her. Like most women in abusive relationships, she tried her hardest to justify and rationalize her husband's behavior. She would do anything but outright blame him.

Growing up in that apartment caused Josephine to grow up with a disturbing view of life and a sense of hatred towards men. She grew to despise her mother for allowing her father to continuously beat and mistreat her. She believed her father was an ungrateful man. He was miserable and didn't deserve her mother's love. Josephine just couldn't understand what kept women like her mother from leaving their abusive husbands.

Coming up, the only thing Josephine sincerely had a love for was school. It allowed her to escape her mind damaging reality at home. She found solace in her schoolwork - particularly reading. Books were like a portal to other worlds for her. She could hide in these imaginary worlds to get away from the screaming of her father and the crying of her mother. It wasn't just the fact that school was her escape that made her enjoy it so much however. Josephine always hoped that a good education would be her ticket out of the gutter. Because of this devotion to learning, Josephine was always intelligent and more mature than her years.

Josephine grew to be a strong woman who had proven her doubters wrong. She was well aware that people allow the ghetto to set limitations on them but she had the will and drive to prevent herself from becoming a victim. She did not allow her environment to victimize her. She graduated from Seton Hall with a GPA of 3.75 and a Masters in Social Science.

Many of her old friends were now prostitutes turning tricks, strippers giving lap dances, and heroin addicts polluting their veins. It was in the benefit of everyone in Josephine's life that she made the conscious decision to avoid being sucked into the suicidal life style that had consumed so many of her friends and pursued her dreams. In reality, it wasn't Josephine who was lucky to have James, it was James who was lucky to have such a good woman who loved him and stood by and behind him no matter what he did. His pride kept him from admitting this aloud but in his heart of hearts, he knew it was true.
Josephine wrapped her arms around James' neck, kissed his lips softly, and laid her head against his shoulder. They embraced for a long time, standing in the threshold of the doorway, staring into the empty living room. She was now sure that this meant James was officially out of the game for good.

"Finally." James exhaled into Josephine's ear as if releasing all 42 years of built up stress and struggle in one, long, and overdue breath.

"You know I never once stopped lovin you Josephine. You and the boys have been my heartbeat from day one. Everything I did, I did it for yall, and just so I could see this day. The day I could retire to a nice house with my beautiful family away from everything."

Josephine was hanging onto James' every word.

"Thank you for stickin by me when no one else would baby." James finished his statement with a kiss on the top of Josephine's forehead. Her eyes were hazy with passion.

"I love you baby." She said, savoring the moment.

Josephine did most of the decorating in the new house; she was meticulous when it came to that sort of thing. Sean got the dog he was asking for - a black and brown Rottweiler. James finally had the peace he had been searching for, for the last decade or so. Everything was going good and everyone seemed to be happy about the new house…everyone except for Mar.

It wasn't that Mar didn't like the house, he thought it was nice. It was big and spacious - comfortable - and he loved how happy it seemed to make his family. Mar missed New York though. He missed Lexi. He missed Chauncy, Brandon, and Nafee. He missed boxing, Prospect

Park and Coney Island. He hated not being able to tell people where he lived now or what his new number was. James wouldn't allow that - for good reason. It made Mar feel secluded and isolated. It was like living in a posh casket or some witness protection program for the rich and famous.

Akron's suburbs were nice but Mar was a big city kid. He missed Brooklyn, the excitement, the beat of the city, the hustle, even the struggle to a certain degree. He missed it all and just wasn't comfortable. To Mar, the kids living in his section of Akron were lames. They had no flavor and no sense of style whatsoever. They all admired Mar and wanted to be his friend but he wouldn't even consider hanging with them. Instead, he spent most of his time around James, who was always willing to kick it with his oldest son.

James took Mar to basketball games and boxing matches, but he really liked to take him out for rides at night. Just the two of them in James' Mercedes, building father to son. One night in particular Mar would never forget…it was the last time he would ever see his father again.

6

James took Mar to Voinovich Bicentennial Park in Cleveland. The park was right on the shore of Lake Erie and had spectacular views of the city's skyline. The lights of the city caught Mar's eyes while the calm of the moon-glittered lake grabbed James' attention. Father and son shared a 5th of whiskey and talked about almost everything. While every sip of Jack Daniels burned Mar's throat - dizzying him more and more - James gulped without wincing a bit.

As Mar sat low in the passenger side of his dad's car he glanced over at James. He was admiring the suave demeanor of the man he felt was the flyest cat in the world. James reached over to the radio and turned Curtis Mayfield's "If There's a Hell Below" down a few more notches so Mar could hear clearly what he had to say.

"You see that world out there?" He asked, pointing to the lights that illuminated Cleveland's nightlife. James began to speak in a slow, steady cadence; pausing briefly between each point.

"It's a cold place…and it's even colder for us…and when I say us I mean blacks. But I don't want you to grow up blamin society for your shortcomings…you gotta stand on ya own two at all times…use them obstacles as hurdles to strengthen you…and don't you trust nobody but cha god damn self, you hear me?"

Mar nodded.

"Cause these jokers is hungry out here…all they got to work wit is scraps. You know how expensive it is to be poor. They'll do whateva it takes to eat…and that mean killin you if they got to. Shit, you would be surprised how many people tried to take ya old man's life. Why? Cause they wanted it and couldn't have it. I aint tryna scare you or nothin, just pullin ya coat…puttin you on point."

Mar was going to add on but James continued before he could say
anything.

"I did a lot in my life Mar, a lot of shit that I shouldn't have, a lot of shit I aint proud of, but nothing I regret. I did it all so I could give you everything I was deprived of as a child until I took it upon myself to get what was rightfully mine by any means. See my pops was a slave. He was a good man with a good heart. Loved his people and never abused my mom, but he was afraid to take the risks necessary for us to rise above poverty. He was a slave because even though he preached pro-blackness and gave seditious speeches against the white man, he was scared to actually rise up against them. Me, I learned from the streets what real rebellion was, it was doing what-the-fuck-ever for financial freedom. He always talked about cats like Nat Turner, Denmark Vesey, the Maroons of the south, Jamaica, and Surinam; the black Napoleon Toussaint L'Ouverture - cats like that. Me, I looked up to the numbers men who wasn't scared of them Italians trying to take what was theirs - the last pennies in Chicago, Detroit, or Harlem; cats like Frank Lucas who used the US army's ships to get that pure Blue Magic over here. Fuck all that don't corrupt your own shit. How in the hell can you corrupt what's already corrupt?" To me, Earl Graves putting that Black Enterprise together, Reginald Lewis making TLC Beatrice International the first billion-dollar black business; Arthur G. Gaston going from a bellhop to a coal miner to one of the preeminent entrepreneurs of the day - that's progress, that's rebellion cause then you in a position to provide jobs, you make people more dependent on themselves and less dependent on governmental welfare programs and handouts. An independent, prosperous, lucrative black nation is the biggest fear of the oppressor - not a bunch of angry, gun-toting revolutionaries who think they can actually kill an evil mindset that has now transcended color. Sure they bombed The Black Wall Street in Tulsa, Oklahoma but how much easier is it to pick off a bunch of cracker-hating, rhetoric spittin' negroes."

Mar listened closely as his father schooled him. James told him about how he was introduced to the game through Biggs, who he still spoke of highly. James told Mar about the pimping, the dealing - all of which Mar already knew all about. James told Mar about everything.

"Dad, can I ask you something?" Mar asked.

"You know you can ask me anything…shoot." James said.

"Why we move all the way out here? We in trouble or somethin?"

James glared out of his window for a second then back at Mar. He no longer felt the need to lie to or hide things from Marquise who was now sixteen - he was old enough to be able to handle the truth.

"Yeah, I did some dirt. I stole some work from somebody back home and of course they want they money. I'm guessin they want me dead by now too. That's why I moved us out here, but don't you worry about nothing. I'ma handle everything."

James heard himself say he would handle everything, but he wasn't sure of himself. He wondered if he really could handle this thing with Fernando and Hector. Though he had told Mar not to worry, he could see it was too late.

The nervousness that had shot through Mar's body was like nothing he had ever felt. He could barely move. Just the thought of losing his father was overwhelming. It was hard for him to imagine what his life would be like without James. Mar just sat there, startled and quiet for a few minutes after hearing James say his life was in danger. The liquor wasn't helping.

The look of worry on Mar's face hurt James deep. He couldn't baby him up though. This was a part of life that James had to give Mar raw and uncut. He palmed the back of Mar's head and made him look directly into his eyes. With James' eyes fierce and serious and Mar's afraid and slightly glossy, James said,

"If anything ever happens to me I want you to take care of Sean and your mom for me, you understand?"

Mar nodded his head but this didn't satisfy James. He needed a firm verbal answer.

"You understand?" James asked again, a little more emphatically
this time.

"Alright." Mar assured him.

"So I got cha word?" James asked still searching for some
clarification.

"You got my word." Mar said coming up out of the temporary shock he experienced. James rubbed Mar's head playfully before turning the radio back up and pulling off. The silent trip home was interrupted only once as James, without even looking in Mar's direction, began reciting a quote.

"When you're on the streets, you learn something every day. The only thing is, you don't get a diploma. Graduation is staying alive."

James left for New York City the next morning and for some reason Mar couldn't stop worrying. He couldn't shake the feeling that something was terribly wrong. He was the only one who really knew exactly what was going on with James, so James leaving for New York had him feeling distraught. On top of that, the way he had said goodbye that morning, it sounded so final, it sounded like James knew his time was up.

7

Fernando, Hector, and four of their men sat quiet in their two inconspicuous black Lincolns in the parking lot of an old abandoned warehouse in Harlem. Impatiently, they waited in dead silence for James to arrive. He was already ten minutes late. They each waited with eager anticipation as car after car passed on the streets that surrounded the warehouse. With each passing car their anger grew.

Fernando had discovered where James moved his family. With their money and connects it wasn't hard at all. They could have made the trip to Akron a week ago and killed them all. Instead, they decided to give James a chance to pay them what he owed. If he did, they promised to spare his family and find a way for him to pay for his disloyalty.

They warned him that if they didn't receive their money by what was now, fifteen minutes ago, they would mutilate his family in order, from the youngest to the oldest, throw them all in the basement, tie James up, and give him the honor of watching his family's bodies rot while he himself starved to death.

The problem was - James no longer had their money or any intentions on paying them. He agreed to meet them at the warehouse in Harlem. Before leaving the hotel he was staying in, James loaded his chrome and pearl-handled Colt .44 revolver, kissed it, and rode slowly out to Harlem.

When James pulled up behind the warehouse, he quickly surveyed the area with the eyes of a hawk. He had already concluded that he would never leave this place alive. He

analyzed the two black Lincoln Continentals. Through the tinted windows, he managed to make out three to four shadows in each car. The parking lot was empty other than that. No witnesses except for the emaciated black cat that just stopped in front of James' car and made eye contact with him. The bright green, glowing eyes were almost alarming James thought as the stray feline proceeded to cross in front of his car on its way into the dark shadow that encompassed the lot.

Fernando exited his car first and scrutinized James' Mercedes Benz - his pitch black eyes piercing through James' driver door window and directly into James' pupils. Fernando believed a man's eyes never lied, if James was afraid he would be able to sense it and if James was up to something, well, he would notice that too.

A chill shot through James' body. It wasn't caused by Fernando - James feared no man but himself - this was a fear caused by the realization that his final hour was at hand and death now awaited.

Regardless of what he felt, it was too late for James to back out now. He was clearly out-numbered, but he would never catch Fernando or Hector alone, they always had shooters with them. James had to take his chances now, no matter how slim they were.

James opened his door slowly. His skin was tingling - anticipating the inevitable burn of bullets piercing it. Stepping out he brushed off his clothes, looked at his adversaries, and then reached back into the car for the duffle bag. He also grabbed his piece off the passenger seat, took one last long look at the picture of his family that hung from the rear-view mirror, then tucked the gun firmly beneath the bag, making sure it wasn't visible. He knew he wouldn't be able to draw it from his waist and still have time to fire, he wasn't Clint Eastwood and this wasn't the movies. James took a deep breath, exhaled heavily, and turned to walk over to Fernando and Hector. He kicked his door closed with his foot.

By this time, the phalanx of soldiers was standing in a horizontal line shoulder to shoulder, with

Fernando and Hector in the middle. James stood in front of Fernando. All of Fernando's men had their guns drawn. All of the men were staring intently at the bag in James' hand, the way he was carrying it made them all suspicious.

"Que pasa amigos." James said with a fake smile on his face. He was standing about a foot and a half away from them. He received nothing but stoned faces and cold, malicious stares in return for his mockery. Fernando had already warned his men that James was a slick talker and that he would probably try to talk his way out of this.

"You got all my money?" Fernando asked. His tone and demeanor were serious. He did not intend to play with James.

"Every last dime." James replied lifting the bag to hand it over. Just as Fernando reached out for it, there was a loud blast and a spark as James' cannon exploded beneath the bag. Fernando dropped the bag and staggered backwards. Two fatal shots went into his chest in a flaming fury that easily chopped through his rib cage and penetrated his heart, which burst open like a balloon filled with blood. Fernando took one strained breath. He was trying to pull in some much-needed oxygen but all that filled his lungs was clots of blood. He collapsed holding his chest and died as soon as he hit the ground.

Rapid fire ensued. Hector and the rest of his goons began shooting at James who stood there returning fire while hot bullets continuously tore through his cloths and flesh. His remaining four shots were enough to drop two more of Fernando's men before he fell to his back, covering the wounds on his chest and stomach.

It was the end of the line for James. His life wasn't lived completely in vain though. He had achieved his goals of providing a better life for his wife and sons, and he murdered the man who had threatened to take it all away from them. James never believed in God the way most people did, blessings and punishments. Something that waited for you after death to bring you home or send you to an eternal blaze of fire to suffer. To James, he was God so besides maybe himself he had no one or no *thing* to make peace with in his final minutes. Instead, he just laid back and began to slip into rest.

"Look at me!" Hector said standing over top of James with his pistol pointed between James' brows, expecting him to beg for mercy. On the contrary, James copped no plea.

"It was business daddy, never personal…" were James' last words before the gun exploded and the hot lead landed in his head and ended his life.

Hector and the rest of his goons jumped in their car and sped off leaving Fernando and Choco in the parking lot swimming in their own blood. Carlos, who had also been left for dead, hobbled into the other Lincoln and peeled out right behind Hector's car.

Back in Akron, Josephine sat nervously by the phone, waiting for James to call or come home. She waited for the second night in a row as the clock went from 3:05 a.m. to 3:06, each passing minute causing more and more distress.

"Tomorrow I'm callin the police and filing a missing-persons report if he doesn't call." Josephine told herself.

Upstairs, Sean - who was accustomed to his father's frequent hiatuses - slept easy while Mar sat up in his bed worrying about James. He couldn't help but think the worst. He had a feeling his dad was dead.

It was enough that James hadn't come home last night but two nights in a row without even calling wasn't like him. Josephine was just about to nod off when she heard a knock at the front door. Of course, since no one really knew where he or she lived it had to be James. But why was he knocking?

"Maybe he lost his keys," Josephine told herself. Carelessly she flung the door wide open expecting to be embraced by her husband, but instead, she was embraced only by her own overwhelming fear and shock as she realized it wasn't James that was standing in front of her.

Hector and the three men accompanying him stared threateningly at Josephine. She screamed and tried to slam the door shut but Hector blocked it with his foot and all four men forced their way into the house. Josephine turned and tried to run for the phone but the biggest of the four men grabbed her forcefully from behind by both arms and tossed her onto the couch like she was a rag doll. She screamed again, and this time Mar jumped up out of his bed.

"Shut the fuck up bitch!" Hector ordered, smacking Josephine across her face with the hard butt of his gun, sending a thin line of blood running from above her right eye. She was momentarily dazed; close to unconsciousness when Hector began choking her.

"Where's my money?" He asked, only slightly relieving the pressure on Josephine's neck so she could speak. She choked.

"I don't know, I swear on my life, he doesn't tell me where he keeps things."

"Well, I guess that's just too bad for you."

Hector ripped Josephine's thin blouse and bra off exposing her bare breasts, she gasped.

"Now, I'll give you one more chance, where did that lying husband of yours hide my money?" Hector licked his lips lustfully. It scared

Josephine, who knew what was about to happen next but was powerless over it. She stared around the room at the three men who in their eyes shared the same look as the one in Hectors'.

"I don't know, I swear to God, I don't know. Please, just don't hurt me; you can have anything you want, anything..."

"Oh trust me, I don't need you to give me permission, I'll take what I want."

Mar had made his way downstairs and was peeking around the corner of the wall that separated the dining and living rooms. Finally, peeking out enough where he could see but wouldn't be seen, he realized what was happening to his mother. The other men with Hector were holding her down while he ripped off her panties and began to rape her from behind.

Josephine was trying to scream but her voice box just wouldn't or couldn't produce a sound. She tried with all her strength to fight the men off of her, but they were just too strong.

Mar's eyes began to water. He felt lifeless but not hopeless. He ran back upstairs as fast as he could without making too much noise. First, he called the police, and then told Sean, who was standing in the hallway looking petrified too,

"Go get in the tub and lay down," Mar figured that would protect him from any strays.

"What's wrong with mom, what's happenin?" Sean asked, his voice was on the verge of cracking as his eyes began to overflow with tears of fear.

"Just do what I said. Go lay down in the tub and stay there."

Sean hurried to the bathroom and did as he was told. Mar ran into his mom and dad's room and grabbed James' .38 revolver from out of the nightstand's top drawer. It was fully loaded. Mar crept silently down the stairs and repositioned himself by the wall.

By this time, the second man was inside of his mother, tearing her faith in God apart with every vicious thrust. She was no longer crying and as Mar looked into her now vacant eyes all he saw was pain.

He dropped a tear then ran out into the living room with the revolver raised. The men in the front room all jumped then reached for their own guns. Just then, the cops pulled up in front of the house, their sirens blaring, distracting the men. All four of them looked over at the front door and as the man inside of Josephine nervously jerked out, Mar shot him in the back of his head, his top split open like a watermelon and he dropped to the floor with a loud thud. As soon as his body hit the floor, the police burst through the door with their guns drawn.

"Freeeeeeze! Nobody move," One of the officers shouted while the others tried to restrain whom they could. Hector managed to escape. On his way towards the back door he passed Mar who was still holding the gun that had just killed his compadre, they exchanged a long stare, both pairs of eyes were filled with the promise of revenge.

The officers apprehended and arrested the other two men that were with Hector and took them in. At the hospital, Mar was asked a bunch of questions that he answered the best he could. Josephine didn't have the strength to answer anything; she was too hurt, too traumatized, physically and mentally. She just sat there staring blankly into space as she waited to be examined.

Josephine's heart and spirit had been damaged severely. Not even time could heal the wounds that night had caused her, and even if it did, it would never cover the scars.

8

While still recovering from the physical and emotional trauma, Josephine and her boys were informed that James' bullet-riddled body had been found in Harlem two days prior. He had been shot twelve times in the chest and stomach. Every shot had hit his torso besides the fatal shot that cracked through his forehead and spilled his brains onto the cement beneath his head. The news numbed Josephine who was already traumatized enough - it completely crushed Marquise and Sean.

A long period of depression followed these two events. The stress just multiplied when the bank foreclosed their house in Akron because Josephine - who was no longer working - was unable to pay the mortgage. This forced them to move back to New York - the very place James had given his life to get them away from.

It was eighty-eight and after it sunk in that they were far from the peace of Akron and back in the slums of New York city, Mar felt it only right that he assume the role of his father as man of the house. Regardless of how young he was, he really had no choice. It was either that or watch his family starve. At sixteen, he was ready to be a man because he had been forced into the role by the physical death of his father and the mental death of his mother. His family was still recuperating and was in desperate need of someone that could put them back on track - that someone had to be Marquise.

Josephine was still in her conscious coma and therefore unable to perform her duties as a mother. This once resilient woman was reduced to a weak, sad, and damaged Isis. She had lost not only her husband - who like Osiris was like her brother, best friend, and soul mate wrapped up in one beautiful package - she had lost her dignity. James had consummated Josephine in every facet of her life and kept her comfortable. Now, back in the cesspool commonly referred to as the rotten apple, in their tiny tenement in Patterson Projects in the South Bronx, Josephine had lost her will and want to live.

Mar watched sadly as his once strong and captivatingly beautiful mother regressed more and more every day. She no longer had pride in her appearance. That, anyone could see by examining her loss of weight and lack of grooming. The indifference she now showed to the vanity that most women cherish was blatant and saddening.

Sean was still emotionally wounded as well. The death of his father and the condition of his mother had severely disrupted the smooth life he had grown so accustomed to. Though always surrounded by it, Sean never really experienced the struggle. He wasn't sure what was going to happen to his family; how they would get by now that James was gone. His young mind was seriously damaged. This was more motivation for Mar, who loved his family too much to just sit back and watch them fall to pieces like this.

One day Mar was staring into the lifeless, unenthused eyes of his mother and baby brother and his father's last words began to resonate in his head.

"If anything ever happens to me I want you to take care of Sean and your mom for me..."

Mar's mind was made up, he would become the breadwinner. He got up that very afternoon and headed over to Brownsville to try to find Chauncy. If anybody had connections that could help him it would be Chauncy.

As Mar walked the beat, he thought to himself that nothing had really changed in New York. After two years, the only things that were different were the slang and the styles. The same sad, dingy faces occupied the same run-down stoops, smoking the same Newport's, drinking the same Thunderbird. *"The game don't change, only the playas,"* James had always said - he was right.

The city still had that stink of hopelessness and that feel of congestion as if the ghetto would burst at any moment because of the mass lumps of people cramped in those tiny tenements on those run-down blocks and squalid skid rows. The city still had that wide range of people; immigrants from Italy, China, and the Middle East had all come over and set up their own communities within the slums. New York being the melting pot it is, you never knew who you would run into. So on this hot summer day in August, it really didn't surprise Mar when he ran into a militant-looking Black Power missionary on his way up from the subway. The man was a devout Five-Percenter named Infinite who for some reason would not stop staring at Mar. Mar felt there may be some tension; he didn't realize that Infinite knew him from a time in his life that not even he remembered.

Infinite was a former associate of Mar's dad and a former heroin dealer from Harlem who after an eye-opening two-year bit in Ryker's Island, had given up his life of crime for the right and just path of a poor, righteous teacher.

Mar, who was in a rush to find Chauncy so he could handle some business, wasn't really in the mood for some Marcus Garvey, back to Africa speech but he could see that the man in front of him wasn't about to let him pass without hearing what he had to say. He decided to listen and just prayed it wouldn't take too long.

"Peace," Mar guessed that was the best response. "How ya old man doin'?" Infinite asked with a smile.

Mar gave him a questioning look. He was trying to figure out why this stranger was asking about his dad. What was his angle?

"Why you askin bout my pops? Do I know you?" Mar said with a bit of hostility in his voice.

"Probably not." Infinite said ignoring Mar's attitude. "You know my dad?"
Infinite smiled.

"Of course I know ya father lil' man, believe it or not I know you too. Little Marquise, the boxer. I used to run wit cha pops a while back in what seems like a lifetime ago, late seventies early eighties. James was a real stand up cat considering our line of work back then. So, how he doin'?"

He had said back then like his dealings with James had been a long time ago. He had bought fifteen ki's from James two years ago. That was before the penal, before knowledge of self, before his change of course. To him his exploits with James had been a lifetime ago.

"He passed away a few months ago." Mar answered, dropping his head. It hurt to think about it let alone speak on it.

Infinite closed his eyes and shook his head disappointed.

"Forgive me god, I'm truly sorry to hear that and I send my condolences to you and your family. I know how losing a loved one feels and I can see that it still bothers you, that's natural. Just try to understand that no man can escape what we have come to believe is death, which is only the transformation of the material body. We all like grains of sand bein blown around by the winds of time, you know what I mean? We all gotta return to the essence in order to perpetuate the cycle of life. You gotta see it like passing on to another life, then you can appreciate death for what it really is, not what we've been led to believe it is - a beginning and an ending. It's not. Sadly, that's the only way some brothas can escape the devil's lasso. You understand?"

"A little bit." Mar said honestly. He didn't get it all right then and there but it sounded and felt right and that's what's most important.

Sometimes the heart sees what's invisible to the eyes. Your heart accepts the truth; your mind will comprehend it later on when the time is right. Still no matter how true Infinite's words of wisdom were, they didn't make the loss of his father any easier. Mar added,

"I don't really know about appreciatin death but I guess it make you appreciate life a lil' more, at least that's what I get from this whole thing,"

"Understandable." Infinite said.

Mar could see that Infinite was smart and had he not been so busy he wouldn't have minded spending the whole day with him. However, right now he had a family to feed.

"I gotta meet somebody, can we finish this some other time," Mar said as respectfully as he could.

"Alright, just let me drop this quick jewel on you and you can be on ya way," Mar listened. Infinite's presence was no longer bothering him.

"This Satanic un-civilized nation is designed and programmed to systematically poison the minds of our youth, youth such as yourself whose ingenuity is stifled purposely and replaced with a trained slave's mentality. They do this through their insidious media outlets, mainly TV and radio through which they make the wrong seem right and the right seem wrong. Righteousness is considered taboo, weird, or for us, some pussy or sucka shit while they train their young to be mechanical and technological engineers. What do we train our seeds to be? Hustlas, pimps, gangstas, hoes, and snitches. Your father was just like the rest of us - a Frankenstein. A product of their diabolical and sinister experiments. Where you livin right now?"

"The Bronx." Mar said, wondering where Infinite was going with this.

"You live in or near some projects?" Infinite asked. "Yeah, I live in Patterson."

"You know what a project is right?"

Mar shook his head no. He knew projects were a bunch of apartments in one building but was precocious enough to know that Infinite's question wasn't a surface query.

"It's a synonym for experiment. The projects we grow up in are experiments at trapping blacks and Latinos in condensed areas for better control. I'm sad that your father - like the majority of us - was unable to deprogram himself before it was too late. You still got that chance Marquise. You still got the chance, youth, and energy to make a change - a difference. The decision's all yours. You gotta decide right now which path you wanna take. The one that made Malcolm X great or the one that killed your father. I mean, if you think about it, brother Malcolm was our Christ and his Calvary was the Audubon. You got a lil' brother right?"

"Yeah, Sean."

"Right, Sean." Infinite said with a smile as a vague image of Sean came to mind.

"Well listen, he ya responsibility now, you gotta be that role-model he need. I'm pretty sure you realize he'll do damn near anything you do - or at least try to. You also gotta decide where it is you plan on leadin him - to prosperity or an early grave. Think long and deep about that cause what I'm sayin to you is that you got his life in ya hands, that's a big responsibility.

"Why don't you and him come by Allah's school in Harlem one day? It's at twenty-one, twenty-two Seventh Ave. And remember, take one step towards Allah and he'll take two towards you, but God only helps those who choose to help themselves. That God is in you Marquise. Peace."

Mar said peace and continued on his way to find Chauncy. Once in front of Chauncy's building he stopped for a second to reflect on all that Infinite had said to him. It was a lot but what did stick the most was what he had said about God only helping those who help themselves. That, and that God was him or in him. Mar took that to mean exactly what his father used to say.

"A closed mouth don't get fed." James would say. In other words, Mar had to make it happen because nobody else was and it damn sure wasn't going to happen on its own.

Mar found Chauncy in the same filthy project building and apartment he had left him in two years ago. Just seeing the building made Mar think about what Infinite had said.

"An experiment..." Mar thought as he glanced around the tall project building.

Nadine was still strung out; hoping heroin would help her escape the harsh realities of destitution and the guilt she felt for the numerous wrongs she had done to her son. Sleeping with men for money or drugs while Chauncy slept in the same bed, spending her child's money on drugs, and not caring.

Two things that Infinite had said came to Mar's mind as he made his way up to Chauncy's apartment and thought about the large number of people in the projects and Nadine's condition.

"An experiment…"

"…In condensed areas for better control…"

This thought was sparked by the large crowd outside and the way the police circled the perimeter.

Nadine didn't even recognize Mar when she opened the door for him. Nadine was dying quickly. Her body was rapidly decaying. It was so emaciated, so skinny that even fellow fiends didn't want to trick with her. She was now stealing and pulling other petty stunts to support her habit.

"Is you holdin youngin?"

"Nah Nadine, I aint doin nuttin." Mar said disgusted. "Where Chauncy?"

Nadine frowned her face.

"He in his room." She said, walking towards her own room. As Mar walked through the apartment, he wrinkled his nose as the smell of old urine stung his nostrils. The scent was coming from that old couch that still reeked and sat in the same far corner of the front room. Mar began to think.

"The reunion might be nice but I better start lookin somewhere else to get on my feet."

Chauncy had his door locked with his music up as loud as it would go. KRS-ONE had just finished dropping his philosophy and had his DJ cut the beat so his final words could sink in.

"When some punk steps up to get beat down Broken down to his very last compound
See how it sound, a little unrational
A lot of emcees like to use the word dramatical
Fresh…for eighty-eight…you suckas!"

The beat to the next song dropped. Mar nodded recognizing the song then knocked as hard as he could. The music came to an abrupt halt and Chauncy barked,

"Didn't I say I wasn't givin you nothin? Get da fuck away from
my door!"

Nadine looked up from her room and Mar just shook his head. The music started blasting again.

"Criminal minded You've been blinded
Lookin for a style like mine you can't find it…"

Mar knocked hard again and again the music stopped.

"Oh, you think it's a game?" Chauncy shouted.

"Damn Chaunc' chill out, it's me G…Marquise."

"Who?"

Behind the door, Chauncy had a look of disbelief on his face. He didn't know whether to believe it or not.

"Mar!" Marquise said.

"Mar? Get da fuck outta here." Chauncy quickly flung the door open. Mar and Chauncy both smiled from ear to ear upon seeing each other for the first time in two years and embraced like two long lost brothers.

"Yo I missed you so much kid…how you been?"

Chauncy was still having a hard time believing his eyes. He thought he would never see Mar again..

"You know…bein me." Mar said coolly.

"Yeah I hear you. It's good to see you homeboy, for real. I got stories on top of stories. Come in."

Chauncy screwed his face up at Nadine who was trying to peek her head into his room. His door slammed shut before she could spot whatever it was she was looking for.

"You hard on ya mom G. I mean, I know she strung out on that rock but yo, that's still ya mom." Mar said taking a seat.

"Man forget that basehead bitch Mar, she aint neva been no mother to me - neva! You tell me what kind of mother would suck dick right in the crib, doors wide open, not even caring if her son watchin or not. You know what that shit do to ya mind Mar? You tell me what kind of mom would let her son go to sleep night after night, starvin, stomach growlin. It's nights, I would cry myself to sleep I would be so hungry. Really hurtin, yah' mean? Would ya mom steal from you, neglect you, shoot dope, snort coke, or smoke crack in front of you? Spend the little bit of money the government givin you on cookup instead of food and clothes so you could look half-descent in school? I highly doubt it homeboy.

"Look at how she let me suffer comin up. And don't front like you aint see the shit cause we both know you did. I know you was feelin everything I was feelin. That shit do something to you. Not just on the outside but on the inside too. I used to be crazy embarrassed."

Chauncy paused and smiled.

"That's why I used to act out like that - not for attention but to direct the attention somewhere else or to let dudes know, 'yeah I might be fucked up, but I can swing these here', you know what I'm sayin?"

Chauncy had his fist balled up and was holding them southpaw in front of his face.

"All she did was open her filthy legs and push me out of that beat down pussy of hers. That's it! And shit, I don't know whether that was a gift or a curse if you think about what I had to go through. The way I see it, Nadine don't deserve no praise for that, cause if it was meant for me to be here I would've came through some other broad. As far as I'm concerned, that rockhead out there that you refer to as my mom don't even exist to me."

"Damn." That was all Mar could manage after what seemed like a lifetime of stress vented in a two-minute monologue. Chauncy didn't want Mar to respond too much to what he had just said anyway. He wasn't sure if Mar would support what he said or criticize him for it. He didn't want Mar passing judgment on him for the way he felt and honestly, as far as Mar was concerned what Chauncy was speaking on was too sensitive a subject for him to touch on right then. His plan was to change the subject but Chauncy decided to first.

"Enough about her though G, I don't want her to ruin this moment right here. How you doin man, it's been a long ass time." That fast Nadine was out of his mind, as she had been for the past few years.

"Same shit really, I wanted to ask you something though."

"Shoot." Chauncy said, changing the cassette in his boom box.

The melodic, Hindu sounding singing in Eric B and Rakim's "Paid in Full" played lowly as they spoke.

"Thinkin of a master plan
Cause aint nuttin but sweat inside my hand So I dig into my pocket, all my money is spent So I dig deeper but still comin up wit lint
So I start my mission - leave my residence Thinking how could I get some dead presidents…"

Rakim had summed up the moment perfectly and Mar just smiled inside at the irony of those lyrics being played at exactly this time.

"You remember when I said, when I came back we was gon get this money, you know, take over all this shit?"

Chauncy was intrigued.

"Of course I do playboy."

"Yeah, well I'm back now and I'm ready to get this money. You tryna get this money?"

Mar asked the question but could see that Chauncy was already reaping the rewards of the drug game. His closet was filled with new clothes and his wall was lined with footwear. Pro-Keds, Filas, and Lottos, were stacked in boxes by the double. Adidas jogging suits, Fila warm-ups, Sergio Tacchini, Prince and Todd 1 sweats hung in his closet. He had a huge stereo with a bunch of cassettes, a big TV, and he had on a rope chain with a Mercedes Benz medallion the size of a saucer with a Gucci link chain beneath that. He had the cleanest fade with a crescent part and a pair of Porsche sunglasses resting atop his waves. There was no doubt that Chauncy was already in the game. That's what provoked the smile on his face as he jokingly mocked Mar.

"You so late you absent. Look, say no more. I either got, or can get, whateva you need." Chauncy smiled confidently and the gold cap on his tooth shimmered.

"Yeah, Larnell be frontin me work - hundred-twenty-five grams a flip. I move it, give him his cash and keep my cut. He treat me good, say I'm his best worker, take me shoppin all the time and shit like that. You see the threads."

Chauncy crossed his arms across his chest and struck his B-boy stance. Smiling smugly, he began personalizing the lyrics to Run DMC's "Sucker MC's".

"I cold chill at a party in a B-boy stance…
rock on the mic and make the girls wanna dance…
Fly like a dove…
that come from up above…
I'm rockin on the mic

and you can call me C - love."

"Yo you silly." Mar said.

"I'm definitely feelin that watch though homie." Mar said, admiring Chauncy's gold Rolex. It was a gift from Larnell.

"If it tick?" Chauncy said knowing his partner would finish his
statement.

"It aint a Roley." Mar said. Mar was galvanized by Chauncy's energy right now. True, he was being slightly pompous, but for a kid from the gutter's gutter - a celebration was long overdue. Chauncy deserved to be able to gloat - to be proud of himself. He was only happy to be able to enjoy the glamorous life after years of living the deprived, impoverished one.

Mar was eyeing Chauncy's wardrobe now and although the clothes were nice and he wouldn't have minded having them for himself, it was the money that he was interested in. He knew Josephine and Sean couldn't eat a Fila Velour or live off a pair of Ballys, they needed the money.

"Yo, how can I get down? I need this paper. You know my pops died. My mom won't work and you know if she don't work me and Sean don't eat. I need this connect kid."

Mar was serious now. As he spoke, there wasn't the slightest hint of a smile.

"Oh yeah, I heard about what happened to ya pops, that shit was fucked up. Ya old man was a stand up dude, for real. You know he was always like a father to me. I'm sorry to hear about that. I heard Fernando and them Dominicans over in Crown Heights killed him in Harlem. You know it don't take no time for news like that to hit the wind. I heard it and I immediately thought about you. I was wondering how you was takin it, but really, I knew you was probably devastated. But listen, that dude Hector still out here doin his thing..."

Chauncy paused, hoping Mar would get the message. He wasn't patient enough to wait and find out. He told Mar exactly what was on his mind.

"If you wanna move on em we can move." Chauncy said.

"And them same dudes that used to run wit cha pops is workin for the motherfucka like he aint just kill they man fifty grand...no morals." Mar studied Chauncy for a minute while he internalized his best friend's statements.

"Yo, my old man died cause he wasn't as ready to go to war with them as he thought he was. These dudes got long money Chauncy. It's hard to touch cats like that. Let's just get our paper right first then we can think about going at Hector. Trust me, nobody wants them dead more than I do, but I can't let emotions get me killed.

That's something my pops used to tell me about my boxing. Whenever I was sparring, he would tell me to keep a cool, clear head or I would act irrational. And every time I fought with my heart and not my mind, I wasn't as sharp. I would just be swingin wild cause I'm mad and tryin to out the cat I'm fightin. But when I was thinking through the whole fight, dudes couldn't touch me cause I saw every punch clearly, mine and theirs."

"I hear you sun." Chauncy replied.

"And as far as them slime balls that used to run wit my dad, I always had a feelin they was snakes. Aint none of dem jokers drop shit off to me and my moms while my pops was up north. One of em even had the nerve to push up on my mom. She never told my dad cause she knew he would've killed the man. Fuck them though, they'll get theirs. That type of disloyalty comes back on a person. My pops always told me, it's four things you don't mess with; a man's money, his woman, his family or his manhood."

Chauncy was finishing the twist on his Phillies cigar.

"You still blow right?" He asked before applying the fire to the tip. The trees burned and the smell made Mar nostalgic.

"Yeah I still blow, it been a minute though." Mar quickly reminisced on the last time he had smoked… it was also the last time he had seen his father.

"Here." Chauncy said, passing the blunt to Mar. Mar took three long drags and passed it back to Chauncy.

"Hit the weed daddy. God damn, these aint joints. That shit aint burnin out no time soon." Chauncy said.

"My bad." Mar said. "So you said Larnell be frontin you work?" Chauncy nodded his head, basking in his buzz.

"The same Larnell you used to hate for messin wit cha dream girl Shanika?" Mar said with a teasing smile on his face.

"That's old news Mar. You gotta get wit da program baby. A lot of shit done changed. Don't forget, you been gone for two years. I grew up in that time. It's coo' though. I don't expect you to know what's goin on in the hood…Lil House on The Prairie ass joker." They both laughed hard.

"Fuck outta here." Mar said, still laughing.

"Nah, but on some real shit, I'm a lot older now homie. Plus, Shanika's a cold whore. When I do get with her, I bust her out and rush her out. She loose. Every dude in Brooklyn - no - New York City - between sixteen and sixty done ran up in that. I think she out in Staten now fuckin wit her baby pops, some clown named Killa. She burnt out though G. I don't be sweatin shorty no more." Chauncy had a real nonchalant look on his face. If Mar knew any better he would realize Shanika wasn't worth the discussion.

Meanwhile, Mar was thinking, 'Money and a lil drama sure can mature you fast.' Not realizing what he was noticing for the first time was how fast the streets snatch a child's most precious gift…their innocence. Now that Chauncy was getting money, his whole demeanor was different. Being as though Mar had lost his father, watched his mother get raped, and been forced to take a man's life; he felt a lot older now. He had wisdom beyond his years. To him, he and Chauncy weren't the same little naïve youngins they used to be. They had goals now and new and bigger ambitions. Most importantly, they both had responsibilities now. Chauncy had to take care of himself because no one else was going to and Mar had a mother and little brother to take care of and provide for.

"So, what ever happened to Lexi?" Mar asked.

"Oh, Lexi, ya boo boo? She still stay in Flatbush. They moved over on Farragut though…over by East twenty-eighth. You tryna go see her?"

Mar's heart beat fast as his insides flushed with nervousness. He had to downplay just how ecstatic he really was.

"I mean, we got time…you think she home?"

"Stop frontin my dude, you know you gassed to go see her. But yeah, she should be home, she barely go anywhere. You know she talked about you the whole time you was…Oh shit!" Chauncy jumped up frantically, knocking the fire and ashes off his lap. The hot cherry of the blunt hit the floor still burning. Mar stomped it out.

"Damn, you see what chu did?" Chauncy said still brushing
himself off.

"Man I aint do shit. You know damn well you can't walk and chew gum at the same time; never could. You gotta be aware of ya strengths and weaknesses bay bro." Mar said while standing up to hold his ground. He had a feeling Chauncy was about to try something. He did. Mar slipped Chauncy's open-hand jab and threw a swift two-piece, catching Chauncy on the chin.

"Yeah baby, I still got it, and I still make it look pretty." Mar said.

They slap-boxed for about thirty seconds then left to go see Lexi.

On their way out Mar glanced in the bathroom and saw Nadine stretched out on the cold floor - her head resting against the porcelain toilet and mouth wide open. She had a needle dangling from her skinny arm and a small trail of blood running down the inside of her forearm. Mar was quick to turn his head and hurry past. He hated staring where Chauncy could see. He wondered if Chauncy had seen Nadine just now but didn't ask. He didn't have to.

"Now you see why I disrespect her, she don't even respect herself."

Even after saying that, Chauncy went into the bathroom, picked his mother up, and carried her into her room. He tucked her in her sheets and as he stared down at the woman that he despised with every cell in his body, his heart cried the tears that his emotionally dry eyes wouldn't.

When Mar and Chauncy got out of the building, Mar's high really kicked in. His eyelids - already low - got even lower and a permanent smile formed in the right corner of his mouth. As his eyes adjusted to the outside, a shiny black and chrome Audi caught their attention. The car was slick but that wasn't why they had both momentarily sobered up and were looking so hard. The car was moving extremely slow and had now stopped directly in front of them. As the window rolled down their heartbeats went up. Larnell peeked out.

"Come on youngin."

"Ooooh shit!" Chauncy said, covering his mouth with a tightly clenched fist.

"This ya new shit?" He asked while Mar thought, "What a coincidence."

"Yeah, this the joint I was tellin you about, now get in," Larnell sounded impatient. Either he was pressed for time or he really liked his watch.

"I got my man wit me…he good peoples. You probably know his pops. Broad…"

"Well both of yall get in, just hurry up." Larnell said checking his rear-view mirror.

Mar and Chauncy hurried into the plush almond beige leather interior of the brand-new Audi. Besides the pine scented miniature pine tree that was hanging from the rear view mirror, the smell of brand new leather was almost dizzying. Mar sat low in the back seat and Chauncy coolly reclined in the passenger.

"This is what I need right here, this shit say Chauncy all over it." Larnell smiled. It was the perfect time for Mar to be plugged in.

Larnell's face and frame were fuller than Mar remembered. There was no doubt he was eating good - food and money-wise. His hair was wavy and his eyes hid behind a pair of Gold-rimmed Armani sunglasses with limousine tint. Mar could see a small chain and a Virgin Mary medallion around his neck - probably more a fashion statement than a religious one. For the last two and a half years, Larnell had been supplying a few small towns in Maryland while running a major part of the Young Terrace projects in Norfolk, Virginia. After a trip to Virginia with a friend that was eventually killed near Grandy Park, he realized Young Terrace was his goldmine.

Larnell liked the state - and the money it generated for he and his family - so much that he decided to move an hour and a half away to Richmond. Besides his home in Richmond, Larnell owned a condominium in Virginia Beach. He was definitely well off. He only came back to New York to drop packs off and collect money. Other than that, he stayed out of the way - far away from the new generation of young and wild hand-to-hand hustlers. He was also dodging all of the drama he had accumulated over the years which included beef with old enemies and one-too-many run-ins with the crooked NYPD.

Larnell had two daughters now. His youngest was two and his oldest was six. He had a gorgeous wife whom he met at The Afr'Am festival at Town Point Park in Norfolk three years ago. They married a year after meeting and now had a daughter together. Larnell was pushing thirty and ready to settle down.

"So how that pack lookin baby boy?" Larnell asked, looking over at Chauncy. Chauncy's head was still spinning from the weed session ten minutes ago.

Larnell continued to supply Chauncy and his Brownsville crew because his oldest daughter's mother stayed in East New York, and this forced him to travel back and forth to Brooklyn. It soon became convenient to be able to pick up twenty-five to fifty grand every time he came to pick up his daughter. Most of that money went to her anyway. The clout Larnell's family had in the streets was enough to keep Chauncy and his squad in check.

Larnell repeated himself. "Wussup wit dat pack?" Chauncy had been daydreaming.

"Oh, my bad, I only got a few caps left." He answered, while at the same time still trying to catch the dream that had just escaped him.

"I'ma need you to run this half a block up to Kaseem as soon as possible."

Larnell removed one of two manila envelopes from his waist and handed it to Chauncy, who stuffed it in his own waist belt."

"I gotchu." Chauncy said.

"It's two-hundred-dollar bills in here for you." Larnell said removing the second envelope and handing it to Chauncy.

"Feel a lil chunky." Chauncy said. The package seemed heavier than his usual.

"Yeah, you been doin right for yourself out here, so we gon double you up. That's a quarter-brick right there. You think you can you handle that?"

Chauncy looked back at Mar who was waiting eagerly to be introduced. Chauncy looked back at Larnell.

"Yo, my man just came back from Ohio, and he tryna get on. I was hoping maybe you could front him the same thing you frontin me. He real good peoples and he mad hungry." Chauncy looked back at Mar and smiled and Mar nodded to show his gratitude.

"Plus, I could use the help right now. I mean, I can handle it, but this shit be movin so fast and I'm hot in the hood right now. Davis already told me he got his eyes on me. I don't really give a fuck about the Jakes cause if they roll up on me I'ma put somethin hot in em, but if I don't have to, it would be better that I aint out here all day every day, nam'sayin?"

Larnell looked back at Mar, who he thought looked somewhat familiar. He analyzed his face and eyes to see if he could sense the slightest sign of fear, weakness, or tepidness. Mar looked determined though, not scared in the least bit.

"So wussup, you tryna get dis paper?" Larnell asked. "No Doubt!" Mar said with crystalline conviction.

Larnell looked over at Chauncy.

"Ight, well yall bust that down the middle. If ya man show ambition, I'll put him on the team. If he fuck up you know that's comin back on you, since you doin all this co-signin for him."

"Don't worry I aint gon fuck up," Mar said, slightly irritated that Larnell was talking about him as if he wasn't there. They had been introduced; he could speak for himself now.

"So you know what chu doin then?" Larnell asked him. "Yeah." Mar assured him.

"I hope so..." Was Larnell's final words.

Just like that, Mar was working for Larnell. Unlike Chauncy however, he was working towards a meaningful goal; to support his family, not so he could afford all the latest "Butters", or superficial materials Chauncy was in it for. The difference was, Chauncy was trying to buy self-esteem, and Mar was trying to buy his family's life back. Never once did his family struggle when James was alive and Mar wasn't about to let it happen on his watch.

Marquise never let the rewards that come with the game blind him and distract him from what he was trying to achieve. James used to tell him to never worship idols; that it was cool to have nice things but to never let those nice things dictate the moves he made.

"...Not the cars, the furs, the diamonds, the women, none of those things," James had said. *"It'll all distort your vision...you hear me... confuse you...have you doin dumb shit...and force you to lose sight of yourself and the bigger picture...you know...the stuff that's really important in life...family and genuine love. And don't ever try to keep up with the Jones' cause the Jones' is never satisfied. What I'm sayin is...don't spend outside of your means to try to live up to a status quo that's always changing. Get*

your bread, stack most of it, and then spend what won't hurt your pockets in the long run."

That was the aspect of his father that Mar missed the most. He had wisdom when it came to his reality - his reality being the streets. He knew how they operated and how to survive in them. He had that wisdom that only experience can teach. That same inherited wisdom would become Mar's guide and blueprint.

Mar was really saving his money and in two months' time was pulling in double what Chauncy was. He had drive and Larnell loved it so he decided to take Mar on a trip to VA.

It was the one-year anniversary of James' passing and Mar could not help but feel the misery in the air or notice how dismal and grim the entire house felt. Mar actually wished his mother hadn't reminded them of James' death anniversary. Nobody was doing much talking. Josephine, along with Sean and Marquise were all reflecting on the individual joys James had brought them. The personal as well as the collective times they had shared with the man who for years held the fabric of their family together. Josephine had pulled out a photo album and began telling Sean and Marquise stories about their father, some they had heard and others were new to them.

Up until this day, Sean had been trying to get better but was still struggling to cope with the loss of his father and Josephine was still dangerously introverted. Due to all the stress she was facing, her face was starting to age rapidly. She looked almost twice her real age Mar thought as he watched her console Sean. In all actuality, she needed the consoling.

Mar was sixteen now but he was a man in every sense of the word. He took care of the house, made sure Sean stayed involved in sports, brought home the groceries, refurnished the place. He was making progress while Josephine on the other hand, was making faint attempts at getting her life back on track. Mar's earnings weren't helping at all. It gave her the excuse to quit after every small failure.

"Marquise will take care of it..." Was Josephine's new mantra. Her once famous intrepidness was now long gone. Mar felt he needed to get Sean and Josephine out of the Bronx and out of New York all together. He thought about upstate New York - Albany, Syracuse - but then decided it might be better to cross the Hudson and move to New Jersey.

"Mom, I need to talk to you for a minute." Mar said. He was tired of seeing his mom looking so pathetic. He tossed an angry look at Sean as well.

"And you need to stop all that cryin, you eleven years old now, you not a baby no more and aint nobody gon be babyin you up." Mar said. He understood why his father tried so hard to toughen Sean up. God forbid he be put in a position to defend himself from trouble. Mar wondered if Sean would be able to survive or would he cower.

Sean looked at Mar with a face of stone. Why wasn't Mar more compassionate? More empathetic to his feelings? In his heart of hearts, Sean knew why however. He knew Mar had to be tough. He could see that his big brother was just trying to take over where his father had left off. Sean stopped crying.

Josephine followed Mar into her bedroom. It had all new furniture thanks to Mar. Josephine sat on the queen-sized bed he had bought for her and glanced at herself in the mirror that connected to the large mahogany dresser. Josephine winced at the sight of her reflection. But before she could once again recoil into that dark internal corner in which she seemed to find so much comfort, Mar began to speak.

"Look at all this mom…look at it." He was pointing to the new furnishing but was referring to everything he had bought for her, Sean, and the apartment. He wasn't saying it to throw it in her face; he just wanted to prove a point.

"I'm only sixteen and I'm doin all this by myself. I should be out enjoyin my youth, pursuing my boxing career, but since you don't wanna work or even help out just a little, I can't do that. You think that's fair to me? Or what about Sean, what if I was to get killed out here, how would he cope, how would yall survive?"

Mar wasted no time getting to the point of the matter. This conversation was long overdue.

Josephine was forcing him to lose respect for her. The pity-party she had been throwing for herself for the past year had caused her to lose sight of her duties, which was to raise, provide for, and care for her two sons. Instead, Mar was doing all the caring and providing.

"I love you more than life." Mar continued.

"You know that. You also know that I would do anything for you and Sean but mom, I need some help. I can't do this by myself; I need you to meet me halfway. That shouldn't be too much to ask. Trust me, I miss dad too, but the truth of the matter is, no matter how much we don't wanna accept it, he aint comin back. Not tomorrow, not never! He gone mom and I'll be damned if I sit around broke, cryin about it. That aint me and really that aint you. You used to be so strong. I never saw you just sit back and let life get the best of you."

Josephine didn't speak; she just listened closely as her son reminded her that she was a woman and a mother and had ignored her maternal obligations. He was right one hundred percent and she needed to hear this. It was a bit of a surprise to be hearing it from her son but honestly where else did she expect to hear it from. Besides the epiphany she was having, she had at that moment realized that James wasn't dead at all, he was sitting right there beside her, speaking through their son.

That day, exactly a year after James' passing and the traumatic event that had momentarily shook up her world, Josephine broke her silence and climbed out of the psychological mausoleum she had trapped herself in. A weight had been lifted that fast and it was all thanks to Mar who was still scolding her before she finally interrupted him.

"Hol…hold on baby, let me talk now." Mar got quiet.

"Baby, I understand everything you sayin right now, completely, and all of what you said is true. You just gotta understand what I've been through this last year. Losing…"

Mar interrupted. "I do understand. I went through it with you but that's not an excuse for you to…"

"Now hold on Marquise," Josephine cut back in.

"You wanted me to talk right? So just let me finish. You couldn't even begin to imagine what it felt like to be helplessly violated like that. That's a very hard thing for a woman to deal with and recover from mentally, some women never recover. Then to hear that your father had been taken away from us; to know that he wouldn't be there to help me get through this, I was hurt, no, I was devastated. I don't want it to seem like I'm using this as an excuse but your father was and still is the love of my life. The only love I've ever known. I was with him for over twenty years. I don't even remember how to live without him. It was hard Mar. My thoughts were so scattered that I really started to believe I was going crazy. It's so much…"

Josephine quickly stopped herself. She could see that once again she was making excuses for the weakness she had shown in this trying time; The weakness that had led to the neglect of her children. For that, there was no excuse.

"You know what, that's all in the past now like you said. Let's just move on. You have my word that from here on out I'll be the mother you always knew and loved."

"I never stopped lovin you." Mar said before hugging Josephine. They held each other tightly. Josephine drenched the shoulder of Mar's shirt with her tears. It felt good to have his mom back. Before this, he was starting to feel like he was alone in this world.

Mar did have Chauncy but it was evident that he and Chauncy were headed in two totally different directions. Chauncy was becoming more and more reckless. He was too caught up on materials and too infatuated with drama and using that drama as a way of getting a name. He felt he still had something to prove and he actually loved the drug game. He had no real plans on getting out of it - not any time soon at least. The game was a stepping-stone for Mar.

For Chauncy it was fun…it was the life. Even more so, for Chauncy, there was nothing after the game. He had already dropped out of school, he wasn't exceptional at sports, he couldn't rap, and he had no trade.

No one in his family that he was in contact graduated from high school. His neighbors were either users or sellers; no bankers, lawyers, or doctors in sight. And if any had emerged from his slums, none had come to him personally and shared their formula for success. Chauncy's only advice came from political slogans like "Say no to Drugs" or "Stay in School". Too bad these slogans alone weren't enough to fend off the drugs and inadequate schooling the people propagating them should have been addressing.

Besides this blind love for a game that would never love him back, a game to which the word reciprocity was foreign unless it came to doing dirt, Chauncy brought a lot of attention, heat, and unnecessary drama on the two of them.

Not only were they under intense scrutiny from local law enforcement but Chauncy now had beef with Shanika's baby father. It just so happened that after all of Chauncy's talks about Shanika being a whore and him no longer being interested in her, he just couldn't stay from between her legs.

"Yeah, yeah, I know what I said, but yo kid, this bitch got the best pussy I ever had in my life! And her head game…oh my god!"

This was Chauncy's reply when Mar checked him about the bullets they had been ducking and shooting because of his infatuation with Shanika - the mother of Killa's son. Chauncy was like a brick wall now. The inertia complacency brings about set in and he was satisfied with his level in life and could care less about rising or changing. There was no talking to him now that he had money and a little hood fame.

"We ghetto celebrities baby…embrace it. This is what we got in the game for playboy…what chu forgot?"

Although that had never been Mar's motivation, he heard this time and time again from Chauncy. That kind of talk, and the deep graze wound on Mar's left ear made him want to get away from Chauncy all together but he just couldn't, he loved Chauncy. Chauncy was his brother.

Mar was always laid back and mild mannered for the most part. Any beef he ever had in his life was always over somebody else - usually Chauncy. Now once again his left hand was shooting for his irresponsible right. Mar knew that this kind of drama could interfere with his money but he had a loyal heart. An enemy of

Chauncy was an enemy of his. With Chauncy, that was damn near everybody in New York City.

There wasn't one borough in the city that they could ride through without worrying about an ambush from somebody's crew that Chauncy had offended. He was known to smack up or spit on a person for trivial infractions when drunk off his Absolut or high off his dust. Because of this very fact Mar was overjoyed when Larnell came to get him so they could take a trip down to Virginia, he needed the break and change of scenery. He needed time to think, Chauncy was making it hard for him to do even that.

Mar looked out of his window to make sure the horn that had just sounded belonged to Larnell's Audi 80 Quattro. As he peered down from the seventh floor, he could see Larnell through the two-way power sunroof saying 'hurry up' and signaling with his hands for Mar to come down. Mar smiled and shook his head.

"Mom, I'm ghost, but I'll be back in a couple days right?" Mar said as he kissed Josephine's cheek.

"You aint even gon stay for breakfast?" Josephine asked, slightly disappointed.

"Another time mom, I promise. I gotta go right now." "Alright, but you be safe you hear me?"

"I promise."

Larnell and Mar made the trip to Virginia in Larnell's car while Larnell's mule, Samone, traveled by Greyhound. She had three kilos taped to her waist beneath an apparatus that gave the appearance of pregnancy. For some reason beyond Mar's comprehension, when Samone boarded the bus she didn't appear to be nervous or afraid in the least bit. Either that or she did a real good job of disguising her fear behind that beautiful smile that had made Mar's heart skip a beat. Samone was a rider and actually, like the hustler that loves the thrill of the hustle more than the hustle itself, she got a rush from transporting work. Mar guessed the amount of money Larnell paid her made the risk worth it.

"The way I see it, it beats trickin." Samone had told a curious Mar before boarding the bus.

"I take a trip, get a nice cut, and walk away with my pussy still intact and uninfected. Not too many bitches can say that." Mar just nodded in agreement. After the bus pulled out of the station, he and Larnell jumped on Interstate 95.

"Ayo Larnell, You knew my pops?" Mar asked as Larnell focused on the highway in front of him.

"Of course I knew ya pops buck, who didn't? The dude's a legend around the way. Ya pops ran wit dudes like Frank Matthews and Guy Fisher. Frank was larger than life fuckin wit that French connection and Guy, that's the cat that owned the Apollo. I bet you didn't even know a hustler owned the Apollo. Nick Barnes, Frank Lucas, Pee Wee Kirkland, Freddie Myers - all these dudes was getting major dope money and they all knew ya pops. They called ya pops Broadway James cause he was always dressed like he was about to got to a show on Broadway. He wore gators to the corner store. You always got the feelin that shit didn't make him though - the money and all that. He was above it. Broadway James was the dude you wanted to get down with if you was a shorty from Brooklyn - him or Frank Matthews. They had a grip on the game out there. Frank just disappeared with millions and ya dad went out with honor. He never ratted, he raised you good, and he died in the battlefield. His inner demons, that's for him and his maker, we all got em, but other than that ya old man was a stand up dude. When Chauncy told me that was ya pops it made me dig you a lil more cause I know you bred from real thorough stock. Why you askin though?"

"Nah, I was just askin. I remember he used to always take trips outta town when I was young. Now I know what he was up to. This shit just got me thinking a lil bit, you know?"

Mar smiled.

"Like father like son, huh?"

Larnell laughed.

"I guess so. But listen, if it's any consolation to you, I lost my ol dad to the streets too. He got murdered right in front of me. We was sitting in the car on Fulton and Franklin about to turn and some cat ran up and blew his brains out right in front of me and my mom. I still remember the smell of the blood and hear the shot from time to time. You just gotta be a G about the whole situation. Trust me, they wouldn't want it no other way."

"I know, I know." Mar said before switching the subject.

"Yo, I'm really tryna get this money though L. It's like, if I don't make it happen aint nuttin gon move in my crib. After that shit happened to my pops my moms had a nervous breakdown. Her and my lil brotha just been spaced out since, so it's like, it's up to me now you feel me?"

For the first time Larnell took his focus off the road so he could look Mar directly in his eyes.

"And that's what you gon get, as long as you pay attention I aint bring you down here for nothin. In less than three years I got chu being in the exact same spot I'm in right now. You got that glow. Just pay attention to the game and what's goin on, and what I'm givin you, keep ya eyes and ears open, I guarantee you'll bubble in no time."

Larnell gave Mar a pound and told him to grab the trees and a Phillie' out of the glove compartment and roll it up. Mar rolled the blunt tight and lit it up. Larnell turned the air up along with The Juice Crew's The Symphony, and put the car on cruise control as they covered the last few miles to V.A.

"Next up… yo I believe that's me
Kool G Rap light up the mic for the symphony
Yo, Marley Marl gives the slice, I get nice
And my voice is twice as horrifying as Vincent Price
Goes deep, til you fell in a spell of sleep
And while I'm countin the money you count sheep…"

10

"Wake up." Larnell said, tapping a startled looking Mar on his shoulder.

"You gotta stay on point! You sleep, you die out here!" Larnell warned. Mar wiped his eyes, yawning. After wiping away the small line of slobber that glistened on the right corner of his mouth, he sat up straight and adjusted his eyes to the new scenery.

"My bad." Mar said still adjusting himself in his seat.

"It's all good, just try not to let it happen again - for your sake. You know they say the only thing comin to a sleeper is a dream. You should be trying to memorize these roads, the exits I'm takin, and the names of some of these towns out here. I got you hittin these same highways and spots real soon and you gon need to know this type of shit."

Mar didn't argue.

"You right, it won't happen again." He hoped he hadn't tarnished Larnell's perception of him.

Larnell and Mar rode silently into Norfolk and parked on Cumberland Street near the Young Terrace projects. There were 752 two- story units covering 36 acres making up what were the largest projects in Norfolk. There since 1953, they resembled the Hall Manor housing projects on the Southside of Harrisburg that Mar's father was raised in from birth until he moved to New York. Mar examined the smiling children - numb and indifferent to their plight - as they made their way from the Young Terrace recreational center. He imagined himself opening a similar center for the kids in his neighborhood back up top. Of course, his would include boxing equipment and lessons. He watched as the kids, with lips stained red, blue, and green from quarter waters began to play the makeshift games poverty creates - stickball, mud ball fights, and freeze tag.

Young girls walked seductively in tight shorts and halter-tops. The dope boys played the corners and as they watched the unfamiliar car closely, it seemed to Mar that a thousand pairs of threatening eyes were staring directly at him. He tightened up just a little. He wasn't scared, just weary of the unknown. Probably a natural reaction he figured as he stared back at the thugs that were analyzing the foreign Audi.

Mar noticed that the majority of them had mouths full of gold when they smiled at Larnell as he stepped out of the car.

"Just be coo' shorty." Larnell told Mar who was watching the sparkling smiles shimmer as the sun's rays reflected off the jewel-encrusted teeth. From what Mar gathered, Larnell was somewhat of a star in Young Terrace. He sat back and watched as no less than twelve hustlers left their posts in and around the buildings and greeted Larnell with pounds and hugs. They ended up shaking Mar's hand as well as Larnell introduced Mar as his cousin. Some of them gave Mar a bad vibe, but he figured Larnell had everything under control. One asked Larnell a question. Mar couldn't make out the question but he did hear Larnell's response.

"Give me about thirty...forty-five minutes. I gotta take care of something real quick and then I'm right at you." Larnell told the light- skinned guy that had asked the question.

"Do ya thing jack, we on ya time. We aint goin nowhere. Neither is these smokers…is yall?" The guy said, intimidating the three crack addicts that seemed like they were growing impatient. All three shook their heads no.

Larnell shook the man's' hand and led Mar to one of the apartments he frequented. It was an apartment he paid rent for. The reason for this apartment became obvious to Mar as soon as they stepped inside. He could tell that the apartment was nothing more than a stash spot. It did have a few pieces of furniture - a sofa in the living room, a cheap wooden dining set in the small space between the kitchen and living rooms. The table and chairs actually created a dining room that didn't really exist. The nicest thing in the apartment was the 34-inch Zenith in the living room.

Larnell took another spliff from behind his ear and lit it up as he and Mar sat on the couch in front of the TV.

"Yo, how you get them to respect you like that? Some of them dudes look shiesty as hell. They know you holdin, aint none of em try to get at chu yet. Aint nobody try to trunk you?"

"I aint getting in no trunk period. Let's get that out the way first. Only way I'ma end up in a trunk is if you knock me the fuck out or kill me. Anyway, I got what they need for a price they can't beat. Who aint in this game to get rich? The stupid thing to do would be to rob me for a couple grand or a couple grams. That shit'll be gone as fast as they got it. A good jux is easy to come across, a good connect aint. So it's all about longevity verse a quick hit. Most cats do the math on that properly. Not only that, I aint come down here as a threat. I aint come down here wit a squad of wild goons on some takeover shit. I came for dolo. Aint nuttin too intimidating about that. I came on some cool shit, got a feel of the city, stayed away from they bitches cause for some reason most cats would rather see an out- of-towner takin his money than they broads, still don't understand that one when most dudes be screamin that M.O.B. shit. But you know, I clicked wit a few thorough locals that dug my ghost and wanted to get this paper and proceeded to get in where I fit in.

"Some dudes just realized how much cheddar we stand to make together, saw that wit my work at my price they could have they projects poppin more than anywhere else in the city, and decided to get it poppin with me. And now the shooters hold me down cause Young Terrace doin the pussy. They all doin they numbers so they all happy. It's simple politics, simple mathematics... Reaganomics baby boy." Mar nodded his head to indicate that he understood clearly. "Always remember this Mar, no matter where you go on this planet, real gon always recognize real and strength gon attract to strength.

That's pure D physics. A purebred is something any real dude can relate to. I don't care if he from Philly or Alaska. And you need to know that too. It's lames everywhere and it's real dudes everywhere...that's just something I keep in mind so I don't sleep. I can respect a man no matter where he from as long as he got integrity and his money aint funny. You straight up and down I can fuck with you, but if you always comin sideways stay out my cipher - it's that simple wit me." Larnell passed Mar the blunt and Mar took a strong pull. Mar was enjoying Larnell's presence.

"Now don't get it twisted or tangled lil buddy, some of these dudes could care less about all that shit I just said and do wanna take what's mine. It's only right. Everything in this game aint as straight as nine-fifteen, matter 'fact, ninety percent of the moves in this game is sideways and underhanded. Some shit jumped off when I first got down here. I brought a friend of mine down here after I had been here for about a month and he got murdered. Some cats from Ida B. Wells - some other projects out here - trunked him and killed him. We went to war, dudes got shot, some got killed, it got real messy. Eventually that shit died down. At the same time, I don't usually be here. I got dudes that handle what I'm about to show you. And nobody know exactly where I rest my head at. For all they know, I shoot back up top every time I leave here. You never let ya left hand know what your right is doin. If shit was to get crazy - like right now dudes is tellin all they homies I'm down here, in the honeycomb wit my lil cousin
- some of these dudes know not to disrespect even if the thought do cross they mind. Some, well, some just love learnin the hard way. But I got so

many shooters on the payroll down here Mar, it's hard for me to be nervous, knowin all I gotta do is drop the money bag off and problems cease. Matter 'fact, remind me to introduce you to my man SK, that's my Luca Bras right there."

Just then, Larnell's pager went off. It vibrated on the table until he grabbed it and checked the number. The number was unfamiliar but the code was Samone's.

"Ight champ, let's get up outta here, it's show time."

Larnell and Mar walked back out to the car after Larnell made sure the small camera on the front door was on and the security system he rigged in the small apartment was activated. As they were about to enter the car, the same guy who had been talking to Larnell earlier stopped him.

"Wussup baby, they gettin impatient." He asked.

"Ten minutes." Larnell said and he and Mar jumped in the car and headed to the bus station. This time Mar took in all the sights and monuments to familiarize himself with the city. Samone smiled when she saw Larnell's Audi and smirked flirtatiously when she saw how Mar was looking at her. It didn't take a genius to see that he had a jones for her. She thought it was cute.

"You good?" Larnell asked Samone after she was settled in the front seat. Mar was now in the back seat where he could admire Samone without her noticing.

"Yeah, I'm good. Aint nobody say nuttin to me. I do wanna get this off me though, I'm startin to sweat."

Samone turned around and smiled at Mar.

"How you doin Marquise?" She said, flirting again. "I'm straight." Mar said, trying to maintain his cool.

The two men that were watching the apartment while Larnell was gone nodded their heads at L and stepped aside as Larnell, Mar and Samone walked into the apartment. Samone wasted no time getting the sweaty plastic filled with coke from around her waist. She sat the three kilos on the dining room table. Larnell grabbed the triple beam scale out of the kitchen along with some baggies and the three of them bagged up a little over twenty-four eighths. As soon as they finished Larnell let a few of the men he knew and trusted come in and cop.

Larnell had been past the hand to hand stage of the game but he wanted to show Mar just how fast good work at a low price went out of town where the competition wasn't as stiff as it was in New York. Mar and Chauncy still had to run up to cars at times just to catch sales. Three kilos was respectable to Larnell but it was big to Mar who watched in shock as close to twenty-five hundred grams disappeared in a matter of minutes. Some came for a half-a-brick some for eighths. In less than an hour he had gotten rid of exactly ninety ounces at one-thousand apiece. Larnell had just made ninety-thousand dollars in a little less than sixty minutes. Amazed wasn't the word to describe what Mar was feeling right now.

With a half-a-ki left, Larnell decided not to be greedy and get out of the projects before the few heartless villains that would eat by all means and hated to see out-of-towners making money in their city - the few that didn't think as logical or rational as the rest - got the urge to see what they could take. Samone and Mar helped pack everything up and the three of them left. Larnell locked up the apartment and slid the two gunmen watching the door a grand apiece and an ounce of kush.

"I just brought this from uptop, this aint none of that backyard bullshit yall be down here smoking." Larnell said jokingly.

"Yeah, alright bruh."

"Nah, I'm fuckin wit yall…don't get too high though, yall gotta hold it down out here. O, I'ma have a couple nines and some Glock .40's next time I come thru, let the squad know."

While they made the drive to Richmond, Mar thought about the nickel & dimin' he was doing back in Brooklyn. What he and Chauncy were doing was lightweight compared to what Larnell had going on in V.A. It made Mar wonder why he even bothered he and Chauncy. He was still ignorant to Larnell's plans.

Larnell dropped Samone off at a Marriot in downtown Richmond then led Mar into a sneaker store that he owned and introduced him to this cousins. After establishing himself in Norfolk he opened a sneaker store, music store, and barbershop in Richmond. Every business was ran by someone Larnell had brought down with him. After introducing Marquise to his family, Larnell drove his bright-eyed partner out to his home in the hills. Mar couldn't get a good look at the house because it was encompassed by neatly trimmed pine trees. In addition, the moon had replaced the sun in the sky.

Larnell jumped out, dropped the rest of the work and money off at the house, and took Mar for a ride. He could see Mar was fascinated by what he had just seen. That type of money in that amount of time would surprise anyone who wasn't accustomed to it. That wasn't Larnell's ulterior motive however. He did want Mar to see just how much money could be made if he played his cards right but he didn't want Mar to get addicted to the thrill. That would ultimately lead to his demise. Larnell's goal was to show Mar how he could materialize those dreams he had spoken of earlier in a timely manner. Mar would have to keep getting out as fast as possible first priority.

"Damn L, you got shit on smash down here." Mar said. He was breaking up more herb to twist in the next blunt. He wasn't ready for Larnell's sudden switch of character.

"Listen, don't be like all these other knuckleheads - glorifyin all the wrong shit. I take these risk and make these sacrifices so my kids won't have to. This is about securin the next generation and puttin them in a better position to secure the one that follows them. That's the goal at the end of the day, don't ever forget that."

Mar thought it made sense, but wondered where this intensity had come from.

"I got caught up in this when I was real young, I aint choose it in the beginning, and by the time I was old enough to choose I was already worth close to fifty-thousand. So, I just decided to get as much as I could and get away from the shit. I was nineteen then. Since then I spent six years off and on in prison, and buried four of my closest friends. I destroyed a lot of lives in the process too, but that's another story.

"This game aint pretty baby boy, it do somethin' to you, make you bitter inside, make ya heart cold you understand what I'm sayin'. You see shit that you shouldn't and I can't front, I only stuck around cause I needed the money, not job money, the type of money I could live how I wanted to live with. My wife get to see the world like she used to dream about, my daughter's don't know the meaning of struggle, not first-hand at least. It's funny to me sometimes cause they'll come home from school talkin' proper as hell, but, I think it's for the better, they sleep easy. If it wasn't for that, I would've left this shit alone a long time ago, it aint fun. Don't you be like the rest of these jokers out here, you smarter than that. That's the reason, the only reason, I brought you out here and not Chauncy or another one of my lil soldiers…you got your head on straight. Don't let what you saw knock you off ya square."

Mar nodded his head. Larnell took a tote of the weed and then
continued.

"I'm bout to let this shit go Mar, straight up. I been lookin for a young, ambitious cat to put on properly. Somebody I can give the game and a lil direction to. That's like my lil personal project before I leave the game. Soon as I met you I knew you was the one. I want to know if you ready though, you think you could handle a lil more responsibility."

Mar wasted no time responding.

"Ain't no doubt." Mar said convincingly. He had waited patiently now it was his time to speak.

"Yo I know you look at me like I'm young, but I done seen and done more shit than some people three times my age. I lost my pops at sixteen, watched my moms get raped, and killed the cat that violated her. It's like, even if I wasn't born built for this shit I been conditioned for it, on some real shit! Now all I wanna do is take care of my moms and my lil brotha, I get them out da hood and it's like, forget everything else."

"I know you ready baby boy, I wouldn't have brought you down here if I thought anything different. And I'ma do everything in my power to make that dream of yours a reality, you got my word."

They gave each other a pound. Larnell gave Mar fifteen-hundred and they rode back to the hotel where Samone was staying.

Samone was just getting out of the shower when Mar and Larnell knocked on the door to her suite. She opened the door in nothing but a dark fuchsia towel with the word "Marriott" embroidered in gold stitching right above her full around breast. Samone smiled and shook her head when she saw the look in Mar's face as he studied her body as if it was a rare sculpture. After letting him get his look in, she led him into her room.

Samone was 5' 6", 130 pounds, thick, big breast and a perfectly round butt that curved then meshed with her smooth legs. The beads of water that glimmered like a thousand little sparkling diamonds on her caramel skin just amplified her natural beauty tenfold. Mar was wide open. Larnell smirked now too, knowing exactly what Mar was thinking about. He had thought about it numerous times himself. He had always come to the same conclusion whenever the thought crossed his mind however; it just wouldn't be good for business. Feelings get involved and people lose focus.

Larnell walked over to Samone and gave her a few stacks of money. She casually flipped through it. By now she knew exactly how five grand felt and when she was sure that this was about the weight. Samone put the money in her orange and palladium Hermes Ostrich Birkin Bag. When she came back, Larnell whispered something to her. She snickered and rolled her eyes playfully at him, then batted her long eyelashes at Marquise. She looked back at Larnell.

"He is kinda cute." Mar could hear her whispering. She let her tongue creep out of the corner of her mouth just a little.

"Yeah, I'll take care of him." Samone said smiling deviously.

"Oh, I know you will." Larnell said. Before he left the room, he reached into his pocket, grabbed a condom, and handed it to Mar.

"Do ya thing baby boy." He said, then left the suite smiling and shaking his head.

There was a second of awkwardness between Samone and Mar when Larnell left the room. They were strangers up until this point. It didn't take long for things to heat up however. Samone went to sit down beside Mar. She wasn't sure if he was nervous or not, so she was going to take it easy on him at first. She was in for a surprise though. Before she could sit down Mar stopped her.

"Nah, come stand right here." He said pointing to the space directly in front of him. Being as though he was only seventeen and she was twenty-five, Samone found it funny that Mar was trying to take charge. His confidence did surprise her but it also filled her with the hope that maybe he did know what he was doing.

"Take ya towel off and let cha hair down for me." Mar said staring at Samone as if she was a piece of banana cake. Her physique was incredible. The towel glided down her silk skin and hit the floor in slow motion, forming a fuchsia puddle of cotton around her slim ankles - right beneath the 4-carat diamond anklet she was donning. Her body was tight and Mar was happy to see that Samone wasn't out of shape and burnt out like most of the females around his way.

Samone came closer as Mar opened his legs and reached out to massage her breast. Her nipples stiffened quickly in Mar's exploring hands. With one finger, Mar traced a line down her smooth stomach, over the belly ring, and down to her pearl tongue, which throbbed with every flick of his moist finger. He put two fingers inside of her and she took deep breaths as he proceeded to stroke her insides until her walls were saturated in a warm satin-like cream.

"Come lay down." Mar told her. Samone laid out flat on her back, opening her legs and rubbing her hands up the inside of her thighs as she did so. She was more than ready for him to enter her now.

"Roll over." Mar instructed.

Samone smiled and nodded in agreement.

"The only way I like it."

Samone flipped over and assumed the proper position - face in the pillow, back arched inward, legs slightly spread, with her beautiful backside high in the air. She played with herself to maintain moisture as she waited patiently for Mar to enter her. Mar finished putting the condom on and pushed inside of Samone slowly and as deep as he could reach. She was tighter than he thought she would be and he laughed when her head spun around fast.

"Damn baby boy," she said full of shock.

"Where you get all that from?"

That was her last words before she went into a long series of deep moans, long sighs, and heavy pants.

After Mar finished, he stretched out on his back with his fingers laced behind the back of his head and his arms spread like wings. He felt like the man right now. To stroke his ego even further, Samone was hugged up on him like that was the best sex she had ever had. Samone wanted to compliment Mar on his size and sexual dexterity for being so young but didn't because the only thing young about him was his age.

"You feel like smokin?" She asked leaning up on her elbows. "I got some weed in my purse."

"Put it in da air." Mar said stroking Samone's head and hair. Samone rolled over to grab her purse from off the floor. When she did this the sheet slid off her revealing the moist flesh Mar had just exercised. Now, not only was he ready to go at it again but he was thinking about making Samone his girl. She was a rider, she was sexy, and she was good in bed. However, he reasoned, he had something to accomplish and right now a woman would just get in the way. Unless of course that woman was Lexi.

"Money first, pleasure second." He reminded himself as Samone lit the kush-filled cigar. Mar decided to make Samone a proposition.

"You know, I'm bout to be the man sweetheart. Larnell ready to give it all up and he want to put me on. He gon plug me in wit all his people; whoever he cop from and whoever cop from him. I'ma need you. I wanna know if you'll ride for me the same way you do for L."

Samone smiled.

"If the paper right…of course. I ride for money baby boy. Listen, L saved my life -

literally. I probably would've died in the hood if it wasn't for him. When I first met L, I was thirteen years old, hot in the panties, and boosting. Aint no doubt in my mind I would've ended up prostitutin or strippin - or both. He took me away from all that though, showed me it was more to life than that. Now I take my lil trips to wherever he asks me to and get paid real nice. I push a Benz and I live in a badass condo. He got my loyalty forever. But I still do me on the side just like he do."

Mar nodded his head.

"Plus I like you." Samone said. The way she bit her bottom lip turned Mar on.

"So I can call you when I need you?"

"Yup, as long as I can get some of this dick on the side." Mar smiled.

"Shit, you can get some now." He said and Samone went down on Mar to get him ready for round two.

The next morning, Samone headed to the bus station and took the earliest bus back to New York. Mar and Larnell stopped at Larnell's house before making their trip back up top. Now that the sun was out Mar could see the house that stood behind the Pine trees. It was massive. Larnell and his family enjoyed five acres of private land. The home was over seven- thousand square feet. It had a sunroom, hot tubs, a three-car garage, indoor and outdoor pools, and every other amenity poor people fantasize about while staring at their small houses and tiny tenements. Larnell's home was even better than the house James had bought in Akron.

Larnell's wife greeted them at the door and his daughter's attacked him in the foyer. Mar watched Larnell's two daughters run over to him and hug his knees screaming

"Daddy, daddy". They screamed. It was almost peculiar to Mar to see Larnell, who from a distance he had watched bubble off crack in the mean streets of Brooklyn, now living like this king in the suburbs of Richmond, Virginia. He could clearly understand now why Larnell was ready to fall back, he had everything he wanted and too much to live for. To go on would be stupid.

Mar now had a clearer view of what he wanted out of this game too. It wasn't fame, or power, he just wanted to live comfortably above the poverty line, make life easier for his family and future kids, and be able to enjoy a few of life's luxuries. Larnell was satisfied because all he wanted to show Mar was that regardless of his purpose for getting in the game, there were benefits to getting out before it's too late.

Back in the Big Apple life was still the same. For one of the most industrialized cities in the world, New York's stagnated ghettos were a complete contrast to the city's progressive working districts and retail corridors. In the brief time he had spent at Larnell's house in Richmond, Mar could breathe clearly. In New York fresh air was a luxury. It took a few minutes for Mar's nose to adapt to the smell of garbage coming from the sewers, incinerators, and trash heaps or the pungent stench of dry sweat, stale beer, weed smoke, whiskey and hopelessness. Ghost-like crack heads and zombie resembling junkies walked aimlessly by him. Crooked cops stared at him for their cars, and con men studied him from afar. Marquise smiled to himself and thought.

"Home sweet home."

Like most people, Mar did have a little compassion for his people and the older he got the more he understood why impoverished people did the things they did. The more he realized their actions were justified by their struggle to get out of their state of poverty and despair.

With so many obstacles, it seemed only logical to cut a few corners to reach your financial goals. Too many people took the honest or long route and never reached their goals or even the comfortableness of not living check to check. Some never even bought a house in their lifetime. Mar contemplated these thoughts among others as he strolled through Brownsville staring at the miserable faces and the unconvincing smiles they wore in an attempt to disguise the pain they harbored inside. He was searching for Chauncy and when he finally caught up with him, he could sense something was wrong.

"Wussup baby?" Mar said as he and Chauncy shook hands.

"Shit." Chauncy answered, the disdain in his heart evident in his tone.

Although Mar knew something was wrong, he couldn't pinpoint what it was. If he could, he would have known that Chauncy was burning with an envy that had slowly evolved into hate. Unbeknownst to Mar, Chauncy had always been a little jealous of Mar growing up; he had always kept that secret though. This last thing with Mar and Larnell was too much however. He couldn't hide it any longer. He had been working for Larnell for more than two and a half years now and hadn't even been further than Manhattan with him, but Mar, who had been working for him for no more than seven or eight months had already been out of the state and to his home in Virginia.

Mar always had it better than him, no matter what it came to - clothes, a family, girls, love, everything - and now Mar was stealing the show again. He loved Mar but his heart hated him because he couldn't be him. It wouldn't have even helped him to know that Mar had plans on splitting everything Larnell was giving him straight down the middle with him, that would have just been something else Mar could throw in his face if he wanted to.

"So you have fun?" Chauncy asked. Mar could sense the sarcasm but tried not to feed into it. He downplayed the trip as much as possible.

"Nah, it wasn't really nuttin', L took care of a few things, we talked a lil bit, and I'm back now,"

"Yeah whateva, well where he at, I got his paper."

"Damn, wussup wit chu? Nah, matter'fact I don' even wanna know."

Chauncy and Mar walked over to the projects and sat on a bench right in front of Chauncy's building. Mar pulled out a White Owl and some smoke and began to roll it. As he gutted the cigar and replaced the tobacco with weed, he studied the scenery. Chauncey's building was a dark dingy brown color and a few stories shorter than the other buildings. Two girls, trying their hardest to look older than they really were, tried valiantly to attract the attention of the boys running back and forth like worker ants, making hand-to-hand crack sells. A woman stood outside of her building smoking a cigarette and keeping her eyes peered on her seven-year-old son who was trying to inch his way away from her tight rein. The other faces were indistinguishable to Mar. He figured the tension was cooling down so he tried once again to talk sensibly to his comrade.

"So wus really good wit chu Chauncy? I know you aint mad at me. Larnell asked me to take that trip wit him, what was I supposed to do, tell him no?" Mar said pausing between the final lick and twist of the blunt.

"Nah kid, I aint mad at chu for that shit, you did what anybody else would've did. You work for main man too, I can't be mad at that. If he just so happened to choose you and not me to show a good time, then hey, enjoy it. Plus, to be honest wit chu Mar, bein ya friend for so long, I'm used to that shit by now, you always had it better than me. Shit swing ya way while I get da short end of the stick, it is what is."

"Damn, so that's what this is all about?" Mar said, more to himself than to Chauncy. Chauncy was looking the opposite way, not at anything in particular, just so he wouldn't be looking at Mar. He really felt that since he was the one who plugged Mar in with his connect; Mar could have told Larnell to take him instead. In his honest opinion that would have been only right.

"You actin real funny style right now. That shit you talkin bout was outta my hands. If you wanna be mad at somebody be mad at God, but don't blame me for the cards he dealt. I know you had it worse than me comin up but look at chu now. You eatin…what's da problem?"

Mar was standing directly in front of Chauncy, forcing Chauncy to face him now. Mar just didn't get it though.

"Aint nuttin up and don't get in my face Mar, straight up." Chauncy said, waving his hand at Mar. Mar was about to say something but figuring he would live to regret it.

"You know what, fuck you Chauncy. You trippin right now, and for the sake of our friendship, I'ma bounce for now." Mar was about to walk off but Chauncy jumped up in front of him and pointed his finger in Mar's face.

"Yo, watch ya fuckin mouth man, shit aint sweet…I'll…"

Mar interrupted Chauncy before he could even finish his threat. He stepped closer to Chauncy, provoking his rage.

"You'll what? What da fuck is you gon do Chauncy? Huh? You feelin froggy than leap." After Chauncy's failed to strike him Mar smiled.

"That's what I thought, you aint about to do a motherfuckin thing. You need to dig yaself homie, seriously, dig ya'self. I aint ya enemy."

Chauncy's pride got the best of him. He shoved Mar, who stumbled backwards three or four steps. Once he caught his balance, he snapped, snuffing Chauncy across the jaw with a short right hook that snapped Chauncy's head to the side and sent a wad of spit and trickles of sweat flying from Chauncy's face. Before Chauncy could even think about countering, Mar caught him with a hook that went wide but brought the same result. Only this time, Chauncy staggered and fell on his back. A burning sensation steamed his elbows and he looked down to see that the flesh was gone after trying to break his fall. He grabbed Mar's shirt to pull himself up but an uppercut made him loosen his grip and fall dizzily to the ground. Before he could even fall however, the pavement came up and slapped him hard on the side of his head. He was dazed.

Mar climbed on top of him and punched him in his face repeatedly, beating his face bloody. By this time, a small crowd of spectators had formed around the two of them and were oohing and aahing as he punched and punched at Chauncy's face and head. Mar looked up long enough to see the crowd and that's when he realized what he was doing. He hated for outsiders to see he and Chauncy in an argument, let alone going fist-to- cuffs. It showed a weakness in their bond. Mar climbed off Chauncy, dusted off the knees of his jeans, and began to walk away again.

Chauncey stood up slowly, holding his sore head in an attempt to suppress the agonizing migraine headache that Mar's fist had caused him.

His face was swelling badly and had three long streams of blood running from a bad cut over his left eye. Through his right eye - the one that hadn't been swollen shut - he stared at the smiling faces that surrounded him. He hadn't experienced embarrassment like this in a long time. He saw girls with teasing smiles, an older woman shaking her head in disgust as the little boy she held under her arm laughed and pointed at him.

By this time, Mar had turned around and was walking back to Chauncy to make sure he was alright. He wanted them to walk away together to show everybody that had witnessed the fight that they were still friends but Chauncy's anger, embarrassment, and confusion led him to pull out his nickel-plated Heckler & Koch 9 millimeter. Something inside of him was coercing him to keep it pointed at Mar's face.

"I'll murder you." This thing inside of him had forced him to say. He clenched his teeth as he made the threat with tears of confusion pouring down his face. It's hard to explain the mindset of a man who can no longer take the internal pressure and this pressure burst his pipes. Chauncy had so much stress built up in him which he had failed to properly vent and now it was coming out uncontrollably and in unpredictable ways. The day before he had beaten his mom unconscious for stealing five-hundred dollars from him and now he had a gun pointed at his best friend.

"If you gon do it, do it!" Mar gritted through his angrily clenched teeth. Chauncy, coming to his senses, lowered his gun and cried.

"I'm sorry Mar, I swear to God man, pain… I got pain in me Mar…I love you man, I wouldn't never try to hurt you…you my brother G…"

Mar walked towards Chauncy who was still holding the gun at his side, though now his hand was shaking. Mar took one more step towards Chauncy and the gun went off.

After giving thanks to fate for not being shot, Mar stopped checking his clothes for bloody holes and began to ponder a thought. There again was that loud ominous blast that over the years Mar had grown accustomed to hearing. In addition, there again was the prospect of dealing with the death that usually followed that stentorian eruption. Chauncy's body jerked forward, his forehead seemed to split open directly in the center and pink pieces of brain tissue and red blood flew onto Mar's face and shirt. Another shot followed echoing throughout the projects.

Mar ducked, knowing the second shot had been aimed at him. When the shooting ceased the paranoid screams and cries of women and children was all Mar heard. He looked up and saw the gunman who was trying to un-jam his gun. It was Killa and Mar could tell he wanted both of them dead. Luckily, Killa got frustrated with the jammed murder weapon and time was of the essence. He tossed the gun and ran off. Mar crawled to Chauncy's side as tears gushed from his eyes uncontrollably.

"Stop standin there, do somethin!" Mar snapped at the few people that had remained at the scene.

"Do somethin…" His command had now become a plea as his own feelings of helplessness kicked in.

Mar glanced up at the darkening sky, with its quickly moving gray clouds and dark blue tint. The downpour that always seemed to follow death was fast approaching.

A faint *"why?"* escaped his lips before he dropped his head and stared at his dead friend. Raindrops began to pour on their heads and wash away the blood. After making a promise to murder Killa that the law would prevent him from keeping, Mar waited silently for EMS to come and take Chauncy's lifeless body to the Brookdale Hospital Center.

Mar, who had stayed at the scene until the paramedics arrived, was taken to the 73rd precinct on East New York Ave. and questioned by Homicide detectives. He would never give them as much as a lead. The Detectives badgered him about the fight they had just had prior to Chauncy being murdered, hoping to scare him with the prospect of him being a suspect. Mar never scared easy however. He stuck to his story. He and Chauncy had fought but they had squashed it immediately afterwards. Chauncy was shot but he didn't see the shooter or even from which direction the shots were fired. Mar refused to turn state.

Mar left the precinct after the detectives realized they wouldn't get anything useful out of him. Before going home, he stopped at Chauncy's apartment to tell Nadine what happened but she wasn't there - she never was. Mar took the subway to the Bronx and walked slowly to his building in Patterson Projects. A gray cloud of melancholy hovered low above his head and followed him into his apartment where his somberness really kicked in.

As soon as he walked in the door, Josephine gasped.

"Oh my god baby…what happened…Are you okay?" She asked hysterically, checking Mar's body for wounds or any sign that the blood that covered his jeans and shirt was his. She was praying it wasn't.

"Nothin." Mar said, staring at the floor. Josephine could see something was wrong and when Mar lifted his head back up his eyes were brimming with tears. She hugged her son close to her.

"Marquise, please tell me what happened." Josephine pleaded, wanting badly to know what was bothering her son and if there was any way she could help. Mar looked in his mother's eyes. He could see she was worried.

"I just need to be by myself for a minute mom, I'll tell you later." "Well at least tell me you're not hurt, you're covered in blood Marquise."

"I know, I'm cool, it's not mine."

"Well who's is it? Why won't you talk to me?"

The truth was, he was traumatized. He had just watched his best friend get his brains blown out; he could barely speak, let alone tell her the whole story. Mar just walked off leaving behind him a confused and concerned mother. Nevertheless, Josephine understood, she knew firsthand how your mind reacts to trauma. He wasn't in any pain physically so she would just back off and allow him to heal mentally.

It was a killjoy considering Josephine wanted so badly to tell Mar about the job she had just gotten as a server in a diner nearby. It was small but it was progress; a step in the right direction. She figured he would be so proud of her but decided it could wait while he recovered. Sean on the other hand wasn't as thoughtful. He followed Mar into his bedroom and proceeded to talk his ear off.

"So wussup…what was V.A. like?" "It was right, but listen…"

"You know mom got somethin to tell you…" Sean said cutting
back in.

"I would tell you but she'll be mad so I'ma just let her tell you, you
know how she get…"

"Hold on Sean, listen, I'ma holla at chu later, I need some time to myself." Mar said, placing his hands on Sean's shoulders. It was just then that Sean noticed all the blood on Marquise.

"What happened?" He asked, now very concerned with his brother's health and well-being.

"Nothin, I'ma holla at chu in a minute, let me get some rest right?" "Ight." Sean said.

He was disappointed but also understood nowwhy Mar was asking to be left alone. Still, he walked away with his shoulders slumped.

Mar shut the door behind his brother feeling bad that he had brushed him off like that. Sean would get over it though Mar told himself as he kicked off his sneakers and flopped back on his bed. He laced his fingers behind his head and stared blankly at the ceiling above him. His thoughts were scrambled and in the midst of trying to collect them, he dozed off. In a matter of minutes, he quickly jumped up out of his sleep, sweating profusely as a loud gun blast sounded and Chauncy's body spun around and his head flew into Mar's lap. Mar looked at the head terrified and dropped the bloody head of his comrade like a hot potato. Breathing hard, Mar sat up in his bed and tried to shake off the nightmare. He told himself it was just a dream but in reality, it wasn't just a dream. Besides the dramatization, that had been Chauncy's fate no more than two and a half hours ago.
Mar glanced over at his alarm clock.

"Damn!"

The clock said "7:45 pm" and he had to meet Larnell at eight o'clock. Mar ran to the bathroom, washed up as quickly as possible, threw on some fresh clothes and walked towards the door quickly. Josephine stopped him in his tracks.

"Hey baby, where you on ya way to? I thought you said we would talk."

"I know, I know but I'm in a rush right now ma, I gotta take care of some business real quick."

Immediately Josephine began to think the worst. Her first thought was that Mar was off to find Chauncy's killer. Mar could sense that and didn't want to completely brush her off.

"Wussup though, you got some news for me?" Josephine smiled.

"Well, I gave a lot of thought to what we discussed and I just wanted to let you know I did find a job." Josephine was beaming with pride.

"That's real good mom, I'm proud of you, just don't lose focus." Mar said hurriedly. He hated the fact that he couldn't be as happy for her as he wanted to; he had a lot going on right now. So that she wouldn't feel bad, he decided to tell her what was bothering him and where all the blood came from.

"Don't think I aint happy for you cause of how I'm acting cause you gotta know that I am, it's just..." Mar paused for a brief second.

"It's just what?" Josephine pried.

"Chauncy got killed today, right in front of me."

"What?" Josephine asked surprised.

"We fought and…somebody came up and shot him in his head," "And that's where all the blood came from? Oh baby, are you okay?" Josephine asked concerned.

"Yeah, I'm good, they aint hit me…but, Chauncy, he dead…"

Josephine didn't mean to panic but she could remember practically raising Chauncy.

"When did this happen? Do you know who did it? Why?" Josephine sent a flurry of questions that came too fast for Mar to answer.

"Look, I gotta go mom, but I promise you we'll finish this conversation as soon as I get back."

"Quise, please don't get in no trouble."

Josephine pleaded with deep concern. Once the door closed behind Mar, she began thinking about how James had also left the house with a vendetta and had never come back.
Sean ran out into the hallway and began begging Mar to let him come with him.

"I gotta handle something right now but I'll be back in a couple minutes, you got my word." Mar could see the disappointment in Sean's face so before he walked away he said.

"I'ma bring you back a lil something too." Sean was a sucker for a gift.

"Ight." Sean said it as if he felt better but inside he was still frustrated. Lately it was hard for him and Josephine to maintain Mar's attention for any extended period of time. The streets occupied the majority of his time now.

Outside, Mar waved down a taxi and told the driver to get him to Fulton and Franklin. On the way over Mar thought about how he used to feel when James would be gone for days and weeks at a time, he didn't want to inflict that type of pain on Sean and Josephine. He promised himself he would dedicate some time to them knowing that once Larnell stepped aside he would have even less time with them.

Larnell seemed to be disturbed by what happened to Chauncy but not at all surprised. Mar gave him the money he owed him and also what Chauncy owed him. It was a long-term investment in his eyes. He knew it would make Larnell happy, and if Larnell was happy, he would be happy.

"I heard about what happened to ya man…shit was deep. I hope you learn from it though. Cause I don't mean no disrespect but shorty brought that on his self. I mean, you aint blind, you could see he had it comin, he was reckless."

Mar didn't take what Larnell was saying as disrespect, it was the truth, he was just reiterating what Mar had already told himself.

"Remember this Mar, experience breeds wisdom. I don't really know his family, so I don't know whats being done about his burial but I'll put up some bread."

"I was gon take care of it." Mar said somberly.

"Well hit me when you figure out all the cost and I'll help you out."

"Good lookin L." Mar said.

"It's nuffin. Anyway, you been thinkin bout what we talked about?"

"All day, Every day." Mar said trying to sound upbeat but unable to disguise his somberness.

"Good, cause I already took care of everything for you. All the cats I introduced you to in Norfolk know you and they know the deal. As soon as I left, I told em they would be seein you for now on. Everybody you dealin wit for now on is thorough. Plus you know where the fam be."

Larnell passed Mar a business card.

"This is my lawyer. He a real cutthroat. If he can't beat it, it can't be beat! If you ever get in some shit, he'll take real good care of you. Just tell him I recommended him to you. Now look on the back."

Mar flipped the card. The name and number on the back was in Larnell's handwriting.

"This my financial advisor. He help me wash that money. The last thing you need is to get caught up for money laundering. He know taxes, he know corporate law, and he know investing. Don't call him till you ready though, he about his money the same way you is. Other than that, if you ever need anything, I mean anything at all, come see me, and if I aint got it I'll point you in the right direction. I 'm bout to buy a boat and start fishin youngin, straight up. I 'm tryna see my daughters get bigger, grow a lil gut and watch sitcoms wit my wiz."

Larnell and Mar both laughed. The irony was, they both knew Larnell was dead serious. He had the look in his eyes of a man that had made up his mind a long time ago.

"We sold all the casinos…all businesses having to do with gambling." Larnell said in an unfamiliar voice. Mar had no idea what he was talking about or why he was talking in that odd voice.

"The Corleone family, partners with the pope…"

Mar still looked confused.

"They may cry blasphemy." Mar had told Larnell he was a movie connoisseur so Larnell was testing him.

"Godfather three." Mar said finally catching on.

"That's my favorite part. I always wanted to be able to say that, I have no interests or investments in anything illegitimate…"

Mar couldn't help but to feel exalted at the moment. It was almost like a crowing ceremony. He could feel power coursing through his veins like smack. He had connected with the right man and now all of his hard work was about to pay off. He was about to receive his gratuity for all of the late nights stuffing crack in the palms of pregnant women, early mornings eluding the long arm of the law, and small-time hustling. He was about to be the man with the weight. How blind he was to the weight that, that weight carried.

"Stick to the plan baby boy, stick to the plan, this shit aint about you it's about your family, the moment you forget that is the moment you'll fall."

Mar just nodded his head almost missing the most important thing Larnell had said the entire time. Thoughts of luxury cars, party girls, jewelry and extravagant clothes circled in his mind briefly but were quickly eclipsed by thoughts of what he considered real importance; starting some businesses so he could employ family and friends like Larnell had done in Richmond, buying some land and real estate like his father had started to do in Akron, securing college tuition for the kids that would come after him like his mother always advocated.

Larnell and Mar did a lot of talking and mainly strategizing those two hours they spent with each other. Larnell was sure Mar had his own plans for how he would go about getting paid but he hoped he wouldn't deviate too much from his own blueprint. He was living proof that it could work if observed properly. Larnell had made over a million dollars his way and he was more than sure that somebody of Mar's potential could do the same.

Larnell gave Mar as much game as possible before the two parted ways that night. He gave Mar his word that he would keep in touch and told Mar to hook up with Samone and come see him in exactly two weeks. He was going to give Mar 10 kilos on consignment when he arrived in Virginia. That would end Larnell's long career in the drug game. He would finally be able to relax, and disappear like one of his idols and first employers, Frank "Black Caesar" Matthews had done.

That night Mar brought Sean a present home as promised. On his way home he stopped at Chauncy's and bought everything Chauncy owned from Nadine for three-hundred dollars. She was more than willing to sell Chauncy's belongings. His room was already cluttered with crack addicts. Mar felt a slight guilt as he walked away from Nadine for the last time, knowing his money would add to her party. Her son was dead and she was having a crack party. She would be found dead the very next day from heart complications.

Mar gave the Nintendo and all of its games to Sean who was
ecstatic.

"See, I told you I would hook you up, don't I always keep my word?" Mar said smiling at his little brother. It felt good to make him happy after almost two years of depression and uncertainty.

12

The day of Chauncy's wake the sun shined brilliantly; it's radiance second only to the overwhelming atmosphere of distress and mourning that hovered like a black fog above the cemetery where Chauncy's body was being laid to rest. Mar was expecting more people to show up at the funeral but he was satisfied with the turn out. With Larnell's help he made sure his friend was buried with honor and not just tossed into some undignified pauper's grave. If he didn't make this funeral happen nobody would have. Mar almost had to beg Chauncy's family to come; reminding them that although he had made a lot of mistakes in his short life, he was still family.

More friends than family showed up. Nafee and Brandon - whom Mar hadn't seen in almost three years - came out to show their respect, along with Chauncy's squad from Brownsville and a couple of the people they had gone to school with. Josephine and Sean came out as well to show Mar support. There was no more than a fistful of Chauncy's blood relatives. They were the few that still showed interest in him and hadn't already written him off as a lost cause. Still, getting them to show up was hard and getting them to put up some money for Chauncy's interment was even harder.

In life Chauncy had burned a lot of bridges, and even though he had set flame to the one that connected he and Marquise, their foundation was just too strong for Mar to ever abandon his comrade, even in death. Mar's love for Chauncy was incorruptible because he understood him. Mar understood that growing up without a mother or father had really affected Chauncy mentally. He had lived his life like a dry leaf in the middle of autumn being blown every which way by every passing wind.

While staring down at his deceased friend - a blank expression on his lifeless face - Mar reasoned that maybe Chauncy was better off this way. Through the waxen face shone an ambiance of peace.

Mar paid his last respects, dropped a rose on Chauncy's chest and stepped to the side. As he walked back to his seat a voice of velvet floated into his ears like the sonance of a finely tuned mandolin. The lovely sound came from behind him as he watched Nafee and Brandon step up to the casket to pay homage.

"Hey Quise, how you been?" The sensual voice asked in an all too familiar tone. Mar turned around to see an angelic face that perfectly matched the angelic voice.

Lexi had grown up a lot. Her seventeen-year-old frame looked twenty-five in development. She stood like a horse now, still petite but perfectly curved. Her chest had grown into nice C cup breast and her honey bronze skin was glistening in the sun as her M.A.C. lip-gloss made her full lips look moist and too inviting.

"Damn, you lookin real good Lexi." Mar said with his eyes still climbing her five foot four frame, only to reach her face in time to see the cute dimples her smile produced.

"You aint lookin too bad ya'self honey." Lexi said. She had already analyzed Mar's tailored suit and the leather hard bottoms that matched it; the precisely chiseled Caesar hair cut; the Movado timepiece and of course his face. He was still as cute as she remembered but a little more mature. Handsome better described him now.

"Chauncy told me you was back in the city, why didn't you come see me Quise?"

Lexi crossed her arms in front of her. Her face reflected disappointment though her heart was overflowing with joy. She had waited eagerly for this day to come. The day when Marquise would come back and make good on his word. She could remember childishly blowing kisses into the wind and praying that somehow that same wind would find Marquise and caress the skin of his beautiful face.

"My word on everything I had plans to, I just been so busy these last couple months I really aint have the time. I had to take care of some shit for my family, then this…plus, I had to get my shit in order before I approached you. You know I couldn't approach you half-assed."

"I don't see why not, money never mattered to us before." Mar stared at his princess.

"And I already know it never will."

Lexi and Mar continued to converse for a while, catching each other up on what was going on with the other in their time apart. They came to the conclusion that through all the years and all their personal perils, the love never died.

After the funeral, Josephine and Sean left in the Lexus Mar had bought Josephine for her birthday. Nafee, Brandon, and Mar talked about old times and promised to stay in touch with each other, then Mar and Lexi took off in Mar's brand new 190 Mercedes Benz.

"Damn Quise, you doin it real big." Lexi said as she examined the inside of Mar's new car.

"So I guess you hustling now." It was more of an accusation than a question.

"I got a idea." Mar said, ignoring Lexi's last comment.

"Let's skip all the small talk and get to what's really important. Is you wit somebody right now?"

"No…not really."

"What do 'not really' mean? Either you dealin wit somebody or you aint, it's that simple." Mar said.

"It's not that simple." Lexi said defensively.

"I'm sayin, you was gone for a while. I wasn't even sure if I was ever going to see you again."

"So what are you sayin Lexi?"

"I have a friend, nothing serious."

"Well I'm back now, is you ridin wit me or do he mean that much to you?" Mar asked. There was no hesitation in Lexi's response when she said,

"You know I'm ridin with you." She wasn't about to turn down Mar's offer. He went on to talk about moving her into a big house in Jersey not far from the one he was about to buy for his mom. He talked about kids eventually, businesses, and a life filled with luxury for her where all she had to do was be loyal to him.

That night they stayed in the Trump Tower in Manhattan and reacquainted themselves intimately. The scratches on Mar's back were reminders of how good the sex was. Mar drank Hennessey while Lexi made mimosas out the orange juice and champagne Mar bought her. They talked about everything from Mar's past troubles to his future plans. He let Lexi know that he wanted her to be a part of everything he did and every decision he made. All Lexi could do was hope that he wasn't selling her a dream like most men she knew.

13

Mar met Samone at her condo in Queens. The plush pad was an eleven hundred square foot condominium in a six-story building in Astoria.

"I got a job for you love." Mar said once inside of Samone's posh condo. The condominium was indeed nice; floor to ceiling windows with breathtaking views, two bedrooms, two full bathrooms - each with Jacuzzis - an up-to-date kitchen with a dishwasher, and a balcony. Samone was right; she was doing well for herself moving work for Larnell. He knew he would have to be just as lucrative to keep Samone happy. She was all ears now however, wondering what Mar needed her for.

"What you need me to do baby?" She asked, a flirty smile on her face.

"Well it's official now, I need you to…what you smilin for?" Mar asked, interrupted by the seductive smile and look in Samone's eyes. She hadn't seen Mar since the hotel in Richmond and seeing his face was bringing back a lot of memories. She really liked Mar.

"Huh? Oh nuttin, go head, I'm listenin." Mar continued.

"Like I was sayin, I need you to take this trip down to V.A. wit
me."

Mar sat back comfortably on Samone's forest green leather sofa with the glass of water she had offered him in hand. He was still wondering what was up with Samone, little did he know the look was lust; she wanted him inside of her as soon as he stepped through the door.

"I can do that." Samone said.

"As long as you keep your end of the deal."

"Oh don't sweat that, I'ma pay you upfront." Mar said reaching into his pocket. He pulled out a thick wad of cash wrapped in a red rubber band. He tossed it to Samone. She caught it, studied it, nodded approvingly, then sat it down on the coffee table.

"That's coo', but that aint what I was talkin bout." Samone said mischievously.
Again, Mar wore a look of confusion. He didn't realize he had any obligations to Samone outside of paying her a handsome tip for her services.

"What chu talkin bout?" Mar asked, honestly unaware of what Samone was hinting at.

"Let's see if this refresh ya memory." Samone said pulling off her panties from beneath her T-shirt. Mar's manhood stood up after watching her nipples harden and realizing that she was completely naked beneath her tee. He now remembered clearly what he had told Samone.

He had said; *"So I can call you when I need you?"*

And she had said; *"Yup, as long as I can get some of this dick on the side."*

"Damn Samone, I got a girl now."

"Listen baby boy," Samone said interrupting Mar. She placed her finger on his lips to quiet him.

"I understand all that and trust me, I feel bad for home girl cause if you givin it to her like you gave it to me, she probably deep in love, but uhh, I got a lil somethin up in me that I need you to get out for me, and no, it can't wait." She straddled Mar's hand and placed it on her spot, it was hot, wet, and throbbing…

Mar got the first orgasm out of Samone in twenty minutes but her sex drive was insatiable. He ended up spending another hour and a half in her cozy bed making her climax three more times. She slept for an hour afterwards. Mar stared at her body the entire time. Samone was like a drug, the euphoria she brought about was pure bliss but too much more of her and he knew he would be hooked for life. He had Lexi now and that's who he wanted to be with. This had to be the last time with Samone. He stared at her breast as she rolled over.

"Damn..." Mar thought staring at her mahogany areoles.

"I saw you watchin me." Samone said. She didn't tell him she could practically read his thoughts.

"Don't worry, I don't want to break up a happy home." "But it's good to know I could." She added.

Samone and Mar got dressed then got on the road. Mar had already let Josephine and Sean know he would be gone for a while but that he would constantly check in with them to make sure everything was everything. He told a broken-hearted Lexi the same thing. She hated it considering they had just gotten back together but Mar had already warned her that very soon he would be taking a trip and that he would be gone for a

few weeks, so, she dealt with it. She loved Mar, so she was willing to accept whatever came with him - even if it did hurt like hell.

Marquise and Larnell made sure the ten bricks were secure between the inner tubes and rims on the tires of the rental Samone would be driving up to Pennsylvania, where Larnell had a buyer set up for Mar already. Larnell was making sure Mar had no problems knocking off the first ten ki's. This would be the first of many big sales. This one was to one of Larnell's cousin who was hustling in Scranton, PA. It was for $180,000. Mar had to control his excitement once more when he accepted that amount of money from Larnell's cousin.

After meeting Larnell's connect and spending $120,000 on twenty- two pounds of coke, Mar was in business. He could've set up shop in New York but had learned a valuable lesson from Larnell.

"Don't shit where you eat or pitch where you sleep."

So, Mar spent most of his time between Scranton, PA dealing with Larnell's cousin and his crew and Norfolk, VA supplying Larnell's Young Terrace squad and the other dealers in that city he supplied. He took a few highway trips and mapped out a few cities and small towns in his route up and down the east coast where the price of powder was double, triple, and in some places, quadruple the price it was in New York.

In only a few months after the initial ten bricks Larnell fronted him Mar was out of town now working with twenty kilos. He supplied his people in Scranton and Philly who supplied dealers in Wilkes-Barre, Easton, Harrisburg, York, and Lancaster, PA. His people from Virginia took care of their people in DC and

Maryland. In New York, the Supreme Team & Fat Cat were flooding the Southside of Jamaica Queens with crack. Howard "Pappy" Mason was protecting Lorenzo "Fat Cat" Nichols' investments and murdering his competition. Rich Porter, Azie Faison, and Alberto "Alpo" Martinez were donning furs, sequin jackets, and sheepskins uptown, driving cars two years before they come out. Rayful Edmond was conducting deals between local D.C. kingpins and his Colombian connects from Lewisburg Federal penitentiary. And in California, Freeway Ricky Ross and Oscar Danilo Blandon were supplying the Bloods and Crips in L.A.

By the time Mar was nineteen he was putting away at least fifty- thousand dollars a month. The only other guy he knew about his age doing the numbers he was doing was Boy George, who at 21 had already put together a multi-million-dollar heroin ring. Mar figured in a year and a half he would have close to the million he was chasing. His quota was to make a million then quit but as his income and bills grew so did his quota. He was slowly starting to get in too deep.

Mar's Cuban connect from Little Havana in Miami - a young Cuban immigrant who had survived his fair share of drug wars with rival Haitian cartels from neighboring Little Haiti - had some of the purest coke to reach Florida. Larnell said he met the guy's cousin while in prison - a runner who used to ship drugs to South Carolina. He got caught in Virginia and was Larnell's tier neighbor in prison. His Cuban connection was thanks to circumstance and timing.

Mar left his product as is. He didn't apply cut because he wasn't greedy. He would rather get rid of the raw quick than stretch his work and have to work harder to off some mediocre product just to make a bigger profit off each kilo.

More important than his product was his tact when it came to his meteoric rise however. For Marquise, an 848 would most certainly mean kingpin and R.I.C.O - something he could ill-afford. So, he was meticulous, he rarely got high any more, and he was focused because he had a plan. He was outsmarting people that got paid to think.

Mar felt none of his success would have been possible without Larnell so no matter how much Mar made, he wired Larnell five grand the first of every month. A luxury tax Larnell had earned for his integrity.

In a year and a half, Mar moved his family to Jersey like he had promised them he would. He bought two houses in a small, quaint, picturesque, suburban town called Avenal three miles outside of Linden, New Jersey. He felt the area was perfect for the isolation and quietness he was seeking. One of the homes he bought was for

Josephine. The house was big and it cost him one-hundred and fifty-thousand dollars. The other house was for he and Lexi and set him back two-hundred and fifty- thousand. Both Lexi and Josephine were extremely happy.

Mar hustled harder to make back what he had spent on the houses and new cars he bought and, in a year, he was up again. Wisely, after a phone conversation with Larnell, Mar consulted John Rutherford - Larnell's financial advisor. John helped Mar open three separate businesses. One was a soul food restaurant in Linden that he had actually opened for Josephine who, beyond all her other talents - was a great cook. She also managed the second of Mar's businesses; a small nightclub downtown. The nightclub gave him the opportunity to network with some of the biggest stars at that time - Johnny Gill, Whitney Houston, Wreckx-n-effect, Naughty by Nature. A host of other musicians and entertainers appeared at his club. Mar felt like heavyweight Champion Jack Jackson, owner of what would become the Cotton Club, getting Duke Ellington, Cab Calloway, Ella Fitzgerald, or Billie Holiday to perform at his establishment.

The third business Mar started was shop he bought for Lexi. They would have to hire a manager with at least three years of experience as a cosmetologist until she completed her schooling. It was a gift for his lady. He did the same thing for the adjoining barbershop that would be run by Sean once he was old enough. Mar collected his percentage off of the annual revenue of each business and besides helping with the barbershop, stayed out of the way to allow Josephine and Lexi to run the businesses as they saw fit. They were both creative enough and seemed to have management mastered. He liked the fact that they were becoming independent. It insured that if he were ever taken away, they would be able to survive without him.

"Now both of you should look into getting a solid education so you can increase your lifetime incomes." John told Lexi and Mar a few months after their businesses were up and running.

"Find something you'll be interested in and go back to school. Nursing, real estate, business management, computer engineering… anything."

"You two seem like you're going to be together for a long time. Get married! And once you get married, stay married! You two live in a neighborhood with other millionaires but you may never know it. You know why, because they could live next door to a person with half of their wealth and not care to show their success. Most of them were married once and are still married. They're compulsive savers and investors always living below their means. And like you most are first generation rich and made their money themselves. So stay away from flamboyance and try not to outshine your neighbors. You're clean now…live and act like it. Like I said, you two get married and stay married. Live below your income. Use credit to your advantage, and to get you started with your investing we'll start you with a few index funds. We'll stay away from individual stocks until you become more familiar with Wall Street."

Mar was twenty-two now but was always mistaken to be older; an easy mistake considering how mature and responsible he was. He carried himself like a man and for that reason; he received a lot of admiration from a lot of people. This admiration was even stronger in Sean.

Sean was getting older now also, and with age came a better understanding of exactly what Mar was into. Mar was like Sean's father now and Sean wanted to emulate him just as badly as Mar had wanted to emulate James. He constantly asked Mar to put him on his feet, to let him work for him and make a little bit of his own money now. The incessantness of this type of questioning nagged Mar who always responded the same way.

"You is on ya feet, and as long as I got money you gon stay on ya
feet."

"You know what I'm talkin about Mar. I'm a man now, I wanna make my own money. What you gon do, take care of me my whole life? I gotta grow up some time, put me in the game."

"So sellin crack makes you grown? You sound just like the rest of these cats…wanna get in the game just to be in it. Listen, this shit aint all glitz and glamour Sean. Dudes is dyin left and right in this game. It's hustlas in the feds wit football numbers on they back. These judges is givin out Star Wars dates…two thousand, thirty-five and shit like that. I aint about to watch my lil brotha get murdered or be sittin in da bing till he old and gray at my cost. Ya blood won't be on my hands. The only game I'm a put you in is basketball at some college somewhere."

Sean hated when Mar treated him like he was still a naïve little kid. He was seventeen now and, in his eyes, old enough to make his own decisions. Besides, Mar started when he was only sixteen, so Sean couldn't see what the problem was. It was hypocritical to him. He knew Mar was just trying to look out for him, but to Sean, being his own man was most important. He was tired of being taken care of.

Sean sometimes dreamed of playing college ball and maybe even going pro. He had a passion for basketball and at seventeen was already taller than Mar at six foot two and a half, and still growing. He had a nice ball game, nice enough to draw scouts from all around the nation to watch him play. He had visions of the NBA but Mar's success in the streets was making it hard for Sean to decide which future looked the most promising. He wanted success now. Crack sells were guaranteed money, the NBA was a dream that was seldom reached by the millions of pro ball hopefuls. He had heard about people getting caught and sentenced to a lot of time in prison or people getting murdered but Mar had managed to avoid both death and incarceration. Sean strongly felt he could do the same.

Sean started off small with a few of his friends from his high school - all of which were naïve street dreamers obsessed with the potential perks of the drug game but blind to the imminent downfalls. Like most youngsters fascinated by the glamorous side of the game, Sean's crew was either ignoring or had no cognizance of the potential consequences. Mar quickly stopped them from throwing their futures away once he caught wind to what Sean was getting himself into. Sean put up an argument, defending his foolish pride, which turned into a scuffle between the he and Mar.

Eventually Sean and Marquise patched things up and had a long talk that appeared to set Sean straight. He promised to focus on school and basketball more, but like most people who get a taste of fast money - he was hungry for more. He did start paying more attention to school and basketball but he just couldn't stop doing his thing on the side. He wanted to prove to himself that he could balance both worlds without Mar ever knowing.

14

Sean was getting work from Gutter - a local hustler in Linden who was quickly making a name for himself. Mar was aware of Sean's dealings with Gutter but was too occupied to entertain it.. He would let Sean learn the hard way. Sean took full advantage of that freedom.

Gutter had money but not like Mar. Though Gutter was two years older than Mar, he had been away for the last three years serving a sentence in Rahway. Gutter didn't limit his trade to drug-dealing however. He also specialized in armed robbery, kidnapping, and murder. You name it and he claimed it. When he found out that Sean was Mar's brother, he realized his young worker was much more than a pawn…he was a goldmine. Sean was a walking ransom and this was just the opportunity Gutter needed to put himself on top.

15

Sean awoke to dense, terrifying darkness. His nose twitched and cringed at the stench he inhaled. It didn't take him long to figure out that the foul odor was the scent of a moist basement. He could hear the thermostat and water coursing through the pipes above his head like blood through veins. Still dizzy and discombobulated he started to remember how he got here. He saw Rock through the reflection in Gutter's eyes but it had been too late. By that time, Gutter's husky cousin was slamming a chrome Desert Eagle against his temple.

Sean tried to stand up and realized he was tied tightly to a metal chair. His heart began to beat rapidly and a claustrophobia he never knew he had begun to kick in as he struggled to loosen his tightly bound arms. His heavy breathing slowly evolved into hyperventilation. He had never imagined, let alone experienced this type of fear. It was a fear he was perceiving with all of his five senses. He could smell his apprehension permeating the entire basement. He could see his fright like heat vapors in the dim light coming from the bottom of the cellar door. He could hear his anxiety pounding like a drum, echoing non-stop from wall to wall and floor to ceiling. He could feel his terror turning into goose bumps up and down his arm. He could taste his horror in his rapidly dissolving saliva.

Sean was too afraid to scream or even move. His heart was beating so hard it felt like it would explode in his chest at any moment. He could only try to catch his quickly fleeting breath.

16

"Lexi, you ready to go yet?" Mar called out from the living room. Lexi was still in the bedroom double-checking her bags to make sure they weren't forgetting anything. Mar had made plans to spend some time away with Lexi in the West Indies.

"Almost baby, give me one second." Lexi said as she tucked her favorite Gucci bra and panties set into her Louis Vuitton suitcase. After five more minutes, Mar got impatient.

"Come on Lexi, you know I hate rushin, our plane leave in a half hour and I don't feel like sprintin through no airport."

"OK, OK, here I come right now." Lexi said rushing out of the bedroom with her suitcase in her right hand while adjusting her Chanel sunglasses with her left.

"It's about time." Mar said holding the door open for Lexi. "Whatever" Lexi replied before kissing Mar's cheek and walking

out to the cab. They threw their luggage in the trunk and headed to the airport. By the time they got there, Lexi's nerves were getting the best of her.

"You aint scared?" She asked in the terminal, then once again as they made their way to their seats in the first-class section of the plane.

"Nah, not really. You?" "Maybe." Lexi admitted.

"Don't worry, it aint that bad baby. I promise. You might like it."

Mar was right. As soon as the plane took off and got over the pocket of air that caused a little bit of startling turbulence and scared her half to death, Lexi couldn't stop commenting on how beautiful the sky and the view from above the clouds was. It was so amazing to her that she made Mar switch her seats so she could sit by the window. That was the thing Lexi loved about Mar the most, he was always introducing her to new things.

"I feel like a bird." She said, not caring how corny she may have sounded. Mar just laughed at her.

"Look how small everything looks." Lexi said full of surprise. She had never been outside of Brooklyn besides the move to New Jersey. When she thought about this fact a tear of joy slid down her face. Mar missed it, by this time he was asleep. The tears fell not only because of the beauty of what she was seeing, but because of the love Mar had for her. He had done so many wonderful things for her without ever asking for anything in return besides her fidelity. She asked him why he did so much for her and he had said, 'What good is havin all this paper and nobody to share it with…not only that…I love you…it aint that complicated…love is what it does…"

Mar told Lexi that not only did he love her but he had a fear of dying alone, and that she was the only female he trusted because she was with him when there was no money. He wanted her to be in his life until death. She felt like she owed him so much more than she would ever be able to repay.

As soon as their plane landed in Montego Bay, Jamaica and their feet touched the rich soil, they were bombarded by Jamaican men and tourist alike, all claiming to have the best weed on the island. One who stood close to six feet four and looked to weigh almost two hundred and fifty pounds forced his way to the front of the pack of merchants thirsty for American money.

"Respect dere lion, da I gwan to dee 'otel?" He asked in his thick Jamaican accent.

"Yeah dred, we gon hit da hotel for a minute before we come out and enjoy the sights. But what you got for me?"

"Well…" The man said, bending down to whisper.

"…me know da I gwan need big bumbaclot spliff to ease da jetlag, yes I?"

"True indeed. Let me see what you got?"

The man pulled a multi-colored bud from his bag and handed it to Mar. The weed needed little examination. Mar bought an ounce and walked towards one of the many cabs. Mar could hear the man saying, *"Jah Bless"* in the background as he and Lexi climbed into the cab and headed for their bungalow.

"You could understand what that man was sayin?" Lexi asked as they unpacked their bags in the deluxe beachside bungalow they had reserved.

"No better than you could." Mar said smiling.

"That's not important though. Right now my only concern is getting you in that shower."

Mar grabbed Lexi from behind.

"Behave Quise, damn, you aint even give me time to unpack yet and you already bein nasty." Lexi said playfully.

Lexi and Mar showered and somehow against both of their wills, managed to not have sex; promising each other they would wait until night to make it special. They left the bungalow after changing into attire more suitable for the island and it's extremely hot climate. They were off to see and enjoy the sights and sounds of Montego Bay.

They rode jet skis and after jet skiing, they lounged by a pool. It was funny to Mar, because there were celebrities vacationing at the same time but the attention seemed to be on the Don and his diva. In a crisp yellow Ralph Lauren polo shirt and white trunks, gold rimmed Mosley Tribes sunglasses, and a rose gold Patek Phillipe, Mar pulled his chair out of the sun and drank the spritzer Lexi had ordered for him. Lexi was wearing the gift Mar had just gotten her - a metallic-green Vera Wang bikini and Pedro Garcia sandals. She looked back at Mar and blew him a kiss then turned and dived in the pool.

Mar didn't appreciate the attention, especially from the Hispanic man that sat across from them at the opposite end of the pool. Mar stared at the familiar face but couldn't put a name to the face. The older Hispanic man seemed to be struggling with the same unfortunate amnesia. Just as Mar was going to approach the man and ask him why he was staring, Lexi climbed out of the pool with the same alluring grace as a dream girl emerging from the tranquilizing fogs of a resting mind. Like some sort of angel, a glow surrounded Lexi while thousands of liquid crystals glistened on her bronze skin and added to her hypnotic appeal. Mar completely forgot about the man. Lexi wiped her eyes then sat down beside Mar and ordered margaritas.

Later that evening they enjoyed a walk along the beach, discussing the beauties of life outside of the crime infested cement jungle they had grown up in and the beauties they had been depriving themselves of by not vacationing more often. Caught up in the moment, they promised to start taking trips more often.

"I just think the world's too big to stay cooped up in some crowded city, or even at home in Jersey, I'm tryna see the world baby." Mar said. He could see that Lexi felt exactly the same.

"I really needed this time right here, not only to clear my mind but to get to know you all over again. I been movin so fast and so much lately, I can't even remember the last time we sat down and ate dinner together, and that's bad cause we own a restaurant. All that runnin'll be over soon though, that's my word. After I make these last couple moves I'm done for good. I'm runnin all my bread through the cleaners and we gon settle down and make them babies we been talkin bout…this aint even supposed to be my life…"

Lexi hung on to Mar's every word. They finished the night at an elegant 5-star restaurant that sat right on the beach. After watching the moon light dance on the surface of the Atlantic Ocean they headed back to their bungalow where Mar had a surprise waiting for Lexi.

When Mar opened the door, Lexi's eyes lit up in amazement. The entire bungalow was covered in yellow rose petals - Lexi's favorite color. The beige candles scented the inside with an intoxicating vanilla aroma. A bottle of Dom Perginon was being chilled in a bucket of ice.

Lexi placed her shopping bags on the sofa in the front room of the bungalow while Mar opened the curtains. The blue light of the full moon added an extra glow to the room while the warm Caribbean breeze modified the temperature and caused the candlelight to dance rhythmically on the walls.

"Lexi, will you marry me?" Mar asked, feeling the time and the mood was just right to propose. From his pocket, Mar removed a radiant cut canary yellow diamond engagement ring. He spent $250,000 on the sparkling diamond ring with it's 8 carat stone and platinum band. Lexi looked shocked and was at a lost for words but she did manage a barely audible,

"I love you Marquise…of course I'll be your wife."

Mar gently glided the ring onto Lexi's finger and she held her hand out, palm down, admiring the resplendent rock. She would have stared at it all night if Mar wouldn't have distracted her.

"Now come here, I been waitin all day to get inside you." Lexi hugged Mar's neck tightly then began to undress. Mar was sitting on the edge of the bed watching Lexi closely.

"I want you to dance for me." He said, leaning back on his elbows admiring his queen.

Lexi stripped down to her lingerie slowly, strip-teasing for Mar the best she could. Her body was moving like a snake and Mar was the charmer.

"Take everything off baby, I want you just how you came into the world." Mar said licking his lips, ready to devour Lexi from head to toe. He sat up and rubbed his hands up the inside of her thighs, his fingers sending sensations through her nerves that caused her love to fill with warm moisture and heat and throb in sync with her pulse.

Mar rubbed two fingers across Lexi's spot, it was as soft as satin dipped in warm baby oil. She grabbed his head and let out a long moan as he slid two fingers inside of her. Mar's weeks on the road showed by how tight her walls were. They wrapped around his fingers as tight as rubber bands.

Mar stood up and backed Lexi into the wall. Lifting her right leg on to his shoulder, he dropped to his knees and gave her lower lips a French kiss.

"Quise…I…I love you…ungh…" She whispered between moans. Then, with one hand on Mar's head and the other massaging her own breast, she climaxed. Mar had to support her as her knees buckled from the loss of bodily control; the orgasm was overwhelming. Mar picked his new fiancé up and laid her on the bed where he would go on to bless Lexi with three more orgasms before she fell asleep, completely exhausted.

While Lexi slept, Mar twisted an L with the weed he bought at the airport in one of the expensive, premium cigars he bought while out shopping that afternoon - a Diplomáticos Cuban cigar. After twisting it to perfection, Mar woke Lexi up to ask her something that had been on his mind and could wait no longer to be asked. Ignoring the air of tranquility that surrounded Lexi as she rested, Mar tapped her shoulder. Lexi didn't awaken immediately, only made a noise and rolled over. So Mar rocked her gently.

"Lexi," he whispered.

"Hmmm?" Lexi moaned softly. A smile was forming on her face as recollection of the soul-ascending love making they had just made came to mind. She smiled but prayed Mar wasn't ready for more, she was exhausted.

"You up?" Mar asked, making sure Lexi would hear him.

"Umm-hmm." Lexi breathed; her eyes still closed.

"Would you kill for me?"

The question startled Lexi who prayed this was just a test and not an actual invitation to murder. She was definitely awake now. Lexi was smart enough to know that questions like that didn't just pop up, they usually stemmed from gut feelings. Lexi paused. She knew she had to give thought to her answer. This obviously meant a lot to Marquise or he wouldn't have wakened her. Lexi stared into Mar's eyes.

"For you I would."

In the brief silence that followed Lexi's bold declaration, Lexi wondered where that courage had come from and hoped it would return in the event she was ever put in the position to make good on her statement. Mar finally allowed himself to believe that maybe Lexi did love him as much as he loved her.

"I know you would, now go head back to sleep…I love you baby."

"I love you too."

Lexi was not able to fall back to sleep that night. Her rattled nerves would not allow it. Nor would her need to know why Mar had asked that question. She would think about that all night. A cloud of worry now hung over Lexi's head.

Mar stepped outside and lit the pre-rolled blunt. He stared out at the ocean and reflected on his life thus far and on the future that lie ahead.

The view from above was beautiful and it had him feeling like the king he was.
Though his mother was doing wonderful, his brother was good for the most part and he and his lady were like Humphrey Bogart and Ingrid Bergman in Casablanca, life was still a complex maze. One wrong move and the beast would be

there to swallow him. If he could just continue to choose his steps wisely, he would find the exit.

The things he experienced could've easily broken another person's spirit and will; especially at the young age at which he experienced them. Mar was a fighter however - in and outside the ring - and if it's one positive thing the streets teach you it's how to survive in the roughest predicaments. Mar finished his weed, shook the haunting image of the Hispanic man he had eye-boxed with earlier, turned up his champagne flute and after drowning the sparkling fluid, he called out into the dark, star-lit sky.

"I hope you happy pops, I told you I would take care of everything and I did."

As Mar walked back into the room he smiled because he could hear James saying,"I already knew you would."

17

Back in Linden the mood wasn't as high-spirited as it was for Mar and Lexi in Jamaica. Not only was Josephine extremely terrified because someone had kidnapped her youngest son, but as she lay in the tub she noticed an unusual lump in her breast. She was morbid. Her mother died from cancer and she was petrified by the notion that she would suffer that same slow and agonizing death. Josephine's apprehension was now double as she trembled from her own fear as well as Sean's

"First of all, I don't even believe ya brova in Montego Bay, or wherever da fuck ya mom said he was but I'll tell you this much, you better hope he back in exactly two days or it's a wrap for you lil man, straight up." Gutter tapped Sean on his head with the barrel of his Glock .40.

Sean could barely lift his head to respond. He was famished and extremely fatigued. He hadn't eaten in days. His soggy pants were filled with his own feces and urine. His muscles had become too weak to constrict and stop his bladder and bowels from running.
From the waist up he was dotted in blood - the drops both old and new. The blood was a result

of his smart comments and the threats he had made towards Gutter. Sean assured him that Marquise would kill him as soon as he got back.

"Two Days!" Gutter said before he and Rock walked away, leaving Sean alone in the basement once again. The tears he had restrained for the sake of not giving his kidnappers the benefit of seeing his fear began to pour when he heard the basement door slam shut. Even though he had told Gutter that Mar was going to kill him, right now he wasn't so sure of that. And even if Mar did find out, Sean was starting to think it would be too late when he did. A spasm of fear shot through his heart as he thought about dying in this basement.

Mar and Lexi's plane landed at exactly 11:17am the next morning. Even though the weeklong trip was over they were still excited. They couldn't wait to tell Josephine about the fun they had and show her all the things they bought her in Jamaica but when they got to her house she had the most disturbed look on her face.

"Mom, wus da matter?" Mar asked running to Josephine's side.

"Somebody took Sean." Josephine said, feeling a nervous empty feeling in her stomach every time she repeated this.

"Took Sean, what chu mean they took Sean?"

"They kidnapped him Mar, he's been gone for a week now and I can't tell the police because they said they would kill him if I did. I just don't know what to do. I'm so scared" Josephine was breaking down.

"Hold on mom, who's they? And how you know he was kidnapped?"

"I don't know who they are Marquise. They said you need to come up with two hundred thousand if we want to see him again. That was seven days ago, and they been callin here ever since. The last time they sounded real impatient, like they really ready to hurt Sean. You gotta do something baby, give em what they want. I can't lose by my baby Marquise. You know I couldn't take that."

Josephine sounded so desperate and it hurt Mar and brought Lexi to tears. Lexi didn't have a child yet but she could imagine what it would feel like to lose one.

Lexi stood there scared, her hands covering her mouth as if she still couldn't believe what she was hearing. She was scared for Josephine and Sean too, but most of all, she was scared for Mar. She could just imagine the lengths he would go to in order to get his brother back. His own death wasn't out of the question.

"Don't worry mom, I'ma take care of everything, you hear me?" Mar was assuring Josephine and wanted to be sure she trusted him.

"You know I can cover the tab but how the hell they know what type of money I got? Six digits aint a number you just throw out there unless you sure the person can handle that. That's a lot of paper. Sean out there runnin his mouth, these clowns shouldn't even know me, I don't deal with nobody out here."
Mar's frustration with Sean was evident.

"That aint even important though, what's important is that we get Sean back, unharmed. How am I supposed to get in contact wit em?"

"They been callin every couple hours or so, they called me about two hours ago, I guess you just gotta wait here until they call back."

"Ight look, Lexi, take mom wit chu to our crib. Mom, look at me." Josephine's fear was causing her gaze to gravitate towards the ground as her disturbed thoughts hung heavy.

"Sean gon be right, he'll be safe and sound by tomorrow, I
promise."

"Please make sure you get my baby back Marquise, they talkin bout killin him if you don't pay that money." Josephine said, still frightened.

"I said I'ma take care of it now go'head with Lexi, relax at my place and try to enjoy the stuff I bought you from Jamaica, Lexi picked out most of it. Like I said, this'll all be over by tomorrow. I love yall."

"I love you too baby." Josephine said. Lexi, who had complete faith and trust in her man, walked over to Mar and kissed him on his lips.

"Just be careful baby."

"Aint I always?" Mar said, smiling that assuring smile he was famous for. Lexi just gave him a look that said, "No, not really, but I'm sure you'll be alright." She winked her long eyelashes at him and walked Josephine out to the car.

Mar wasted no time getting on the phone. He drove to the nearest payphone and called an old friend of Larnell's named SK.

"Yo K, what's good?" "Who dis?"

"It's Mar, yo listen, I got a job for you, it's real serious to me and it's a nice amount of paper involved."

"How much?" "Twenty thousand."

"That sound about right. Who, what, and where…I don't need to know why."

"I'd rather give you the particulars face to face. How soon can you be up here cause this shit gotta be handled A-sap."

"Few hours, I can be there by the evening."

"Aight cool. Listen K, this shit about my family. My lil brotha been gone for a week now."

"I got chu bruh, I aint never let chu down before did I?" "Nah, you aint never let me down before."

"Well I aint about to start now, you got my word. Now I should be up there in a couple hours. I'm leavin the crib as we speak."

"My man." Mar said satisfied. "I'll call you when I get to Jersey." "Ight G, peace."

Mar sat back on the sofa and contemplated the predicament he now found himself in. He couldn't find anybody else to be angry with but himself. Like his father, he hated that his actions had placed his family in this situation but he knew that whoever it was that had kidnapped Sean would slip just enough for him to get the drop on them.

Mar laid back on the couch, impatiently waiting for the phone to ring. At exactly 3:23 pm…it did.

"Hello?" Mar said quickly.

"Who dis?" The disguised voice on the other end asked. "Who's this?" Mar shot back.

"Listen homeboy, I don't think you realize the seriousness of the situation. Cause if you did, you would know you aint in da position to be askin questions and you damn sure aint in da position to be actin tuff."

Mar swallowed his pride and immediately regretted it. Pride tasted worse than anything he could remember.

"It's Mar."

"I figured that. Listen I don't know you, you don't know me so this shit definitely aint personal. I'm bout my business the same way you is. I prefer business over bloodshed so I'm hoping we can get this shit over quick and easy. You got what I ask for?"

"Yeah, but I need to know my lil brother's still alive."

"Hey lil man, pick ya head up, ya brova on the phone."

Mar, more furious than he could ever remember being, listened close as Sean pled for him to help him.

"He here. Like I said, I'm about business. I don't just snatch lil niggas up and kill em for the fuck of it. This about bread."

"Where you want me to drop it?" Mar said. He too wanted this over as fast as possible.

"Downtown, in front of the Hampton…by the airport."

"Too many people. What if somebody see us; me passing you a bag and you passin me my brother. I got a better idea…"

Gutter Just listened while Mar told him he would drop the money off in an alley near Gutter's section of the city. After a brief debate, Gutter agreed. Once Gutter got the money he would tell Mar where he could find Sean. After they hung up the phone Gutter looked at Sean.

"Your brother come thru wit that ransom...you can go."

Mar and SK met up at the train station on the New Jersey Transit's North Jersey coastline. Mar noticed another guy in the car with SK.

"Who's this?" Mar asked, inquiring about the unfamiliar man SK had bought with him.

"This Truck, he good folk." SK said confidently.

"Wus good." Mar said shaking the huge hand of the Silverback gorilla SK had just introduced as Truck.

"I see how you got cha name big fella." Mar said in regards to Trucks size and weight. Truck's face remained almost expressionless as he shook Mar's hand and nodded his head.

"A man of few words, I like that." Mar said. The comment was directed mainly at SK.
"You know how I ride bruh, now wus up wit dis job you got for us?" SK said crossing his tattooed arms in front of his chest.

"Somebody kidnapped my lil brova. I'ma be dropping a bag full of money at a spot near where they be at. All I want you to do is park there in advance so yall can see who it is and follow em. I gotta wait for em to call me and tell me where my brova is. Once they call me, I'ma call you and yall can do what yall do. Can you handle that?"

"Of course. I aint think it would be that simple." SK said
confidently.

"Just be careful G, I know ya work. I wouldn't have called you if I didn't think you could handle this shit for me."

Mar made sure he told SK and Truck everything they needed to know. Once he was satisfied that he had done that, he drove them to the same Hampton Inn that Gutter wanted to meet at beside the Linden Airport.

After leaving SK and Truck at the hotel, all Mar could do was wait. The clock moved unusually slow. He couldn't sleep and after what felt like an eternity the sun began to rise along with his anticipation. He never meant for Sean to get dragged into his life and now all he wanted was to get his brother back. He planned to watch the news but the news ended up watching him. His focus was entirely on Sean.

Seven pm rolled around and Mar was more than ready. He called SK again.

"You ready G?"

"Born ready bruh." If it was one quality Mar loved about SK it was his reliability.

"Ight, I want yall to come meet me."

"Where?" SK asked.

Mar gave him the directions to his mom's house in Avenal and in a few minutes they were out front beeping the horn.

Mar - carrying a black and gray Nike bag - followed SK and Truck to their car, spoke to them for a minute then told them to follow him. He climbed into his own car and led them to where he would be dropping the money off.

Mar sat the bag up against the dumpster and covered it slightly with the old piece of newspaper he found on the littered ground in the alley. After seeing that it was secure he checked his watch.

"Seven forty-five". He said to himself reading the numbers.

Mar nodded gently towards where SK had parked and headed back to his car. He knew SK would be happy when he saw that there was actually two-hundred thousand in the bag. He had to put the right amount of money in the bag in case SK slipped up or tried to burn him for the twenty grand he had given him up front. At the end of the day, he would pay that ransom to get his brother back. No material thing came before his family.

Ten minutes after Mar pulled off Gutter, Rock, and Sean pulled up in the alley. Gutter looked up and down the narrow street. He was starting to think it was a bad idea to drop Sean off and pick up his money in this dark alley. He was going to take Sean somewhere else after counting the money but decided to get it all over with right now. Nervously, he looked around a second longer and after feeling comfortable that no one else was in the alley, he had Rock jump out and grab the bag. Rock was slightly nervous also and he clutched his Mac 11 tightly, almost desperately, as he made his way towards the dumpster. After a few seconds of searching for the bag he found it. Rock stood up with the bag in his hand, glanced around quickly like a mouse making it's way through the dark, then scurried back to the car.

Inside the car they counted the money while Sean watched. His mouth was gagged so Sean couldn't exhale the fear that was escaping his lungs like air from a punctured tire. He still felt the joy however. He was finally about to be released.

"It's all here." Gutter said to Rock. He turned to Sean. "You free to go lil man."

"Let him out." Gutter told Rock. Rock got out and picked Sean up. Sean was hogtied so Rock had to carry him. After tossing Sean to the ground beside the dumpster, Rock jumped back in the car and Gutter pulled off. As soon as they made the left out of the alley SK was on their tail.

Once Mar saw SK and Truck pull behind Sean's kidnappers, he pulled around the block and back into the alley. Mar got out and quickly untied Sean who broke into tears.

"I'm sorry Mar, I swear to God I'm sorry."

"Just c'mon, let me get you home to mom. We'll worry about everything else later." Sean and Mar both looked up when they heard the screeching of tires.

"Hit dat mothafucka K! Hit em!" Truck barked. SK slammed into the driver side of Gutters Saab 900, sending Gutter and Rock crashing into the back of a parked SUV. Banged up, Rock reached for his Ingram Mac 11 but it was too late, shells from Truck's Winchester .30-30 were flying through the window. The Downpour of bullets was relentless. After the first 7 rounds Truck stopped shooting. His aim was deadly from years of hunting deer in the woods of Virginia with his father. Hunting these non-aiming jokers was nothing.

The few nightwalkers, hustlers, and addicts that were out watched in fear from their hiding spots as Gutter crawled out of the car only to collapse on his face. He was covered in blood from neck to thigh. Rock was slumped over against the dashboard, blood running from a giant hole in his head; the chunk that used to cover the hole lying beside him in the seat. Truck was about to reload but when he saw Gutter die, he grabbed the gym bag full of blood money off of his shoulder and ran back to SK's car. SK mashed the gas and they were quickly in route for Norfolk.

A teary-eyed Josephine was overjoyed to have her son back. Of course Sean - who was still shook up - was happy to be out of that basement and out of those filthy clothes. He was happy to be back in the presence and safety of his family.

Spending seven and a half days in that dark basement with no food, no shower, and strained sunlight had taken a toll on both his mind and body that would not be soon forgotten - if ever. After a nice hot shower and a hot home-cooked meal he was a little better.

"Now you see why I don't want you in this game?" Mar asked Sean as they sat on the back porch that night talking.

"Yeah." Sean said humbly. He was both ashamed and embarrassed. Not only because of what he had put his family through but because he now realized that what Mar had sad was true, he wasn't built for that life.

"Yo, my bad Mar, I should have just listened to you from the jump."

"You right, you should have. But you know, you live and you learn the hard way, that's what life's about."

"Did you really give them two-hunded thou'?" Sean asked curiously.

"That aint important, just know I would've gave them everything I own to get chu back. You definitely dug a unnecessary hole in my pocket though."

"I know, my bad." Sean said full of shame.

"It's all good, anybody can get robbed or kidnapped, you just made it too easy for em. I'm just happy to have you back though. This shit is a minor setback, nothing more, nothing less." Mar said brushing the whole thing off. He was ready to forget about this whole mess now, or at least put it behind them.

"Just remember that I love you, don't put me thru no shit like that ever again."

"I won't and yo…I love you too Mar."

18

A week after Sean was returned and the remembrance of his scary ordeal began to fade, Josephine was scheduled to see a doctor in regards to her discovery of the lump in her breast. After extensive testing it was determined that she did indeed have breast cancer.

As if Mar hadn't already experienced enough, life was testing his strength and resilience once again. When Josephine stepped out of the doctor's office, she didn't have to say a word; her expression said everything.

Mar walked over to his mother and hugged her tightly. He could feel her warm tears falling onto his neck and shoulder and fought back the tears that were welling up in his own eyes.

"C'mon mom, let's get outta here." Mar wrapped his arms around Josephine's shoulder and led her out to his car.

"Don't worry mom, we'll fight this just like we fight everything else…together." Mar was trying to soothe his mom as much as he could but Josephine could barely hear him by this time; she was completely ravaged mentally and spiritually.

"I'm not leavin ya side until you better, I swear to God, everything else in my life can wait."

"No baby, don't do that. There's no need for things to change. I'm strong and I will get well, let's just continue living how we were. If we don't then I probably will lose to this. To change my lifestyle would mean I already gave up in my mind. I'll get better."

Mar never doubted his mother but if his eyes weren't open before they were now. He saw that nothing in life was promised and that the things and the people that he loved and cherished could so easily be taken away from him. This made his decision to stop hustling narcotics concrete now. He needed to put all of his time and energy into helping Josephine overcome this illness, no matter what she said. He had to make sure Sean stayed straight and would be able to get into the college of his choice with or without the basketball scholarship.

Mar knew he had told Lexi that he had one more move to make but now decided against it.

"It's always that last move that gets you pinched." Mar reminded himself. Besides, even after the set back with Sean, he still had close to a million dollars in dope money and a hundred thousand in dope. That was on top of the business, legit money, and real estate. Mar felt that doing any more dirt would just be stupid and greedy. Two things he wasn't.

Like Larnell, he fronted the last few kilos he had to one of his best customers and fell completely off the scene. Mar plugged the guy in with his connect in Little Havana and pulled the same 'Frank Matthews' Larnell had pulled. The same disappearing act his father had tried to pull but was unsuccessful at.

Mar focused his attention fully on his legal businesses and didn't invest another dime in drugs.

Mar also took this time to make one of his dreams a reality. A dream that had been inspired by the youth center he had seen in Norfolk when he first went through Young Terrace with Larnell. He opened a non- profit organization and after filing for tax-exemption, he opened a recreational center in his old neighborhood of Bed-Stuy where kids could go to learn, eat, exercise, and hang out after school without getting into trouble; a move motivated by Sean and Chauncy's curiosity and lack of constructive alternatives to running the streets. The way Mar saw it, inner city kids had way too much unsupervised idle time on their hands and a lack of positive role models that could teach them how to shatter the imaginary limitations placed on them by cultural economic gaps, therefore they got into more trouble and made less progress in society.

After getting the city to donate him a building that had been abandoned since he was a child, Mar turned a dilapidated building in Brooklyn into a beautiful safe haven for ill-nurtured kids. A great portion of the rec' center was dedicated strictly to young, aspiring boxers. The walls were lined with pictures of Joe Louis, Marvin Hagler, Sugar Ray Leonard, Ray "Boom Boom" Mancini, Hector "Macho" Camacho and of course - Muhammad Ali. The ring was professional size and all the equipment - gloves, head gear, heavy bags, speed bags, weights, jump ropes, etc. - was brand new. Every day, sweaty bodies ranging from the ages of ten and thirty could be seen honing their skills.

Mar was there when he could be and those times, he couldn't he hired local ex-boxers to run the center.

Friday nights in the rec center were for boxing tournaments. It was a vision of his to get kids and parents alike off the streets. It was too late for him to fulfill his dreams of becoming a professional boxer, but this boxing club was a way for him to live his dreams vicariously through a bunch of kids that were headed for one of the two yards that embraced inner-city youths with welcoming arms - the prison yard or the graveyard. Mar told the children that attended the rec center to come to the center with their family and friends on Friday night for the first annual boxing tournament. It was the first night he was holding the event and he asked that the children bring as many people with them as possible.

That first night the small gymnasium was packed with different people from the neighborhood. After filing into the gym people were seated, fighters were clothed and everybody waited for the tournament to begin. Inside the professional size ring Mar stood beside a district judge and a member of city council under a bright light. Sean watched from the shadows as Mar stated the rules and prepared the two hundred people in attendance for the first of fifteen three round bouts. Sean laughed at the irony of who Mar was standing beside and the fact that they had no idea who Mar was. It was a testament to his brilliance.

Mar was pleased with the attendance. The greater majority of the people there were between the ages of fifteen and twenty and this satisfied Mar. He knew that while they were at this event, these kids wouldn't be on the corners, in the buildings, or on the pavement, drowned in their own blood. There was a registered nurse ringside. The district Judge was one of the judges and the city council member refereed the bouts. At the end, no one was hurt and Mar's Boxing Night was a huge success.

The success of Mar's recreational center was bittersweet because it couldn't be fully enjoyed. Mar was forced to keep the majority of his attention on Josephine's progressing sickness. They were both worried - Josephine more so - about her losing her breast. So, Mar had John Rutherford consult the best cancer experts throughout the United States and all around the world if need be. Josephine had heard about a procedure called a lumpectomy that could remove the cancerous growth alone in her breast. But, three of the best cancer specialists in the United States very carefully considered Josephine's medical file and strongly recommended that the breast be removed. Each agreed that this particular strain of cancer was very aggressive.

After going through chemotherapy, she got better, to a certain degree. In her remission, she added a few pounds and her skeleton wasn't as visible as it was only weeks before. Josephine slept and rested a lot. She couldn't leave her house but was always energetic whenever Mar or Sean would come to see her - every time appearing to be stronger and healthier. Those days were some of their best days together. Mar bought her all kinds of gifts, they went for walks, had long thought-provoking discussions, went out to see movies, and ate out together frequently.

Mar showed Josephine all the love he had inside for her, knowing her time may be short and his love wouldn't mean a thing when she was gone. On top of this Josephine took up a new hobby, painting. She used acrylics and other paints but most of all she liked water colors.

Josephine seemed to be getting so well. For weeks their walks through the
park continued and her remission was giving Mar the inspiration he needed to really peak in all facets of his life. He appreciated life so much more now. Then, one day after coming home from a trip to Atlantic City where he and John were working on constructing a hotel and a co-op, he saw that his mother was sick again, this time worse than before. This devastated Mar who had just began to think the treatments were beginning to work.

Mar and Josephine met with her doctor in the unusually empty corridor of the hospital and the doctor told them bluntly that Josephine was going to die and that there was nothing that could be done to prevent it.

Josephine broke down and without a word left to be alone in the car. She didn't want to hear or believe that she was going to die.

Mar stayed around to talk to the doctor who explained that Josephine had stage 4 cancer, meaning the cancerous tumor had spread beyond her breast, under arm and internal mammary lymph nodes and was now in other bones, her lungs, and her liver. He told Mar that holes were forming in Josephine's bones that would soon lead to the collapse of her skeleton. He compared the effect to termite-infested wood. She had small tumors in her brain that would unavoidably expand in time, and her blood was rapidly producing toxins that would very soon kill her.

Although she had heard that her death was imminent, Mar didn't feel it necessary to tell her all the details the doctor had explained to him. He put together as much money as he could, as much muscle and influence and he did everything he could to prevent his mother's death.

After a series of hospitals and experimental drugs, they were forced to give up and allow nature to take its sometimes-cruel course. They decided to make their last days together enjoyable. It wasn't easy with that ominous black cloud of inevitable death hanging over their heads at all times.

Mar had some business with John in New York to handle so he made plans to spend the weekend in the city that never sleeps with Sean, shopping, talking, and enjoying a concert that Mar was sure Sean would love.

"Where we goin?" Sean asked as Mar's Mercedes Benz glided through the Holland Tunnel from Jersey City into New York.

"I figured we'd do a lil shoppin, plus, Nas and Wu Tang performing at the Apollo tonight."

"Word?"

"Yeah, but first I wanna take you to meet somebody." "Who?" Sean asked.

A guy named Infinite, I met him a while back. He ran wit dad back in the day but he on a real positive vibe right now. He asked about you, and I told him I would bring you by one day to meet him. Anyway, you know I proposed to Lexi while we was in Jamaica right?"

"Yeah?"

"No doubt. She been to hell and back wit me. She put a lot of work in to solidify her spot. I can't really see myself wit nobody else."

"She got chu." Sean said smiling.

"She got me? What chu mean she got me?"

"You know, she got chu cashin in that playboy card, never thought I'd see the day."

"Shit, I aint even gon hold you, she did that a long ass time ago. Who you seen me wit since we left Akron? Exactly! I knew she was gon be the one when I first laid eyes on her."

"Damn, that's deep. You know I'm happy for you." Sean said. When he thought about it, Mar deserved happiness more than anyone he knew.

When they reached 7th Ave. in Harlem, Mar took Sean to Allah's school so he could meet Infinite. Mar had promised Infinite that he would bring Sean around one day and he liked to keep his word. Not only that, although Sean had been staying out of trouble lately, Mar wanted to make sure it would stay that way. He was hoping Infinite would become like a tutor for Sean.

Sean looked at the Black and Gold flag in the window. A sun with a black number 7 in the middle, a Black star to the left and a Gold crescent behind the 7, eight points on the sun each divided in two, one side being black the other being gold. Around the sun read:

"In The Name Of Allah."

Sean was puzzled.

"What is this place?" He asked.

"It's a school…Gods and Earths...I want you to meet somebody."

Sean and Mar were greeted by a tall, brown skinned man who introduced himself as Asiatic.

"Peace to the gods, what can I help you wit?" Asiatic asked. "Yeah, I'm lookin' for Infinite, you know where I can find him?"

From the look on Asiatic's face, either a lot of members went by that attribute or no one did. Mar tried to describe him the best he could.

"It's been a while since I last saw him but, he about 5'8, 5'9 maybe; slim built, light-skin; probably about 35, 36 now."

"Infinite God Allah?" Asiatic said. "Yeah that's it, he around?"

Asiatic looked down at his feet then back up at Mar, his eyes told a thousand stories.

I'm sorry but brother Infinite was murdered almost a month ago. He was fatally beat down by two police officers in Pelan, excuse me, the Bronx. They murdered him in cold blood...all for speaking the truth." Asiatic's voice faded.

Mar shook his head in disgust. Police brutality in New York and all over the United States was getting out of hand. The worst part was nothing was being done to stop it.

"I'm sorry to hear that." Was all Mar could come up with, even though what he was thinking was enough to write a volume of books and discourses on racial inequality and profiling.

"Don't matter if you righteous or you evil in this wilderness they call North America, if you black you in danger. If you're original man, woman, or child, they could care less how high you are on the corporate ladder or how low you are in the gutter, you black and they want to murder you, especially if they can't enslave you. They launched an all-out genocide on us here in America and at home in the motherland, got the natives over there thinkin they administering drugs to help them and they putting AIDS in their systems. Over here they put the poison in ya head with decadent TV shows, and they aint gon stop until they slay every brotha and sista in this cesspool, or until we kill each other, whichever comes first."

"Look, here's a stack." Mar said, handing the man a thousand dollars.

"I Hope this can help with any bills or anything around the school, I really commend yall for the message yall tryin to get out to the youth, the self-esteem and the whole nine, I can dig that, and I support it a hundred percent."

"Thanks a lot brotha, and believe me, anything is plenty," Asiatic said gratefully.

"It's not a problem, listen you take it easy right." "Alright brotha, peace."

"Peace." Mar said before turning and walking back towards the
car.

"Who was Infinite?" Sean asked, but before Mar could answer something caught and demanded his attention. A jet-black Lincoln Continental drove slowly up the street, almost coming to a complete stop when the driver noticed Mar.

"Go get in the car." Mar said to Sean without taking his eyes off the Lincoln.

"Nah, I…" Sean was trying to protest.

"Man, go get in the car now!" Mar ordered as the car came to a very brief stop right in front of them.

Mar's eyes remained intently focused on the car as he prepared to draw his gun. The back window of the car was tinted but whoever was inside either wanted Mar to see them or wanted a clear, unobstructed view of him, because the window began to roll down slowly. Once the window was far enough, Mar could see the face of an older Hispanic man whose eyes were fixed on Mar's.

Mar watched the malicious stare with his hand on his hip like a cowboy in a western waiting to draw his six-shooter. Eventually, the man in the car cut his eyes at Mar and stared directly ahead as the window rolled back up. The Lincoln pulled off and that was that.

Mar let out a deep breath and readjusted his Rosco in his waist belt. He walked slowly to his car when it hit him. That was the same guy who had been staring at him in Jamaica. Now his head throbbed as he tried to remember the face. Jamaica wasn't the first time he had seen the guy. He knew he had seen this face before Jamaica but for whatever reason, he couldn't put a name to it. He climbed inside his black Benz and checked the rear view, making sure the Lincoln hadn't circled the block. When he was satisfied that they were gone, he pulled off.

"Who was that?" Sean asked as Mar pulled from the curb. "Nobody, they probably thought I was somebody else. But let me tell you somethin, when I tell you to do something just do it, don't question me. This is the second time you did that shit and them couple seconds of you tryna debate wit me could've got chu killed. What if they would've started shootin just now?"

"I'm sayin, I wasn't just gon let nobody do somethin to you wit 'out helpin, I could see somethin was goin down." Sean said in his own defense.

"I appreciate you carin and all that but chu aint superman, bullet's won't just bounce off ya chest Sean, and you aint got no heat on you so like I said, what was you goin do if they would've started poppin off?"

"I guess I would've just had to die wit chu." Sean said, running out of arguments.

"Yeah, that's real bright, and force mom to mourn over the loss of both of her sons, huh? Just leave her wit nuttin I guess. Yo, you need to learn how to start thinking things all the way through first before you do shit like that. If I tell you something, it's for your own good, so do me favor and just listen from now on, right?"

"Ight." Sean said, fresh out of comments to come back with.

Hector looked up at his driver in the rear view. He was sure the man he had seen in Montego Bay, and just now on 7th Ave. in Harlem was exactly who he thought he was.

"That's the sonofabitch that killed Felipe." Hector said. Tony looked slightly confused, he was having a hard time remembering.

"You remember that fuckin punta James, the one that burned us for the money and moved to Ohio?

"Yeah, I remember him." Tony said

"Remember his wife and that little boy…That's the little boy that shot Felipe."

"Oh." Tony said.

"Now make sure you don't let him out of your sight, you follow him to wherever he's going, because he's dying now…to-day!"

"I'm on him." Tony said, never taking his eyes off of the black Mercedes Benz two cars ahead of him. The car looked to be slowing down near a fast-food restaurant.

"Yo, you think we can stop and get somethin to eat, I'm hungry as hell." Sean said noticing the White Castle that was coming up on the right side of the road on 7th Ave and West 125th street. Mar was still trying to figure out why he felt like he knew the face in the Lincoln.

"Yeah, we can do that." Mar said, pulling into the restaurant's parking lot. As soon as Mar turned off the engine, he remembered the face.

"Hector…" He said out loud.

"Who?" Sean asked but Mar had no time to respond to him. As soon as he reached for the key so he could start the car back up he saw somebody standing beside his door out of the corner of his eye.

Mar turned to face the figure and was staring directly down the barrel of the .357 Magnum revolver that was pointed at his head. For a split second all sound ceased and Mar couldn't hear Sean yelling at him, telling him to duck, or the click of the hammer outside the window. All Mar heard was his heart beating fast and a surge of blood rushing through his veins like river rapids. He took a deep breath that sounded a thousand decibels louder than normal. Then, the barrel erupted - loudly. He saw the spark then a bullet shattered his window and flew through his cheek in a flaming fury. Mar could feel his cheekbone crack and chip loose. By the time he had grabbed his face, a second bullet tore through the thick muscle tissue in his right thigh and once again the lead found it's mark deep in his bone. Another shot followed right behind that one hitting the same leg three inches above the knee.

Mar bent over in agonizing pain, but not for long. A fourth shot busted through the back of his shoulder blade. The impact of that shot sent him snapping backwards in his seat. His back arched inward until a fifth shot penetrated his stomach, sending him forward again where he laid with his head in his lap. A sixth and final shot was aimed directly at Sean's face but it missed wide, shattering his window as well. Out of bullets, their assailant ran off, jumped back in the Continental, and sped away.

Mar crawled out of the car looking like he had just taken a blood bath. He looked around the parking lot then fell on his chest after his weak arms gave out. He strained his lungs trying desperately to pull in air. It was the most difficult breaths he had ever taken in his life. While struggling for oxygen, he choked and gargled clots of blood and saliva. Sean ran around the front of the car and to his brother's side.

Everyone in the restaurant had made their way outside by now. As Mar looked through glossy, dimming eyes at them, he was terrified by the horrid looks on their startled faces. None of them looked like they believed Mar would make it and it made him feel like he wouldn't. maybe they were right…maybe he was going to die.

"You gon be right." San said. He was even more afraid than Mar was. His tears dropped to the cement that was already saturated in Mar's blood. Mar continued a painful journey in and out of consciousness, while Sean pleaded with him to stay alive.

"Just hold on Mar…the ambulance is on its way…" Mar tried to respond but the only thing that proceeded from his mouth was more and more blood, a sign of internal bleeding. Seeing the blood erupt from Mar's mouth and spill down his neck made Sean throw up. Mar managed to stay around long enough to hear the sirens of the EMS…then…he heard nothing else.

19

The black Lincoln swerved dangerously past the slower moving traffic on Adam Clayton Powell Jr. Boulevard before Hector told Tony to slow down.

"What chu tryna do, get us pulled over?" Hector asked.

"I was just tryin to get away from there as fast as possible, it was a lot of people out there." Tony said in his own defense as he turned left onto West 116th and headed towards Lennox Ave.

"How far away do you wanna get? We're five blocks away, slow down. Anyway, did you make sure he was dead?"

"Are you kiddin me…" Tony Thought.

"…the way he was slumped over in that seat."

Tony looked up at Hector through the rearview mirror.

"Trust me, he's dead."

When he finally opened his eyes, Mar's vision was still slightly blurry and his head was still dizzy and sedated from the pain killer the I.V.'s were pumping into his veins in heavy doses. The doctor walked from beside the bed and Mar - still shaky from the shooting - jumped at the sight of him. A rush of pain jolted through his body that made him grimace.

"Oh, I'm sorry sir, I didn't mean to startle you. I didn't even realize you were awake." The middle-aged doctor said, barely looking at Mar. The doctor was still checking the charts and files that were clipped to his clipboard.

"You know clinically, you actually died on us twice." The Doctor finally lifted his head to look at Marquise, whose entire face was bandaged besides his eyes, mouth, and nose.

"You're one hell of a fighter though. I have to be honest with you, there was really nothing else we could do for you. Even with all of our medical expertise we were basically helpless. Yup, the only thing that saved you Mr. Jackson was your will to survive."

Mar remained quiet, just listening. The reconstructive surgery had his face extremely soar; it was throbbing with pain. The doctor continued.

"I can see why you didn't want to leave yet. You have a very beautiful and supportive family and now that you're awake I'll send them back in. for your own comfort I suggest you keep all movement to a minimum. I'll be back to check on you later." With that, the doctor left the room.

Shortly after the doctor left, Lexi came through the door smiling and crying at the same time. She was followed by a subtly smiling Josephine and a bright-eyed Sean.

"Hey baby." Lexi said walking to Mar's bedside. She backed up once to get a good look at him. She quickly wiped away tears of joy and leaned over and gently kissed her fiancé's lips.

"I'm so glad you didn't die on me Quise. I don't know what I would have done without you." Lexi said.

Just the thought of her living without Mar made more tears rush to the sides of her eyes then out and over her smooth cheeks. She wanted to hug him so bad but could see that he was still in a lot of pain.

Mar just nodded his head and managed a faint smile. In his condition it was all he could muster. He couldn't talk even if he wanted to. The surgeons had operated on his jaw and repaired the roof of his mouth and for now his jaw was wired shut.

The bullet that went into his face had caused some damage that would leave Mar's jaw slightly disfigured. Luckily, it wouldn't be noticeable without a lot of scrutiny. Being as though the gunman was shooting downwards, the bullet went down through his left jaw and out of his right cheek, instead of up towards his brain.

After Lexi stepped aside, Josephine came and stood beside her son. She looked down at him and smiled that comforting, motherly smile that expressed no matter how old he got, he would always be her baby. Instead of showing pity, she showed him love and the type of security only a mother could give.

"Baby, it aint the mountain ahead that wears you out, it's that little pebble in your shoe. You just keep fightin for me, you hear? I want you to hear something." Josephine was rubbing her first born's hand.

"Sometimes our internal fire goes out but is blown back into a flame by someone else, and each of us owes our deepest thanks to that person who has rekindled this fire within. You know, I read that somewhere and it really struck a chord with me. I immediately thought about us. For me, you're that person. You rekindled that flame in me when I gave up on myself. You gave me that strength to go on and I owe you. Please don't rob me of the opportunity to repay you. Stay away from that game Marquise. Don't let them streets take you away from me. I love you so much and I don't want you leavin this earth before I do."

Josephine could feel a warm, salty puddle forming right behind her eyes so she excused herself and went into the restroom. She didn't want Mar to see her crying. She felt as though she had to be strong enough for the both of them.

Sean came and stood by Mar with a big cheese on his face but at a loss for words. He just knew he was happy that his brother was still alive. For Mar, Sean's presence alone was more than enough.

Once Mar was finally able to leave the Harlem Hospital Center, he spent most of his time at home with Lexi. Four days after he was released, Lexi surprised him with the news he had been waiting for, for a long time now.

"Quise, I'm pregnant," She said as they lay in front of the TV. She wondered, like most women, what his reaction would be. She knew he always wanted a child but the dream of a baby was always different than the reality of one.

"Are you sure?" Mar asked. He didn't want to sound like he didn't trust Lexi, he was just surprised and wanted to make sure this was official considering it was something he wanted more than anything.

"Well I wanted to make sure I was before I told you I took another test this morning, boo that's my third test, so unless the tests' are wrong then yeah, I'm positive."

Mar's face lit up, he hugged Lexi tightly and she smiled brightly. The nervousness of how he would respond subsided. They both had gotten a little carried away and realized it when

Mar grimaced and sucked air through his tightly clenched teeth. His torso was still in pain.

"Damn." He said still making the hissing sound through his teeth. "I'm sorry baby." Lexi said.

"It's nuffin, but I guess we got a lot of plannin to do." Mar said pulling Lexi back in close to him, only slower and more cautious this time.

"I guess so." Lexi said fantasizing about how it was going to be to have this baby. What it would look like? Was it a boy or a girl? Which one did Mar want the most? The one thing that wasn't a question was how much they would spoil it. They talked about it deep into the night but as soon as the morning rolled in, Mar was back to the seriousness that had been scaring Lexi for the past week.

As Mar reflected, he noticed that Hector had become a lifelong enemy of his. He was responsible for James' death, for Josephine being raped, and now for him being shot and nearly killed. Of course, he was compelled to kill Hector himself. But Mar preferred wit over emotions. He couldn't allow his anger and vindictive feeling to force him into some irrational decision. Anger is one letter short of danger. His next move couldn't be sloppy. He had a baby to think about now, and he had finally made a way where could sit back and enjoy his prosperity without slinging another bird in his life. He couldn't allow his thirst for revenge cause him to do something stupid and jeopardize it all. His money was long and Hector's was too. The stakes were up. The moves were never direct or overt when real money was involved. So, instead of reacting to being shot illogically, he wisely separated his thoughts from his feelings.

As soon as he was able to leave the house he did. He rode directly to Brooklyn looking for somebody; anybody that he might remember from his childhood or have alliances with; a gun that was looking to make a quick buck. Nafee's name popped into his head. Even though Mar had been away from BK for a while, besides checking on his recreational center in Bed-Stuy, he always kept his ear to the streets and from what he was hearing, Nafee was a real gunslinger nowadays. He would be perfect if Mar could just find him. The problem was, Mar didn't know where to begin looking for him. And then he remembered hearing Brandon was running with a squad from Marcy Projects now.

After a two-hour drive and not spotting one familiar face that he trusted enough to handle this situation, he was starting to feel like his search would turn out to be futile. He was just about to head back to Jersey when he spotted Brandon on Myrtle Ave., posted up by himself. He had always hung around Marcy when they were kids and Brandon was probably the first one in their crew to sell crack. When he was twelve, he started selling packs of crack for Danny Diamondz's crew, the Marcy Posse. At the time, Mar, Chauncy, and Nafee were still virgins when it came to the crack game. As Mar studied Brandon from his car, it looked like Brandon may had been still pitching which would be good news for Mar. Bad, that his old friend was still making hand to hands, but good because it would mean he was still hungry. He would most likely kill for the money Mar was about to offer…Literally.

The tint on Mar's windows were almost pitch black so when he pulled up on Brandon, Brandon reached for the Brazilian firearm on his waist. Mar had to roll the window down quickly before Brandon shot him and his new car up. And if Brandon was still how Mar remembered, he wouldn't have hesitated to do just that.

"Yo, you got like two seconds to make yourself known or we gon start the fourth of July early out this mufucka." Brandon said showing Mar the butt of his Taurus.

"It's me." Mar said. He admired Brandon's courage. It was just what he needed right now. Squeeze first, ask questions last. Brandon only let his guard down because the voice in the car sounded so familiar.

"Who's me?" He asked, letting his shirt fall back over the thick handle of his gun.

"It's Marquise." Mar said dropping his head a little further so Brandon could see him better.

"Marquise? Get da fuck outta here…Mar?" Brandon walked over to the car and looked in.

"Oh shit Mar, where you been at baby?"

"Aint a whole lot to it, bobbin & weavin, tryna get even." "I here that, so wussup B, what chu need?"

"C'mon let's go for a ride." Mar said hitting the locks. "I see you keep the thing on you." Mar said.

"This shit like wearin' a belt for me playboy, it's part of the outfit. Accessorizing, you understand me?"

Mar smiled as Brandon tucked his Taurus into a brown leather shoulder-holster.

"Plus, you know my motto; I rather be judged by twelve than carried by six, smell me?"

"Yeah I smell and You smellin kinda good right now." Mar said sarcastically.

"Oh dat? Dat's just my medicine…shit keep me on point out here. But fuck all da small talk, what brought chu back to the jungle. Oh, but before you say somethin, I heard about what you did for them kids out where you used to stay, that's some real positive shit. You doin right by keepin em away from a nigga like me. You don't want em learnin the crafts I picked up you feel what I'm sayin?"

"Yeah, I figured they could use a little somethin like that." Mar said. It felt good to be appreciated.

"And what's this I'm hearin about this mansion you got out in Jerz?"

"Nah it aint no mansion. Just a lil somethin outside the city where me and the misses can feel safe. The real reason I'm here though is cause I need a favor."

Mar had learned over the years to downplay his achievements. "I'm all ears." Brandon said. He sounded intrigued.

"I see you already doin ya thing out here, but what would twenty- five stacks do for you right now?"

"Put me right where I need to be, so who I gotta jam, and I aint got no picks." Brandon said seriously.

"I don't need you to jam nobody, it's a lil more than that."

Mar allowed the silence after his statement to clarify his proposition.

"Listen B, you aint sayin' nuttin but a word, who is it?" "You know Hector from out…"

"Out Crown Heights." Brandon chimed in, already knowing who Mar was talking about.

"Yeah I know him. Everybody know him." He finished.

"I need him in the dirt ASAP!" Mar was dead serious. He never wanted someone dead as bad as he wanted Hector dead.

"Well we aint got nuttin else to discuss, give me ten grand up front and the rest when I bring you his necklace, by that time you'll already hear about it in the news. His necklace is a gold and…"

"Black onyx something." This time Mar cut in. He remembered seeing the necklace when Hector drove past him in Harlem.

"Right." Brandon said.

"It's a little portrait of his dead homie Fernando inside of the gold and black onyx locket medallion. Him and homeboy used to be real tight B, like me, you, Nafee and Chauncy used to be back in the day, ya' mean?"

"Yeah, we was inseparable back then." Mar said, his mind momentarily drifting down memory lane.

"It aint shit baby. People get older younahmsayin? Different roads. As long as we all straight it's like we still together."

It was as if Brandon had read Mar's mind and Mar felt a quick second of guilt for leaving. He had to remind himself that it had all been for the best. Besides, Chauncy had gotten murdered, Brandon had drifted to Marcy, and Nafee, well the last Mar heard about Nafee, he was on the run for a body - nobody ever saw him.

"Ight, I'ma meet you right where I picked you up tonight at nine, with the ten stacks… I trust you Brandon."

"C'mon Mar don't do that to me G, I got too much love, not to mention, respect for you to pull a stunt over ten thousand dollars. Plus I aint no dickhead, I aint about to run off wit ten gees when I stand to make twenty-five. I got chu homie. Just give me a week, a week and a half to get in with this joker, cop off of him once or twice and I guarantee homeboy'll be out cha way."

Exactly a week after Mar's meeting with Brandon, the people of Crown Heights were alarmed, but not at all surprised to see Hector crawling out of his building bleeding excessively from a gunshot wound in his stomach. A masked gunman followed him from inside and shot the back of his head on the cement. Hector's brains beat his forehead to the ground.

After the shooter removed Hector's necklace, he quickly fled the scene in a dark blue Chrysler 300M. Mar got the news the next day and the necklace two days later.

20

With Hector out of the way, and no other strings to tie him to his former life, Mar wanted nothing more than to spend this Mother's Day with his ailing mother. He knew he may never get to do it again. It was May 10th, 1997 - the day before Mother's Day. Mar called Josephine and told her that he wanted to do something special for her and Lexi. Their time together was again starting to become scarce with all the things business wise that Mar had to handle on the day-to-day basis. With Josephine's condition the worse it had been since she had been diagnosed with cancer; Mar had to run the restaurant and the nightclub until he could find someone else to manage them. The time they did have together wasn't very enjoyable. Josephine was severely sick and slept most of the day.

The cancer was eating away at her body rapidly and nothing was helping; not chemotherapy or any of the medications she had been placed on. Every day was a battle for Josephine. Just waking up seemed like a task.

"Sure honey, I would love to spend the day with you and Lexi." Josephine said before sending Mar her love and hanging up the phone.

She took one more sip of her cooling chamomile herbal tea and made her way up to her bedroom.

"All that fighting to lose to this." She said to herself at the top of the steps. The twenty something steps to the top felt like a hundred to her tired bones.

It was hard for her to maintain her faith in God at times like this. Sometimes she cursed him and other times she reminded herself of Job and the trials and tribulations he faced only to be blessed ten-fold in the end. Was that history or myth she asked herself as she grabbed the antioxidant supplement pills and other naturopathic medicines she was supposed to take. She poured the pills and medicines into the toilet along with a few of her own salty tears.

Josephine looked up at her emaciated face in the mirror and her already sick stomach turned at the sight of the monster that stared back at her through the mirror. She snatched off the wig that covered her baldhead and shook her head in disgust at the woman staring back at her through the mirror. Josephine wouldn't have to watch death consume her anymore, that night she drifted off into an eternal sleep. Her detachment of spirit and flesh was one free of pain and agony.

It seemed as if Josephine knew she was dying that day, she felt it, so she was ready for it. She didn't make a fuss about it, just closed her tear- flooded eyes, never to open them again.

"Hey mom." Mar yelled from the living room of Josephine's house. He was ecstatic about taking Josephine out, it had been so long.

"C'mon now mom, I don't want to be late, I got us reservations at this restaurant, and I got another surprise for you." Mar made his way to the kitchen.

"See, here you go, I don't know who's worse, you or Lexi."

Mar poured some orange juice on to the ice in his glass and drunk the whole thing in one thirsty gulp.

"Women." He said to himself. After a few more seconds of waiting and no response from Josephine, Mar headed upstairs.

"I'm comin up so I hope you decent." He said on his way up the steps. Mar looked in through the open door and could see that Josephine was still lying in her bed. He thought she was sleep until he noticed how limp her arm looked hanging from the bed. His heart fell out of his chest.

"Mom?" He walked slowly into her room. His worse fear was slowly materializing. It didn't take him long at all to realize that she was gone. Mar sat down in the chair beside her bed and stared at what to him was still a lovely face.

For a minute he thought so much that he thought nothing at all. He just stared blankly through lost eyes that eventually filled with tears.

He kissed Josephine's forehead then sat back in the chair; his elbows on his knees and his head in his hands. It was the first time in his life that everything he had done had meant nothing. His money meant nothing. His connections meant nothing. His smarts meant nothing. All of it meant nothing because none of it was enough to save his mother.

21

Even after the doctors had confirmed Josephine's belief that she had breast cancer neither Sean nor Marquise believed their mom would die this early in her life. Marquise believed she was too strong willed to let cancer beat her and Sean simply couldn't fathom losing her. After all she had been through there was no way she was supposed to be experiencing more heartache. Where were the blessings?

The doctor had revealed to Sean and Mar that though black women were less likely to be diagnosed with breast cancer, they were two times more likely to die from it than white women. Statistics weren't in her favor. Often it was the lack of funds that hindered black women from receiving adequate care. Sean was sure that wasn't going to be his mom's fate. Mar had enough money to see to it that their mother got the best treatment available.

Of course, Mar did spend plenty of money on treating his mother's illness but it all turned out to be worthless. Her body was unable to fight off the overpowering sickness and she indeed passed away.

There are certain moments in a man's life that completely changes how he views everything; from the world and social issues to his own individual life; moments that spark a change and a newer, more mature way of thinking. For Sean it was the death of his mother.

As Sean stared down at his stiff, pale, dead mother he had an epiphany. He realized that the only certainty was that nothing was certain…besides death. Death was a reality and life was a hoax, a mirage… a trick. A trick that God played on all of humanity. Good or bad, rich or poor, none of that mattered. It didn't matter how you lived, in the end you died…like everybody else. It wouldn't matter if you were rich, when you die, they throw you in the same dirt as the poor, they just lower you in a better box.

Death was the medium that showed just how equal all of life was. Man, woman, animal, and everything else. Seasons come and seasons go. The same sun shines on every generation. These were Sean's thoughts as he studied the work of the mortician - whose job it was to try to make Josephine look as alive as possible.

Mar was thinking pretty much the same thing. He was questioning some of his own motives and values. He came to the realization that a lot of his moves were motivated by shallow desires. Life now looked like a giant dog chasing its own tail. It was moving fast but going absolutely nowhere. What was the meaning?

Lexi had held Mar's hand nearly the entire time and while staring in his eyes, she saw two things she had never seen before, two things that had been foreign to Mar before this funeral…confusion and fear. Not only did Sean notice this as well, he felt it.

Sean and Mar continued to glance over Josephine from the seats at the front of the funeral. They planned to use every second with her before she was lowered into the ground forever. She didn't look that bad they had concluded. The mortician had actually done a good job of making her not look like a soulless mannequin. She was swathed in a violet silk dress. Mar had hired a professional seamstress to make sure the dress was stitched and hand-rolled with precision.

Unlike Mar, Sean thought Josephine had died without ever fully reaching her potential or maximizing her life. It seemed she was cheated by God. That she was never rewarded or blessed for her pure heart. Sean felt she had died too soon. Mar on the other hand knew it didn't matter how long a person lived but how well. In his eyes their mother had, lived a good, fulfilling life - hard times included.

Sean stared at Mar as the preacher read the eulogy. Mar's face seemed saddened, but still it maintained its normal sternness. Sean knew that even if Mar wanted to cry, he wasn't going to have to. Not right now, not with all of these people watching. Mar was always conscious of those waiting for him to show weakness...he would never give them that satisfaction. That discipline and self-control was what Sean had always admired about his brother. He exhibited strength and poise no matter how serious the situation.

22

Seven months later Lexi, who was new eight months pregnant, Sean, and Marquise went to celebrate Christmas with Lexi's mother in Flatbush.

Lately, Lexi had also neglected to spend time with her mother like she should have. Seeing Mar lose Josephine made her realize how precious every moment with someone you love is.

Christmas with Lexi's mom was just what Marquise, Sean, and Lexi needed. Her mom cooked collard greens, black-eyed peas, sweet potatoes, baked macaroni and cheese, turkey, and corn bread. It was clearly evident that she had missed her daughter's presence. The four of them exchanged gifts that morning and that afternoon they enjoyed the cooking and company of Lexi's mother.

"Mom, me and Mar gettin married right after I have the baby." Lexi said as they sat around the table.

"Well, it's about time baby, yall been together since yall was babies."

Mar and Lexi both smiled.

"I always knew this was gonna be the man you would marry; it better had been the way he came and took you away from me like that." Mar blushed.

"Don't get all shy on me now Marquise, you know what I'm talkin about." Patrice said. She almost reminded Mar of Josephine.

"Nah, I don't know what you talkin bout Ms. Patrice." Mar said teasing her.

"Uhh, Huhh, it's okay though, you just promise me that you'll take care of my baby."

"I promise." Mar assured.

"And yall could come see me more often, it aint always gotta be no holiday, I do get lonely."

"You got my word on that too."

After the festivities of the day were over and the mood mellowed, Sean asked Mar if he wanted to go out for a drink.

Sean and Mar drove over to Bed-Stuy to one of James' old hangout spots on Franklin Avenue between Monroe and Madison. The bar was a cool little swank joint back in the day; an off the books after-hours club in a townhouse basement. Situated behind a locked gate, it was now a respectable spot for nostalgic old-timers who hung on to the memories of how swingin the joint used to be. They reminisced about their glory days when they had the streets of Bedford-Stuyvesant on lock and all the party girls hung on to their fur coattails, while popping in quarter after quarter in the jukebox to hear Sam Cooke and Al Green.

Once inside, Sean and Mar sat at the bar and ordered a few drinks - shots of Silver Patrón with ginger ale. Between sips of tequila, they reflected on their lives. It had truly been a long and hard road from childhood to now. They were the sons of a drug czar whose lifestyle had put them in harm's way more times than they would like to remember and a woman whose strength - though tested more than the average - carried her until death. They had now grown into men; which was now a remarkable feat for black babies born into an atmosphere of poverty and crime.

Sean had set out a year after high school. He had plans on trying out for UConn however, since he didn't get the scholarship he and Mar were hoping for. Mar promised him if he would just attend college, he would pay for it. Sean would just have to be a walk on; he would have to prove himself even more so now. Mar had already began looking for a house in Delaware and buyers for the businesses he had established in Jersey. It felt good to have been up against all odds and overcome them. Through all they had been through - losing their father, struggling while their mother recovered from being raped, living on both sides of the poverty line, being shot and nearly killed, held for ransom, the drug game, eluding federal indictments, friends being murdered in front of them - they had survived.

Luckily, besides being kidnapped and somehow not being touched by the six bullets Mar's shooter had pumped into Mar and the car, Sean had experienced the evils of the game secondhand. But, as he told Mar:

"All the shit you went through might as well had happened to me. You don't know how scared I was when you got shot up. I felt every bit of your pain. All I kept thinkin was, please don't let me lose my brotha the same way I lost my dad."

Sean took another sip of his Patrón. He picked up the icy glass, ignoring the napkin that was stuck to the condensation on the bottom of the glass, and sucked the rest of the tequila through the thin straw.

"I know, that's why I held on baby boy." Mar said. Sean just nodded his head then continued.

"I know it might've seemed strange that I aint cry when mom died but believe me, it hurt Mar…real bad." Sean's eyes began to water just thinking about Josephine and the day they lowered her body into the ground.

"It hurt so much I couldn't cry. I wanted to but that day, when you called me and told me you found her dead, the only thing that cried was my heart. I loved mom more than I can say. In time

you kinda took over the role of pops but mom, nobody could ever replace her."
Mar placed his hand on Sean's shoulder.

"It's gon be right…trust me. I know you loved mom, we all did, but life gotta go on. Let's just try to celebrate the fact that she passed on to smoother seas." They both threw back two more shots and Sean left the bill and a nice tip on the counter.

As they walked out of Tip Top a man in his drunken haste bumped into Mar. Sean reacted quickly. He shoved the man hard and gave him a warning.

"Watch where you goin."

The man turned around to face them. This drunk, with his foul odor and ragged clothing turned out to be Brandon.

"Mar?" He slurred with the filthy stench of cheap wine on his
breath.

"Maaar-quise…" Brandon said stretching Mar's name annoyingly
and hugging Mar's coat.

"What chu doin out here, you must need ya boy again, huh?"

"Nah, I'm visitin Lexi's mom for the holidays." Mar said, struggling to get Brandon's arms from around him. He was surprised by Brandon's condition considering he had just given him twenty-five thousand dollars no more than eight months ago. Only if he knew that the day, he met Brandon on Myrtle Ave. the weed he smelled had been laced with crack. Somebody had turned Brandon onto turbos and his addiction to cook-up had been growing even back then.

"You lookin real bad champ." Mar said as he backed up a few
steps.

"Aww man, aint nuttin wrong wit me B, I'm cool as a fan in a
blizzard baby." Brandon said trying to shake off the insult.

"Whateva you say." Mar said unable to contain a small chuckle. How could Brandon actually believe he was cool. He looked like Pooky from New Jack City.

"I am man, I'm straight as nine-fifteen doggie."

"Yo, you killin me wit da fly ass sayins fam…you *not* cool or straight, you doin bad and you look worse. What chu do wit da bread I gave you?" Mar asked, even though he already figured out what the answer would be. Brandon, embarrassed as he was, glanced over at Sean then back at Mar.

"Man it aint no secret. I fucked it up B. I start bumpin that flake, next thing I know my man got me smoking woolies, and now…man, I'm fucked up right now Mar. That's what chu wanted to hear right? Well dere you go, Brandon's fucked up!"

He announced the last part for the whole bar to hear. Mar just shook his head in disappointment as everybody in the bar watched the confrontation closely.

"Nah, that aint what I want to hear, I grew up with you since this high…" Mar used his hand to show just how little they were when they first met.

"…Why would I want to hear you doin bad? But what's real is real, you twisted and it's showin."

"C'mon sun, don't judge me, I don't need that right now. I get that all day every day, motherfuckas judging me dat don't even know me. If anything, I need some support."

Mar had a good heart - sometimes too good - but he was tired of helping people that didn't want to help themselves. Not only that, he was starting to wonder if the people he helped would do the same for him if he was in need. He highly doubted it. Mar looked down on Brandon despondently.

"All I got is some advice for you Brandon. When ya ditch get too deep stop diggin."

With that, Mar walked past Brandon and out of the bar. Brandon ran out right behind them and grabbed Mar's arm to turn him around. Sean jumped at Brandon but Mar grabbed Sean before he could strike him.

"My bad." Brandon said after he realized he had just put himself
in danger.

"Look out for me, you see what kind of condition I'm in." Again, he was pleading.

"What you need, a ride to the rehab? I'm not givin you money so you can spend that shit on some hard." Mar said.

"You know what…fuck you then B, come around here actin like you all holier than thou, man you aint no better than me Mar. You sling that dope, you get people killed, shit, you might be worse than me."

Mar slammed his fist into Brandon's face hard. Brandon's eye socket shattered on impact and he hit the ground hard. Sean began to stomp his face into the pavement relentlessly. Mar had to grab Sean before he killed Brandon. It looked like that was Sean's plan by the way he was stomping Brandon's face into the ground with no remorse.

Brandon curled up on the sidewalk like a bloody fetus. He was squirming and grimacing in pain; dizzy from the force of Sean's stomp against his head. His skin was scraped to the white meat on the side of his face that laid against the ground. His jaw was now out of place. Mar and Sean jumped in Mar's 600 and fled the scene.

"I can't hear what the fuck you're sayin, speak clearly." Tony barked angrily into the phone.

"Man, they stomped my fuckin face…sssss….aaahh…it's hard for me to fuckin talk…Listen….sssss…..I said Marquise…the one that killed ya man, ya man Hector….he on his way to East Twenty -eighth and Farragut in Flatbush right now. He in a ninety-eight Mercedes Benz CL6000...shhhhhit! The car's silver…"

Brandon was pissed and he wanted Marquise dead. He had to pay for his disrespect, and for dislocating his jaw.

After Brandon murdered Hector, Tony took over and in Brandon's transition from pusher to user, he started getting his work off of Tony's people who still had some of the rawest fishscale in the city.

"Where at on Farragut?" Tony asked.

"It's the first or second house from the corner. You should see his car though.

"You better not be lying to me."

"Why would I…ahhh…why would I call you just to make some shit like this up? Just hurry up before you miss him because if he get back to Jersey I can't help you."

Tony wanted to do this himself because he felt responsible for Hector's death. If he would have made sure Mar was dead Hector would still be alive. To Tony this was unfinished business. As he made his way to Flatbush he reminded himself to make sure the job was finished this time.

"He won't live through this one!"

23

Marquise had been shot a few months ago. He then tragically lost his mother to cancer so the day he and Lexi went to visit her mother on Christmas, Lexi was overjoyed. Mar was happy because he needed a distraction from all the turmoil in his life. Sean was just happy that Marquise was happy. As pregnant as she could be without bursting, Lexi had a good time at her mother's and was happy to see Mar enjoying himself as well. Hard times had flooded his life like a cascade and she knew how much he needed to enjoy himself. He needed a reminder of why life was still worth living.

After opening presents and eating a nice meal prepared by Lexi's mother Patrice, Sean and Marquise had gone out for a drink and Lexi helped her mom straighten up.

"I'm just so happy for you baby." Patrice told her daughter as she rinsed off the dishes and passed them to Lexi to be put in the dishwasher.

"You know," Patrice continued.

"I really like Marquise. He's smart, he's sweet, good to you, respectful to me…he's a man's man you know? I think he'll make a real good husband."

Hidden behind Patrice's comment was a bitter feeling as she began to compare Lexi's deceased father and Marquise. Women despise an irresponsible man and that's exactly what Lexi's father had been while he was alive. He squandered his money in squalid pool halls and speakeasies. He gambled it away in basement poker games, and as long as he lived he never held down a job more than six months. Lexi's father had lived and died in debt. So many times Patrice wanted to tell Lexi the truth about her dad but didn't because Lexi adored her father and it would break her heart to hear exactly who her father really was. No matter how much Patrice despised Lexi's father she didn't want Lexi to as well. She found it more peaceful to let Lexi enjoy the fantasy of her father being this great man. Just thinking about him was starting to anger her.

Marquise was no fantasy however. He was the real thing and he was good for her daughter. Patrice was proud to tell Lexi this.

"I think he'll be good for you."

"I know he will mom." Lexi responded, placing the last of the plates in the dishwasher. Mar always provided for his family. He wasn't careless with his money. He wasn't a drunk, and

he never put his hands on Lexi. He treated her like she was the queen of Sheba.
As Lexi and Patrice finished the last of the dishes and made their way back into the living room Mar and Sean burst through the door…a little too fast. Their haste interrupted the talks of men and marriage and alarmed both women.

"Lexi, c'mon…we gotta go." Mar said hurriedly. Patrice couldn't conceal her concern. Her eyes were begging for an explanation for the frenzy. Lexi was just as worried and put up a bit of a fight. She wanted to know what was going on.

"Look, I apologize Mrs. Patrice but we really gotta get back to Jersey…somethin just came up." Mar said as he kissed Lexi's mom on the cheek. The kiss was a little rougher than he intended.

"Wait Quise…What's wrong baby, what happened?" Lexi asked, frightened by the way Mar was acting.

"I'll explain it to you later Lexi, right now we gotta go." Mar said, grabbing all their things and hurrying Lexi out of the house.

"Thanks for the food Mrs. Patrice, everything was good." Mar said as he kissed the warm cheek of Lexi's mother one final time.

"Okay baby, I'm sorry yall gotta leave so soon and in a rush like this. You just make sure you drive safe and come back to see me soon, alright?"

"I promise." Mar gave his word then he, Sean and Lexi headed out to the car. Mar and Sean were forced to cater to Lexi's slower pace.

"Baby, what's goin on? Please talk to me." Lexi said as Mar helped her into the passenger seat. Sean climbed in the back behind the driver seat. Lexi needed extra room for her belly and the baby boy it held inside. She looked like she would deliver at any moment.

"Let me just get us outta here and back home and I'll let you know what this is all about."

It had been such a nice day. A nice Christmas spent with her mother and fiancé. Why did it have to end like this? Lexi thought as her trembling hands clutched tightly at her purse. Scared didn't begin to describe the fear she was feeling. She watched through the rearview mirror as Mar made his way to the driver side door. He opened the door but before getting in he bent down and looked directly into Lexi's eyes.

"You know I love you right?"

"Yes I know that Quise." Lexi said, slightly confused. "And you love me right?"

"Of course I love you baby." Lexi said, Mar's questions just adding to her worry.

"Would you just get in the car so we can leave, you startin to scare me." Only if she knew Mar's behavior was starting to worry Sean now too, and he knew what was going on.

Mar stood straight up to slide his feet in first. Just then, the screeching of tires made Lexi's heart skip a beat. Out of instinct, she immediately cradled her stomach as the black car pulled to a screeching halt right beside Mar. Mar spun towards the car. A man jumped out of the car and ran up to Mar and from point blank range shot him dead in his forehead. Sean and Lexi both felt nauseated as they watched Marquise's blood splatter against the windshield. The shooter fled after that single shot.

Sean jumped out of the car with a sickening feeling of déjà vu and Lexi let out a long, high-pitched wail. Slowly that wailing became eerie shrieks of terror as her worst nightmare materialized right before her eyes. Being with a hustler, Lexi had grown accustomed to the fact that Mar was always in danger and that something like this could happen at any second. From flirting with the penal system to possibly being killed because of jealousy, he was always at some form of risk. It's a haunting feeling but her love for Marquise had overshadowed all fears of his dangerous lifestyle.

As Mar began to slowly detach himself from a life of crime Lexi pondered with dread how torn she would be inside if his past would come back to disrupt the paradise they were creating for themselves. Here and now those unshakeable nightmares were manifesting. Her fiancé and the father of her unborn child was dead and she didn't have to get out of the car to know it. She felt it. The maggots had already begun to eat the dead half of her heart. Lexi got out of the car slowly and kneeled beside her lover, secretly praying for the angel of death to come back and take her as well.

Lexi's withering heart hung unbearably heavy and she could barely see through the salty mist that covered her eyes. Even worse, it was apparent that her baby could sense her pain and the loss of its father as a pang of hurt rose up from her womb. Not a pain, but a mental hurt. By this time Patrice was on her way over to the car to console her daughter. Lexi was no longer screaming, just rocking Mar's head back and forth in her lap and crying. Her eyes had no signs of life but she was still moving. She looked down at the man who had revealed to her the truth of love, life, and now death. The man who had rescued her from a life of petty hustling and grinding poverty.

Lexi brought her face close to her beloved's and placed her mouth over his cold lips. She could feel his soul ascending and her cries grew heavier. Sean and Patrice cried too until Lexi glanced up vacantly in all directions around her. It was as if she was looking for someone or something to blame, something to take her frustrations out on - the boys with pockets full of crack and drug money, the amateur graffiti filled with the names of ghost and what seemed to be a space reserved just for Marquise. These streets were to blame. As Lexi glared at the project buildings, and hustlers, and prostitutes, and con-men, and other low-life degenerates she cried loudly, in piercing agony. Her screams were like gust of icy wind that cut through the still of the night as they sliced with equal ease through the hearts of all that heard it. It was a scream that would haunt Sean and Patrice for the rest of their lives. They could no longer cry as Lexi's own lament made them realize their sullen songs of sorrow were nothing in comparison to hers.

Lexi's hysterical voice rang through every corner, alley, street, side-street, and building in Flatbush, echoing into the ears of all within earshot. As if in a trance, people began to exit their cars, stoops, homes, and hideouts and walk closer to where Lexi and Mar were lying in a growing pool of blood. As they approached the tragic scene and stared in shock at Lexi weeping over Mar's body, they backed up in fright. No one but Sean and Patrice dared come any closer. It was as if the stream of blood running from beneath Mar's body and the hysterical screaming of Lexi had paralyzed them and frozen the marrow in their frigid bones.

Horrified women and children gazed upon the horrible scene and cried frightfully. The older men tried to comfort their wives, daughters, and sisters, and the younger ones who knew Marquise or of him were in shock as much shock as the women. As Lexi began to regain some focus, she prayed one more time for God to accept the breath of life she was offering and let her follow Marquise into the sun and out of the darkness of this cold world. Everyone who had witnessed the tragedy or the aftereffects of it could see as clear as day that half of Lexi's being was lying dead on that frozen concrete and that she would never be the same again.

GET IN, GET OUT
Love and the **GAME** II

FORWARD

When Saleem Little wrote Love and The Game, he produced a novel that crosses genres in its appeal to raw human emotion. From urban fiction to historical fiction to thriller to romance to action and adventure, Love and The Game is a full literary experience. Little writes with an aptitude that surrounds the reader with the sounds, visions and spiritual connectivity of a New York City hustler's lifestyle which toggles convincingly between the moral and the amoral.

Love and The Game is much, much more than a Scarface rags-to-riches knock-off in book form. Love and The Game digs deeper. This book puts you inside a drug dealer's family and forces you to look at their world through their eyes. From that view, it's not so easy to say "this is bad" or "that is good".

There is a progression that led Marquise "Mar" Jackson to lead the life that he leads, and Little digs deep into Mar's family history to give it to you. After reading Love and The Game, you see the how Arthur G. Jackson inadvertently opened the door for his son James to get that life-changing taste of a hustler's life as a teen. You see how immersion into that lifestyle progressed into the cold-hearted criminality that spanned almost three decades, transforming James into the person that Harlem dubbed "Broadway James", a legend in his own time. You see how, in turn, James' son Mar did not blindly insert himself into his dad's lane but still ended up taking a similar path in life.

Mar is not your typical drug dealer, and he's definitely not in it for typical reasons. Mar is in the game of drug dealing by blood, not gullible admiration. Like his father James that had a good run in the game before him, Mar was mentally forged for the drug trade and all of the horrors and trials that come with it. He analyzed his friends as they went from boys to junkies and/or dealers. He witnessed the women he desired as a boy become lifeless sex toys for anyone with money, drugs or both. Through it all, his goal was to maintain control and make enough money to get in and get out unscathed.

The rise to fortune is never easy, especially if ill-gotten. As Mar applies his energy to a trade that leads to many deaths, you get a better view of the complexity of his world. From his recollection of a murder dealt by the hands of his father while Mar was still a preteen, past the moment he partially avenged his father's death and mother's rape, Mar can hold a reader's attention with a warm heart and a cold grip.

Initially for the survival for his mother and little brother, Mar's involvement in drugs slowly drowns him in all of the foibles that illicit activities eventually bring to light. Drug dealing eventually endangers the family he tried to protect. As he rises in rank, his best friend's jealousy become unbearable. His love for his girlfriend is tested by his lust for drug runner. Life is simply complex with no signs of letting up.

Along for the treacherous ride is Lexi, Mar's first and last love. Little give her a depth that makes her involvement in the Love and The Game easily counterbalance Mar's adventures. Lexi's love for Mar is singular, but she is far from a trophy girlfriend. This almost forgotten little girl from Flatbush unfolds an aspect of the game that is chilling, yet equally feminine. The direction that Little took this character caught me off guard, but I was definitely impressed and enlightened by the various stations in life Lexi was able to achieve. From poverty in the ghetto to suburban life and eventually European extravagance, Lexi fitted perfectly in the intricate plot twists that Little brings to this novel.

-Joey Pinkney June 25, 2011

"Sometimes our internal fire goes out but is blown back into a flame by someone else, and each of us owes our deepest thanks to that person who has rekindled that fire within."

-Josephine

1

"Regrets"

Sean glanced around his cell in Allenwood Federal Penitentiary and for the first time he realized just how alone he was. True, Marquise and his mother were both gone, but Sean had brought most of this on himself. No one really wants to be affiliated with a rat and this is the stigma Sean brought on himself when he signed that 5K1 and became an informant for the U.S. government.

One of the most disturbing things to Sean was the treatment he was receiving for his cooperation. He was putting his life and integrity on the line for them. Maybe if this was the sixties, maybe even the seventies he may have been tucked away in some witness protection program, in some suburban neighborhood, working a nine to five for the rest of his miserable, guilt-ridden life. Not nowadays though. Snitches were too common, to plentiful to placate with huge deals and witness protection. Sean got on the stand and testified against seven different dealers from New York to New Jersey...He got twenty years for his cooperation.

Was it worth it? Hell no! To him, getting back in the game wasn't worth it. After all he had watched his brother go through, after being kidnapped and threatened with murder, after realizing then that he wasn't built for the game - to touch a drug period wasn't worth it. The snitching was far down his list of regrets.

Lexi wasn't speaking to him at all anymore. So, here he was, with no contact whatsoever to anybody. He had nobody; nobody but his own antagonistic conscience eating him up on a daily basis. There were those thoughts of hanging up from time to time but the thing he thought about most was how he ended up here.

Seven months after Josephine's funeral Sean, Marquise, and Lexi made the trip to New York to celebrate Christmas with Lexi's mother. They had a real good time and the climax for Sean was being able to treat Mar to a few drinks at their father's favorite bar. Being able to be alone and talk man to man with Mar had been the highlight of the day for Sean.

In Mar's final hour, Sean really got to express his feelings on all he, Mar, and Josephine had been through. The time alone with his brother had been nothing but enjoyable until Mar's old friend Brandon stumbled into the bar drunk and bumped into Marquise as they were making their way out of the Tip Top. Sean didn't really remember Brandon but he remembered he and Mar used to be friends as kids. None of that mattered once Brandon began to get disrespectful. After Mar put Brandon on his back pocket Sean blacked out. He began stomping Brandon's face repeatedly. Had Mar not grabbed Sean when he did he may have killed Brandon. That moment would cause the fastest chain of negative events Sean had ever seen. These events would haunt Sean for the rest of his life.

After Mar's funeral, Sean was looking for someone to lean on and this time there was no one. He was never as good at holding himself up as Mar was - being independent was new to him. His mother had spoiled him as a child and Marquise had supported him from then on. This was the first time he was being put in the position to depend on himself.

The month following Mar's death, Lexi gave birth to Marquise Demarcus Jackson Jr. Lexi immediately began calling him Quise - the same thing she used to call Marquise. Sean and Lexi's mother Patrice were in the hospital when Quise was born. They were the only support she had now and even early on she realized it was nothing like the support and security Marquise gave her while he was alive.

Sean left for college two months later. He would be attending a major four-year university in Connecticut where he would major in business. He promised Lexi he would stay in touch as much as possible and help out as much as he could. It was the least he could do for his brother who had done so much for everybody while he was alive. Mar had done so much for Sean personally and now all Sean wanted to do was make his brother proud by going to college and becoming somebody and helping to make sure Quise could do the same.

College was a new experience for Sean. It had been a long time since his life had, had real structure. He adjusted well though. After falling behind in grades early on, he got his GPA up to a 3.4 and Lexi and Quise seemed to be doing just fine according to Lexi. In Sean's sophomore year things started to fall apart however. He began to lose focus. His money was drying up and the urge to be popular was getting the best of him. It was around this time that Lexi was being forced to sell the businesses she inherited from Mar and handling litigations in her battle with the city to keep her salon. She had reached out to Sean but there wasn't much he could do, especially financially. The money Mar had left him covered tuition and that's it. Tuition and fees were $31, 985 and Room and Board was another $7,842. On top of that was the couple hundred he had to spend on books. Most of the remaining money had gone to Lexi and Quise. Josephine's house was his but there was no way he was going to sell that. The house had too much sentimental value. He planned on living in the house when he finished school.

After contemplating long and hard about what he could do for money, Sean soon discovered college could be a goldmine with the right amount of coke and pills. It was in his sophomore year that he began to realize that college was slightly overrated. A big majority of the kids were there for the party. He realized a lot of them went to school because their rich parents had saved the money so they might as well see what Spring Break was really all about. It didn't hurt that they got the new Porsche or Mercedes to drive there in.

Sean used to think the crack fiends and junkies in his old neighborhood were bad but when he thought about it most of the crack heads he knew just sold scraps and committed petty stunts only to beg a dealer to give them a ten dollar bag for the seven they came up with. These kids were in their late teens and early twenties and rich, they blew thousands on drugs. They were doing drugs he had never seen or heard of - Special K, meth, oxycontin, mushrooms, codeine, Percocet, hydrocodone, LSD. You name it, they did it. Sean couldn't resist the urge to supply that demand.

Sean hadn't gotten the athletic scholarship everyone had hoped for and after assuming he just wasn't good enough, he never even tried out for the team. Instead, he allowed his childhood fantasies of mega-contracts, super endorsements and a Michael Jordan-like career fade away. Business & Economics was a little more realistic. The economic side of his course was arduous but overall, he knew it would pay off. The problem was, the distractions in Seans' life were becoming stronger than his focus.

College parties were actually orgies where wine, liquor, and beer flowed like water. Drugs of all sorts were being done in every room and this is exactly how Sean got introduced to Jimmy, a twenty-year old Irish kid from Boston who promised Sean he could get him some pretty good coke for a good price.

Sean started with a group of five people that snorted coke and would buy for themselves or collect their friend's money and bring it to Sean. He had another small group of clientele that bought ecstasy from him. Some of the people he sold powder to rocked it and smoked it. Seeing this changed his whole perception of college in general. Nothing was ever what it seemed. Here he was in a prestigious university and a quarter of the student body were drug addicts.

Sean's circle began to expand and his supplier had to introduce Sean to his connect because he could no longer fulfill Sean's orders. The more money Sean made, the less interested in school he became. At the beginning of his junior year, he dropped out. He kept his apartment near the campus so he could still supply his clientele but school no longer served a purpose for him. It was also at this time that Lexi called about her problems.

"I don't know what I'ma do Sean. They taking my salon, my money's getting low, I tried to cop from somebody else but they burned me."

"For how much?" Sean asked angrily.

"Twenty-five." Lexi admitted reluctantly.

"Twenty-five thousand?"

"Yup."

"Who was it? And why you aint just come to me?"

"I don't know. I didn't even know what you was really into. Plus, I wasn't sure if you would help me. I'm thinking you gone tell me I don't need to be hustling and that you'll help me with bills and all that. I really wasn't trying to hear that Sean. I don't like depending on people to take care of me and my son."

Sean thought about what Lexi was saying.

"You right, I am going to tell you that you don't need to be hustling."

"Neither do you." Lexi said defiantly.

Sean brushed Lexi's comment off.

"That shit is dangerous Lexi."

"I know that Sean, did you forget how long I was with your brother?"

"Nah, I didn't. But you see how that turned out for him, why would you wanna go that same route?"

"I don't know no other way right now."

"What are you talking about Lexi, you don't know that way either. You think just because you was with Marquise that qualifies you to sell drugs successfully? Are you serious? Listen, I ended up selling mom's crib in Jersey, I'ma stay out here in Connecticut, I aint really tryin to go back there, aint nuttin in Jersey for me. I got a pretty penny for that house. I'll send you half of what I got, it's nothing."

Sean was trying hard to dissuade Lexi from getting involved with drugs. He would have done anything to get her to rethink her decision, even if that meant giving her half of the $375,000 he got for the house Josephine left him.

"And then what happens when that money runs out?" Lexi reasoned.

"Am I supposed to keep coming to you for handouts?"

"I don't care if you come to me for the rest of my life. You my sister as far as I'm concerned and I'll do anything to see to it that you and Quise straight."

Lexi was starting to get frustrated. This is exactly why she hadn't gone to Sean in the first place. Why did everybody think they knew what was right for Lexi?

"I'm perfectly capable of making my own decisions." Lexi said to herself.

"Sean, you don't know how long you gon be around. I can't depend on nobody but me, Mar's death showed me that.

"Yeah, but Lexi what I'ma give you is a nice amount of money, at least a buck-fifty. You could invest that in something legit for yourself, maybe another salon or something."

"I tried another salon!" Lexi said effusively. She took a few deep breaths to get her anger under control.

"Look, I apologize for calling you, I knew this was gonna be a waste of time. I'ma ask you one more time then I'm hangin up. Is you gon give me some work or not?"

"Lexi, you know if Mar was here he would kill me if he knew I sold you some coke. Shit, he would kill me for selling the shit myself."

"Well, Mar aint here no more is he?" Lexi said. It was the first time her contempt for Mar for leaving her alone in this cold world had surfaced.

"Still," Sean said, still trying to reason with Lexi.

"Still nothing Sean, you…no, you know what, it's cool, I don't even need ya help. I'll take care of it myself." Lexi said preparing to hang up. Right then it was evident to Sean that Lexi was determined to hustle and that was with or without his help. Now he felt the need to at least protect her by introducing her to someone he knew wouldn't take advantage of her.

"Hold on Lexi." Sean said, the defeat in his tone pleasing Lexi's ears, but filling her heart with guilt. She knew Sean was only trying to do right by Marquise, and here she was making him compromise his morals just so she could get her way.

"We do what we gotta do..." She remembered Shanika telling her as they sat in their old Flatbush apartment discussing the struggles of single mothers.

"Whatever we gotta do! Being broke and tryna do this shit alone...that's why we boost, steal, trick, or whatever...we be driven to that shit...that life of crime or whatever you wanna call it...it's our children's needs that force us into it..."

If a little guilt was all she had to live with to make sure she and Quise were provided for then so be it.

"What Sean?"

Sean sighed a breath of frustration.

"Listen, I'ma plug you in. My people stay in Boston, that's about two hundred miles from where you at if you willing to travel that far. It's about three and a half to four hours up and back, depending.

Lexi was smiling on the other end.

"How I'ma get in contact with him?"

"I'ma put it together. Just be patient. Give me like a day or two and I'ma let you know when we on deck." Sean stopped. A thought arose.

"You know what you doin?" He asked Lexi.

"Yes, I know what I'm doin." Lexi said, her irritation returning. Why did men always underestimate women? How hard could selling drugs be? They practically sold themselves.

"So just give me till tomorrow or the next day and I'll hook something up, you can wait that long right?" The last thing Sean wanted was for Lexi to venture off in search of a connect again. He had to look out for her now because it was obvious she was going to get involved with drugs regardless of what anyone had to say about it.

"Yeah I can wait but I can't see why you don't just give me some work." Lexi said, stating what she felt was the safer and faster route.

"Cause, we family and I don't want this shit to come between that. I don't really wanna give you the connect Lexi, but I can see you dead-centered on flippin some coke, so I'ma point you in the right direction…you know, put you in a good situation and then I don't really want nuttin else to do with it."

"That's cool." Lexi said. She was satisfied Sean was going to make sure she got what she wanted. Lexi did get exactly what she wanted and before long she was growing accustomed to nerve-rattling highway trips with work, budgeting, and ducking the insidious traps of the numerous law enforcement agencies breathing down her neck. Lexi was in the game.

Exactly one month after introducing Lexi to his supplier, Sean was preparing to make one of his own routine runs to Boston. His route quickly came to mind. "I-95 N to Providence…Exit 12…I 93...Beantown!"

Veronica, a 24-year-old woman of Italian descent; with wavy brunette hair, and azure-blue eyes watched Sean as he counted a stack of money for the second time and rewrapped each stack. Her scrutinizing eyes looked like two azurite stones set in porcelain, but they were anything but beautiful. The stones were blemished and the porcelain was stained.

Veronica was finely built with a thin, olive face. Her thin nose was now a permanent repository for cocaine. Sean met Veronica in New London shortly after dropping out of college. She had been one of his customers until the money ran dry and her parents didn't have any more credit cards for her to steal and charge to the max. Now she worked as a mule to support her habit. It was a symbiotic relationship - she didn't have to pay for coke and Sean didn't have to transport it.

"How much is in the bag?" Veronica asked as Sean placed the last stack of money away. Sean threw a quizzical look at her.

"Since when do she ask questions like that?" Sean's conscience asked him. Before he could take the time to answer his anger took over and he barked at Veronica.

"Don't worry about what's in the bag…just drive…mind ya fuckin businesses too."

"Jesus Christ, Ok, I'm sorry Sean."

This would have to be her last time Sean thought. She was becoming too nosy. Not only that, she had made this trip too many times already, it was time for he and Veronica to part ways. But not before she made this last trip.

Sean's life was riding on this trip. He was spending everything he had on what he thought would be enough work to give him enough money to last him while he spent three weeks in Morocco with his girlfriend. Altogether, he had over three-hundred thousand in the bag. That Three-hundred grand would be buying him fifteen ki's of flake, ten thousand ecstasy pills, and five new Glocks. Three Glock .40s and two Glock 19s. This was also the biggest shipment Veronica had ever moved.

"We don't have to go over it every time Sean, I know the routine, I know what to do."

Veronica said as Sean ran down the rules for the umpteenth time. When she first met Sean she would have never talked to him with such indifference but with time comes comfortableness. Too bad comfort tends to make way for disrespect when lines are crossed or limits are tested.

"Yeah we do cause I stand to lose too much if you fuck up. And watch ya mouth too, you startin to get real loose with the tongue. Pump ya breaks a lil bit."

Sean zipped the bag closed then he and Veronica made their way outside to Veronica' s Envoy. Sean sat the bag on the back seat and shut the door feeling content. He was satisfied that everything was precisely where and how it needed to be. More importantly, he had no bad feelings whatsoever. This would be a quick trip with no hassles.

Following Sean onto the highway, Veronica reached in her pocket and pulled out a small bag of coke. It was all she had left but she tossed it anyway. It was odd even to her. She never threw coke away - she spent her life chasing money so she could buy coke. But, she had to. These last couple trips had really bothered her conscience which rattled her nerves, leaving her incapable of driving properly. This was too much and she just couldn't wait till it was all over.

"Fuck." Veronica grunted, pounding her palms against her steering wheel. She hated the position she was now in and wanted it to be done with. She couldn't take the pressure and felt like she would fold at any moment. She wondered if Sean knew.

"How could he know?"

"How could he not know?"

"These people are big, high-tec…they said there's no way he'd know."

"Sean's smart though, he picks up on everything…maybe he's going to have you killed when you get to Boston…will they be there to help you?"

Veronica's mind was racing and it was making her crazy. She literally screamed into the wind as her GMC rode a smooth seventy miles per hour. The scream did nothing but gave her a bigger headache.

When Sean and Veronica reached the hotel in Boston, they went through their normal procedure. Sean waited as Veronica got the room in her name, then escorted her into the room where they sat - usually in silence - for ten to fifteen minutes before Sean took Veronica's keys and left for his connect's house in her truck.

Nothing unusual.

Sean rode to Ruck's house and made the exchange - a fairly quick one considering how many times this had been done. It was now routine. Sean trusted his work would be top notch, and Ruck was sure all of his would money would be there. A simple exchange of bags and subtle pleasantries was the most either party extended before Sean and Ruck parted ways - both pleased with the profits of their arrangement.

Sean left the house and scanned his surroundings like a hawk. As usual he was suffering from the same nervousness he felt every time he handled large sums of work. Still, everything was normal and that calmed his nerves to an extent.

Sean pulled into the motel's parking lot and back into the same spot he had pulled out of. As he went to reach for his door, he noticed a figure in dark clothing running up alongside his car. It didn't take long for him to make out the bright yellow initials…then the gun headed towards his head…then…urine… running down his legs.

"Put your hands on the steering wheel…Now!" The federal agent holding the gun to Sean's head shouted.

Sean's heart was in the pit of his stomach…beating wildly. He looked around frantically like a small animal at the mercy of the hunter's rifle. His fear was forcing what he soon realized were tears to run from his eyes.

"Don't fuckin move again asshole!"

The agent opened Sean's door slowly and told him to get out. Like the flashing camera of the paparazzi, ten to fifteen black pistols focused on

Sean as soon as he exited the car and laid face down on the ground. His embarrassment rang loud as agents made fun of the fact that Sean had pissed himself. He didn't speak - not out of honor but because his fear had momentarily made him a mute - he simply complied with every order. Once the cuffs were on his trembling wrist, he knew it was over.

2

Surprise

Friday night at eleven o'clock pm, federal agents broke down Lexi's door. After scaring Quise and Lexi both half to death, the agents found twelve-hundred grams of coke and arrested Lexi for possession of a controlled substance with intent to deliver.

Saturday morning Lexi was on the phone with her lawyer. Eight hours later she and her Lawyer went to her prelim where her case was bound over for court. She was given a five-hundred-thousand-dollar bail. Not even seven hours later the FBI persuaded the judge that evidence existed to prove that Lexi's home had been used to store and mix drugs - specifically cocaine. Next came the property forfeiture. The FBI and DEA acquired liens against the house and it's contents. Federal Marshalls evicted Quise and the female friend she had called to come take care of Quise after she was taken into custody. The Marshalls allowed Quise's sitter to pack only a few articles of clothing. They then immediately changed the locks and posted guards at the property. They served the Notice of Intent at the same time they were evicting Quise and his sitter. Lexi's lawyer told her that in ten days she would get to go in front of a judge and argue against the forfeiture. They seized all of her bank accounts as well, including checking, savings, CD's, and all brokerage accounts which included her stocks, bonds, and any mutual funds she may have had. And after asking over and over again what was going on, she was told she had the power to make all of this go away, as long as she agreed to testify against her brother-in-law Sean.

3

Eye In The Sky

The feds had been watching Sean for 3 months now. They had watched him trail Veronica from Boston to New London on five different occasions. Veronica had been well aware of the investigation on Sean, she was the reason for it.

Three months prior, Veronica had made a trip to Boston alone. She picked up five kilograms of cocaine, nine ounces of heroin, and two-thousand double-stacked ecstasy pills. The only reason she knew this was because it was what the F.B.I. had told her she would be charged with if she didn't give up her boyfriend or whoever it was, she was transporting it for.

After snorting a line of coke on her way back, Veronica's driving becoming slightly reckless and she was pulled over by State Troopers. It didn't take long for the officer to realize that she was under the influence of something. After she admitted that she had done a line of cocaine but that she didn't want any trouble, the search began.

"Why would you get any trouble?" The officer had asked.

"And why are you moving around like that…you nervous? I'm gonna have to ask you to step away from the vehicle…as a matter of fact…"

The officer handcuffed Veronica and made her sit on the side of the road. It didn't take long for the Trooper to discover the drugs. The case was turned over to the Feds, who paid Veronica a visit. It didn't take her long to reveal everything she knew. Veronica told Sean she was pulled over and arrested. She told him since the car wasn't in her name, they called the rental company who discovered the person they had rented the car to had actually passed away two years prior. If whatever was in those bags was discovered no one had said anything about it.

"What was I supposed to tell them, wait I can't let you take that car, there's a lot of drugs in there that I really need to get to someone or they'll be mad at me…I was just happy that they didn't find it and locked me up…just think, I could be doing a lot of time right now Sean if I would have tried to save your drugs."

Beyond her belief, Sean had gone for it and charged it to the game. Over time, he put it behind him and began sending Veronica on trips again. He was going to make her work off her debt.

From the day the Feds let her go, she wore wires, got him to incriminate himself in conversations, and she delivered knowing that federal agents were tailing Sean as he tailed her.

After helping with the case with Ruck, taking the rap for the work found in Lexi's house and securing a deal that got her off, Sean testified against six other dealers and would now spend the next twenty years bouncing from one jail to the next afflicted with guilt and shame.

4

Back At It

It took some time for the ordeal with Sean to blow over. Sean and Ruck were both gone and once again Lexi didn't have a plug. Eventually some normalcy returned to her life but she realized she was once again spending money that wasn't returning. She had to do something but she was really starting to believe it just wasn't meant for her to sell drugs.

A man named Emilio de la Cruz owned the delicatessen Lexi found herself in one warm day in April. Emilio was heavy in the drug game but he had no need or urge to extend his business to anyone else. Lexi had tried before to plug in with Emilio but he refused. Lexi was here today for two reasons; they had the best hoagies in town and to see if a friend of hers who ran the deli would give her a job.

The deli - though fairly lucrative - was nothing more than a front for Emilio's illegal activities. He owned several other businesses that served the same purpose. His nephew Juan ran the place. Juan was fond of Lexi but their relationship was purely platonic. She was a regular here and Juan always took good care of her.

Juan and Lexi chatted for a minute while she watched one of Juan's nephew wrap her foot long sub. She asked for an application but Juan told her not to be foolish. If she really wanted a job she could have one but if she was looking for a connect today was her lucky day. Another one of his uncles had just gotten out of prison and would more than likely do business with Lexi.

"He's in the back, let me introduce you to him."

Juan wiped his hands clean and took off his apron. He only worked in the deli because of his parole. He still dabbled in crime but unlike his uncles, he didn't deal in drugs. He liked quick lump sums of money. He was an arms dealer but now he specialized in heists…jewelry stores, gun & munitions stores, banks - Juan would take anything from anybody. He took the deli seriously however because he realized the benefits of some legitimacy and his uncle promised him the store would be his one day.

In the back room of the deli sat Jose, a large man with pig-like features and an obvious lack of scruples. He was drinking warm rum at twelve-thirty in the afternoon. He looked like he was one drink away from drunkenness.

"Lexi, this is my uncle Jose."

Jose took a sip of his rum, gargled the fiery liquid, then swallowed it before shaking Lexi's hand and asking her how she was doing?

Jose's infatuation was evident immediately. He licked his lips as he observed Lexi. She was immaculately beautiful he thought to himself. Her skin was like honey, she was petite but built like an hourglass, and her eyes were diamonds. She was incredible. What could a woman so fine want with a man as vile and unattractive as him? Cocaine of course.

"She lookin for a connect." Juan said, interrupting his uncle's fantasy - a fantasy which had already boiled over the pot of admiration and into the internal fire of chronic obsession. Lexi just studied Jose, she wasn't sure if that was her cue to speak or if she should just wait for Jose to respond to his nephew's comment.

"Sit down, sit down." Jose said patting the chair closest to where he was seated. Lexi glanced over at Juan who motioned to her that it was alright and to go ahead and sit down. Jose examined Lexi critically, his dark eyes narrowing to slits. The look on his face was incredulous, scrutinizing, analytical. He was checking her for weakness, seriousness, or anything that could be told about her just by studying her eyes and demeanor. Though dim-witted he was sharp when it came to his craft - reading and judging characters and moving whatever his brother or cousins put in his hands. He also had a great deal of common sense.

"So you sure you wanna fuck wit me…wit this?" Jose asked.

"I mean, I think I'm sure."

"What do you mean, 'I think I'm sure'." Jose repeated in mocking tone.

"You're either sure or you're not." Jose glanced over at Juan, then back at Lexi. This time the look he wore was a questioning one.

"I mean, part of me wants to give that shit up and get a honest job. Sometimes I feel like this game isn't meant for me. I lost my fiancé and son's father to this. Now his brother just got twenty years. At the same time, I got a nice amount of clientele, and I'm used to that fast money. I know what I want. I want another connect, a few more birds, and my phone to start poppin again, but sometimes I wonder if it would be better for me and my son if I just got an honest job and lived an honest life."

"Honest job…what the hell is an honest job? And what do you consider an honest life?" Of course Jose's defensiveness was a reaction to what he felt was an indirect criticism of he and his line of work.

"You know…a regular nine to five, pay my taxes, obey the law…"

Jose didn't even let her finish.

"You think the people that make these laws you talkin bout obeyin, you think they actually abide by em?"

Jose wasn't giving Lexi time to interject, it was time she listened, because it was obvious that, though she had obviously sold some dope, she was still naïve to the ways of the world.

"They make them laws so they can take the focus off them and put out this image of a good country wit some rules. All bullshit. While you runnin round thinking this drug dealer or this thief is a crook or criminal, they robbin us all blind. If you looking so hard at the crook and making sure he fit the description of the usual suspects, you can't see that the fast-talkin lawyer in his suit and tie, or that middle-aged IRS man in all black is the one robbin you blind."

Jose shook his head, the weight of his disappointment in America's society and it's hypnotized citizens adding emphasis to his head shakes. Jose explored more grand conspiracy theories, before asking Lexi if she was sure once again. This time Lexi assured him she was.

"Tu muy bella…" Jose said, again falling victim to the amnesia Lexi's beauty usually induced. That fast he almost forgot what he was saying and wanted only to remind Lexi of how beautiful she was.

"You're very beautiful." Jose translated, realizing Lexi hadn't understood him. Lexi blushed. The blushing wasn't caused by any attraction to Jose but because she could see right now that because of her looks alone Jose would not only not be able to say no to her, but she would probably be receiving special treatment for as long as she dealt with him. His obsession was evident, all she would have to do now is entertain his crush from time to time, lead on that maybe she could someday look past his repulsive face and see the last iota of beauty that remained in his dark insides. As long as she fostered that false hope, he would continue to pursue a sexual encounter and she would have the power. This usage of these innate powers couldn't be viewed as a deceitful game she felt. Exploiting beauty was simply a byproduct of ages of a ubiquitous male chauvinism that prevented women from rising above menial positions in society. Using their God-given allure has been women's one steady source of bread and butter since the beginning of time. Lexi had to do what she had to do. If seduction worked, then so be it. She left that deli with a purchase price seven to eight grand cheaper than the twenty-five she had grown accustomed to paying with Ruck.

Lexi was back in business.

5

Spirit of a Hustler

After what felt like an eternity, the second light in a long list of obstacles destined to make Lexi late for her appointment with Jose turned green.

"Bout time."

Lexi accelerated quickly, her tires making extra revolutions because of the slick surface. Finally, after many attempts at gripping the road, the tires began to tread water like propellers on a speedboat. Lucky for Lexi, the cop at the last light had made the immediate left and the congested flux of traffic that had slowed her down earlier was far behind her and unable to see her subtle fishtailing. She had the road to herself now and she planned to take full advantage of that.

Lexi had made her mind up that Jose's pad would be the last stop in her route. First would be the grocery store, then, her cousin's house where she had to take this work. Both places she would be able to get in and out of with no hassles. Jose's spot wouldn't be that easy.

"What a bad bitch." Jose thought as he waited for Lexi to arrive. He glanced at his ugly face in the mirror he held in his hand. He had real bad skin, full of craters and acne scars. His eyes were small and sunk in like a pig's, his nose was excessively large and his hair was oily. He was a lazy, overweight, obnoxious indolent and the only reason he had money was because of who he was related to. No matter how sloppy and bad at managing money he was, he was in the slums where his more polished brother needed him. Jose still knew how to distribute coke.

After cursing his obese mother for giving him a face only she could love, Jose snorted the thin line of white powder he had been using the mirror to support.

"Aaaaaahhhhh…." Jose moaned after three quick inhales to clear his eroded nostrils. He wiggled his nose and said aloud,

"See, that's why they love you Jose, you got the best shit in the city."

These soliloquies were now routine. Jose didn't trust many people and his ill-mannered, antisocial behavior forced people to keep their distance. He knew he was ugly - something most women couldn't see past - so no women really loved him for him, they liked the money and the gifts, never him. And he wasn't the most honest, trust-worthy person in the world so most men shied away from a friendship with him. The bottom line was, anybody who claimed to like Jose were people who bought cocaine from him. It was that simple. That, or the ladies he spent money on. Knowing this made him cynical of everybody he came in contact with. On top of that, the coke was slowly starting to rattle his brain and dementia was slowly starting to settle in. Now, most of his comments were directed to - and answered by - himself. A reality Jose was growing to be just fine with.

"Who da fuck needs friends…a bunch of liabilities…more people to get close to you then do you wrong…can't be betrayed if you aint got no friends…fuck em all…"

A thin stream of blood began to run from Jose's nose, over his top lip, and onto his awaiting tongue. As the burgundy liquid filled his mouth with a disagreeable bitterness, he thought about Lexi - his pure little angel. He viewed Lexi as some kind of angel who the winds of misfortune had blown from heaven and into hell; an angel who was just trying to do the best she could in an unfamiliar world. Lexi was the only person Jose truly loved.

"Muy bonita." Jose said slowly as the coke began to take effect. His blood was rushing now, his heart issuing surges of blood to his bloodstream so fast his heart pounded and fluttered. Jose began to rub his genitals until a painful erection formed as he envisioned, he and

Lexi making love in beds of cocaine. His dementia even permeated his perverted sex life. He imagined himself snorting lines of blow off of Lexi's succulent, honey-bronze skin - licking it off of her pubic hairs as his tongue made its way to the moist slit between her thighs.

Jose knew Lexi was capitalizing off of his infatuation with her but didn't care. She wasn't the only one. Cocaine was nothing to him. All his brother wanted was twelve grand a ki; eleven whenever he brought them over himself. Jose didn't have to do much. He waited for his brother to bring a shipment back, or for his cousins to ship it themselves from home. He would get a call and a bag full of raw cocaine. He could cut it as many times as he wanted as long as he paid what he owed for each brick. So, though Lexi thought she was getting over on Jose, she wasn't. Coke wasn't a big deal to him. Getting Lexi was however, and if allowing her to believe she was getting over on him would get her, he would play the game as long as it needed to be played. One remarkable quality Jose did have was his unwavering patience. He knew Lexi would crack long before he would.

Lexi spotted the bright orange sign she was looking for. She quickly pulled into the GIANTS parking lot. She didn't bother to find a spot. Lexi pulled up to the entrance of the store and turned on her two-ways. She hurried through the store grabbing a few boxes of mashed potatoes and a couple cans of corn. She grabbed two of the biggest boxes of assorted Kool-Aid she could find and hustled to the self-check out line. Of course, she only scanned one item and threw the rest in the bag. No matter how much money she made, and how deep in the boondocks she lived, that little poor girl from Brooklyn was still in her.

Outside, Lexi jumped back in her Infiniti and headed to her cousin's house. Again, she laughed at the irony of her situation and the change of events in her life. A few years ago she was running a hair salon and now she was running drugs. She still found it amazing from time to time. She was actually about to drop five-hundred grams of powder off to her cousin and walk away with the average American's yearly income. All of this would take about ten minutes. If adversity introduces people to themselves then Lexi had the spirit of a hustler in her all along.

6

Choices

"Nice doing business with you Ms. Davis." The sound of this was really starting to annoy Lexi. Luckily, this would be the last time she would have to hear it. She was finishing up the last bit of paperwork she had to sign before handing over the last of Mar's business or breaking the leases on the office and storefront space he was renting. This final transaction was with another fast-talking Irish man who wanted to turn Mar's sports bar into an Irish Pub. He too was robbing her blind like all the others had. The liquor license was in her name so it wasn't hard to turn over, the hard part was the price she was letting it go for. Lexi knew she was cheating herself but she was getting desperate. The businesses were becoming too complicated for her to manage on her own. She was presented with the prospect of hiring a managing company but figured it would be easier to just sell them, and get enough to invest in a few interest-bearing accounts.

The one business she did know how to run and planned to keep was the beauty salon Mar had opened for her. There was no way she was going to waste the money spent on cosmetology lessons and the certificates she gained. She and Mar had put a lot into making sure she would be fully-equipped for that field. This business in particular had a lot of sentimental value. However, like Murphy's law, her bad luck just kept coming and anything that could go wrong did. The city decided to knock down the two adjoining buildings that housed Sean's barbershop - still managed by Lexi - and Lexi's salon in order to gentrify the neighborhood.

Lexi really believed that the salon would be her source of income for a long time to come but when the city decided that the block that housed Lexi's salon and several other small businesses was prime for redevelopment. Lexi's salon was in a prime location in the retail corridor of the city. Lexi called on the only person she believed was able to help her - John Rutherford.

"Hey Lexi, how can I help you baby?" John said after realizing who he was talking to. Her voice was actually a pleasant surprise. This was the first time he was hearing from anyone in Mar's family since the funeral.

"I need to know how to stop the city from knocking down my salon. They're saying my salon is located right in the area of the retail corridor that they want to occupy in order to gentrify the neighborhood. I don't want to move. Now I got a few other small business owners out here that'll sign a petition or whatever but I really need to know what I have to do."

Lexi sounded desperate. She had a plan but it was almost as if she knew deep inside a petty piece of paper with a few names on it wasn't going to save her salon. She really needed legal help.

"I have to be honest with you Lexi, when a city secures a developer to say…revitalize a neighborhood, broaden a street, or build like…a recreational park or some type of shopping plaza that they believe will generate income for the city, there's really not much renters, small business owners, or landowners can do."

John paused to allow Lexi to speak or show any signs that she didn't understand. She was silent but definitely listening. John went on.

"They have what are called Eminent Domain laws. Now, Eminent Domain gives each state the power to take private property for its use or a public use by a city, person, association, or corporation. Why can I run this down like this, because I'm dealing with the exact same thing in Virginia right now. I don't know if you remember Larnell."

Lexi shot a quizzical look in the sky.

"Of Course I do, He used to date my older sister a long time ago."

"Well, that's who introduced me to Mar. He had bought an eight-unit condominium in Richmond and now some corporation is trying to buy the land where his condos are to build who the hell knows what."

There was nothing but silence on Lexi's end of the phone.

"I'm very sorry Lexi but your options are very limited right now. The one thing that you do have working in your favor is that the city has to pay you equal market value for your property. But frankly, you can either take that buyout package and get out of the way of the demolition crew or you can wait for the city to condemn your property and force you out. All I can say is be smart Alexis."

John was frank. He was a straight shooter and that's what Mar had always liked about him.

"Take the money, and as soon as you find another place to set up shop, you give me a call and we'll make it happen."

"I invested too much time, blood, sweat, and not to mention money into this salon. I gross close to three-hundred thousand off of this salon John. And Mar bought this for me, you know that." Lexi lamented.

"I know, I know. Believe me, I realize how unfortunate this situation is." John said, the grief in his tone now equaling the amount in Lexi's.

"I aint about to just walk away from this without a fight." Lexi said angrily.

"And opening another one might backfire. One of the reasons I make so much money is because of my current location."

Lexi continued to argue her point but got nowhere with John and nowhere with the city either. Eventually, she took the buyout package that financed a new salon. The new salon forced Lexi into bankruptcy in the first year. She also grew frustrated with how long it took for legitimate investments to mature. She occasionally thought back to a time where money was no object. Where all Mar had to do was make a sale and the proceeds from just one of his sales could finance any and all of her material desires. She hated budgets. She hated interest because it took too long to accumulate. Yet, she was a woman, and thanks to Marquise a very spoiled woman. She still loved to shop.

She continued to splurge, never minding that her income would never support what she was spending. Lexi had an addiction to spending money. She learned the hard way that the addiction to spending cures itself because soon there's nothing left to spend. Before she realized it, she was down to seventy-five thousand dollars. So, she chose to invest that in something that she knew from experience would double it's worth quicker than any other investment she could make at the moment - coke. She was now in the same game that had killed Marquise four years earlier.

7

Jose

When Lexi Finally got to Jose's apartment, she was extremely tired and he was his normal inconsiderate, horny self. The groping began almost immediately - his chubby fingers with their hairy knuckles grabbing Lexi's slim waist, fondling her breast and pinching her butt. Lexi twisted and turned trying to get out of his clutches but did let him get his occasional feel in without protest just to secure the two bricks for the thirty-five-thousand-dollar price tag he promised her.

"Damn mami, when you gon stop wit da mind games and let me fuck dat pretty little pussy? You know you want me to." Jose said confidently while standing in the middle of the living room holding his crotch, making sure Lexi noticed his erection.

"I'll tell you what," Jose continued before she could say no.

"You don't even gotta let me fuck you. Tonight, all you gotta do is let me lick that cuchi and I'll be satisfied."

"See, why you gotta talk to me like that? Like I'm some two-bit whore or something." Lexi said. At times she could care less about what Jose said, but other times she took offense.

"Maybe if you tried talking to me like a lady, I might think about it. Why don't you try to be a gentlemen, talk to me like you respect me, not like you want to fuck me and forget me. It's offensive Jose. Can't you be romantic?"

Why did Lexi always expect from random men what Marquise would have given her with no questions asked. She had been with the best, anything else for the rest of her life would be less.

Jose stood there for a minute, giving serious thought to what Lexi had said. He did respect Lexi. He didn't look at her like the other broads he had in and out of his life. She was different and he did owe her that to keep that in mind.

Jose took a puff of his cigar and exhaled the smoke slowly. His eyes were squinted like he was contemplating a chess move. He was a real character - narcissistic, no matter how fat and hideous, loud, flashy, flamboyant and pompous. Lexi felt sick just thinking about his filthy, cigar-scented tongue on her body. Just when she began to wonder what he could have been thinking about he began to speak in the most charming voice he could muster.

"Yo te quiero, por tu mente, no solo tu querpo, por que tu eres, bella por dentro y por fuera." Jose smiled gallantly after he finished. Slightly puzzled and slightly amused Lexi asked Jose what he had said to her.

"It means I love you for your mind and your body because you're beautiful inside and out."

Almost childlike, Jose awaited approval and instead of laughing in his face, Lexi grabbed Jose's chin as if to say how cute.

"See, I knew you could be sweet. That sounded so much nicer than what you said at first. Still, I gotta pass for the night, I have to get home to my son."

"All your words are lies…truth is the fire in your eyes." Jose said, before laughing at himself and leaving to get Lexi her work. He respected Lexi too much to press her any further tonight.

"Here you go baby girl." Jose said after returning with two packages.

"Be safe." Jose said, relighting his cigar. Lexi hated the smell of cigar smoke.

"Thanks baby." Lexi said, handing Jose his money and tucking away her coke as he counted it.

Lexi left the house satisfied and Jose felt he had done his moral good for the day. Now he was ready to get a hooker, a bottle, and a room.

The smell of pot roast was pleasing to Lexi's nostrils. It was a pleasing reminder of the normality she would now be able to settle into. No coke deals, no police, just her and her beautiful son. She wished life could always be that simple.

8

Love at First Sight

After three months of doing business with Jose, Lexi would finally meet Emilio de la Cruz for the first time. Emilio was like the phantom. He was seldom seen but always talked about, something that added to his lure. Because of this mystery he sometimes seemed larger than life. Lexi would soon find out that like most stars he was human, just slightly more disciplined and discreet in his dealings.

Lexi was making one of her routine stops in the deli when in walked the sharpest, Dominican man she had ever laid eyes on. His face was serious - stern even - but very handsome. His eyes were dark and dangerous-looking, but attractive. A small scar outlined the corner of his left eye. His face was slim and defined. He wore a three-button wool Brioni suit with a silk pocket square, a cotton Ermenegildo Zegna couture shirt, a silk Canali tie and a pair of leather Santoni loafers. He was sharp and Lexi noted that not only was the calculator she was using to appraise Julio's diamonds and outfit working, so was the sensitive side of her heart. Blinded by some primal inferno of passion, her insides were going crazy and it was scary to her. This was the first time her body had actually reacted this way to a man since Marquise. The now foreign feeling was causing her wires to tangle. She wanted to run to the restroom for fear her crush was seeping out of the pores on her face like the sweat forming under her arms.

Upon noticing Lexi, Emilio was just as dazed by her attractiveness and immediately walked over to her and introduced himself.

"Hello gorgeous, my name's Emilio…you are?"

Her mouth was sensuous, with luscious lips, perfectly set teeth and an enticing tongue that occasionally traced a thin moist line across her top lip. She had soft, slanted eyes that wrestled with Emilio's will as they had done with every other man who dared to stare directly into them.

Lexi's response was hesitant. Emilio's eyes, charm, and confidence had overwhelmed her. Finally after running through a list of names in her memory bank she finally pulled the one she recognized as her own and told it to Emilio.

"Alexis…but people call me Lexi."

"Lexi…why do I know that name?"

"Because…Juan asked you to do something for me and you denied me." Lexi hoped she didn't sound too curt.

"Well…I'm glad you didn't ask me yourself, I would have never been able to look into those eyes and say no."

"Why didn't you tell me she was so beautiful?" Emilio said, turning towards Juan who simply shrugged and proceeded to concern himself with something else in the store.

"Please…you have to let me take you out?" Emilio asked.

"Now?"

"Why not? You haven't eaten yet." Emilio said noticing the sub on the table in front of Lexi.

"I know a great spot here in Linden…La Galicia. I eat there every time I'm in town. It's over on Wood Ave. It's a Spanish spot…well, Portuguese. You like Spanish food?" Emilio asked.

"I haven't eaten it enough to say that I do or don't"

"I promise you, you'll like it…but…we can order you something a little more American, you know…just to be safe."

"It's alright…I like trying new things." Lexi said allowing Emilio to take her hand and help her up. Emilio took note of Lexi's flirting and she took note to his manners.

After Portuguese cuisine Emilio and Lexi shared a bottle of Moscatel Roxo.

"You know they don't bring this stuff out of the cellar until it ages for twenty years?" Emilio said trying to make conversation.

"This is Portuguese too?" Lexi asked.

"Yeah…well anyway, I want you to know that I think you are very beautiful Alexis. I want to get to know you and I want you to get to know me. But I want you to stop whatever business you're doing with my brother. As my lady you'll have to be clean. Besides, you wont need for money…trust me." A confident smile accompanied Emilio's statement.

"Your lady?" Lexi thought. Maybe Emilio was getting the wrong impression because he was definitely speeding. It was too early to discuss commitments so Lexi gracefully shifted the direction of the conversation.

"Don't you think I should get to know you a little better before we get into the deep stuff? Besides the deli and the obvious, what exactly do you do?"

"Well I don't deal with the obvious anymore…too much hassle, too many lawyers and litigation fees. I run a clean operation baby. Real Estate's my Racket. An old friend of mine named Tony started a real estate firm and asked if I wanted a piece of the pie. He already owned a nice amount of Brooklyn."

"What part of Brooklyn, I'm from Flatbush." Lexi said. "Crown Heights mostly…You'll probably meet him one day, he's a close associate of mine. Other than that though, I own a construction company as well as a landscaping company and I like to think I'm a pretty good investor. My portfolio's nice. Now look, I hate that you made me do that…I sound pretentious don't I?"

"A little." Lexi said smiling, her head bowed, lips wrapped snuggly around the rim of her glass and those beautiful deeply expressive eyes glaring up at Emilio. Her eyes looked liquid, like running syrup - syrup that had glued his stare to hers. The arresting stare of those compelling eyes now rattled Emilio's nerves and swelled his heart with emotion.

"So you don't hustle anymore at all?"

"No I don't officer." Emilio said jokingly.

"No, I'm just saying, a lot of people are saying otherwise."

"You shouldn't put a lot of stock into gossip."

Lexi was silent.

"Just know that I can provide for you." Emilio said.

"I have a son that I'm raising alone." Lexi said, her attitude slightly more serious now. If Emilio was gonna run, this would have been the time.

"Do you think I couldn't provide for both of you?"

"I don't doubt that you can but a young man needs more than money and gifts."

"Hmm...I understand. No, I'm probably not the best father but I have principals, principals that keep me moral and grounded. As long as I'm those two things, moral and grounded, I'll be a harmless presence in your son's life. I may even help him in some ways."

Emilio gave Lexi time to think over his remarks. He understood her concerns as a mother and respected her even more for the screening.

"I said I like you and I meant that, that's whatever comes with you. I know and understand that every rose has it's thorns, I got shit with me I'm hoping you can deal with as well. You seem worth whatever comes with you though and I hope I am to you."

At that moment, Lexi looked down at her lap in silence. She needed a brief moment with Marquise so she could apologize, explain, and hopefully get his blessings. Her mind was made up, Emilio was what she needed right now and oddly she felt Mar would approve. He wasn't a bum. He was smart, he was charming, and he was enterprising. Not to mention good-looking

"Have you ever been in a serious relationship?" Lexi asked, thanking Marquise for the appropriate question.

"Never met a woman I could trust."

"So no then?"

"Well, there was one. Three months. I thought it was something. Turned out to be nothing. You ever know someone who knows the price of everything but the value of nothing?"

Lexi nodded her head.

"Didn't go anywhere though."

"So no then?" Lexi insisted.

"No, I guess not. Not yet at least." Emilio answered honestly. He hated the question because that empty feeling he had felt for so long was returning.

"What about you, ever been in a serious relationship?"

"I've only been in one relationship to be honest with you. The father of my son." Lexi said.

"What happened, how long ago did you two split apart."

"He was murdered a few years ago."

"I'm sorry." Emilio said.

"It's okay. I've learned to deal with it. You know the hardest part about it?"

"What's that?"

"That face…the face of the guy who did it. It haunts me."

There was a long moment of silence. Emilio didn't know what to say and Lexi's mind had left La Galicia and returned to that bloody scene in Flatbush.

"So," Lexi said, bringing herself out of her awful vision. "How do I know you know how to treat a real woman. I mean you do know it takes more than a fancy restaurant and an expensive bottle of wine to keep a woman. That may get any woman but it won't keep a real one."

"Do you actually believe I don't know how to treat a…Listen, I know that if you're a go-getter, you get out here and you prosper, you establish a good home, you love your woman with passion, and admiration, you feed her well, put her in the finest of fabrics and the rarest of jewels, caress her, soothe her - mentally and physically - strive to fulfill all of her wishes and desires, keep in mind that she's a fertile field or a delicate rose, be gentle, a man, stern but not brutal; if you keep in mind that charm, manners and royal treatment will influence her more than force, don't humiliate her and make sure she don't have to rely on nothing or nobody outside of you, she'll be compelled to stay in your home and be loyal to you."

"Lexi quickly filled her glass and took a drink. She didn't have anything to say. There was nothing else to say…

…passionate, highly skilled love-making ensued…the uniting of their bodies was marked by stimulating heat and arousing perspiration; heightened sensual perception and a lost passion that burned like the flames atop the candles that gave glow to their glistening naked bodies. After Marquise, her body had become an impenetrable fortress. She had no need or want for a man. Many tried but to no avail…Until now. Emilio had gotten her to drop her guard.

With his hand nestled comfortably on her warm pubic mound beneath the blanket of humid satin that covered it, Julio's exploring fingers caressed the throbbing opening and fondled in search of the fleshy pearl tongue. Lexi completely surrendered to Emilio's touch and allowed herself to get lost in his magic…without feeling guilty for it. Instead of fighting back, as he positioned himself between her thighs and led his manhood to her slit, she reached down and guided the warm, erect organ into her moist opening. Lexi moaned and cringed like a virgin as Emilio stretched the elastic of her walls and entered a place that hadn't been entered since the death of Marquise.

9

The Pieces

Lexi's juvenile romantic ideals had survived the wonder years of prepubescence and the tumultuous identity search of adolescence and evolved into the fanciful ideals of love that she now clung desperately to as a mature woman. She had truly believed however, that Marquise's death had also murdered those ideals because for years she had given up on ever finding love again. She had always felt a bitterness towards God for teasing her the way he had. Sending her an angel she thought she would have for life then brutally taking him away from her. She no longer wanted to get too attached to a man. What would stop him from sharing Mar's fate and her world being crushed again?

Just as she thought this Emilio's voice startled her.

"Every blessing ignored becomes a curse." He said. It was then that Lexi realized Emilio was watching her and she wasn't even aware of how long. She had been staring into space for over twenty minutes now and to himself Emilio had joked that she may have been blinded by the morning sun had his ceiling not been above her head.

"Don't second-guess anything." Emilio went on.

"I'm not here to hurt you. I understand you lost a man that was close to you and I'm willing to be patient."

"It's not that." Lexi said.

"He wasn't trying to hurt me either. That didn't stop me from getting hurt though."

The strain escaping her voice resembled the oceanic winds trapped in a beached sea shell. The winds of her past would never escape her shell until she too ceased to exist.

"That's life Alexis, you take chances, some pay off, some don't. Either way, you learn and you continue to live. You don't shut down after one tragedy."

Just as Lexi prepared to respond Emilio placed his lips over hers. The kiss was passionate and took her breath away. After regaining her air, she again went to speak but he shushed her.

"I want you to come to France with me." Emilio said. He stood up and Lexi stared at his naked body, admiring the semi-erect appendage she now knew so personally. Her blood rushed.

"France? For what?" Lexi asked as Emilio walked into the bathroom and turned on the shower. The steam drifted back into the room as Emilio told Lexi that he wanted her to meet his partner.

"My friend I told you about, his name is Tony. He found this hotel that's supposed to be like, the classiest place in the world. The Trianon Palace in Versailles. Every year we take a vacation to a place in the world we've never been. This year it was his pick and that's what he came up with. Last year it was my idea to go to Morocco. We get together to discuss business too"

"When do we leave?" Lexi asked. She didn't have to be asked twice to visit France. She had never been there before either.

"Today." Emilio said before jumping in the shower.

"Oh - Kay." Lexi said to herself after realizing the trip had already been planned and she had better get herself ready. Lexi wrapped the sheet around her body and walked into the bathroom.

"There's some extra toothbrushes under the sink." Emilio said as Lexi watched his Silhouette through the condensation on the shower doors.

"You're welcome to join if you want to." Emilio said sarcastically. Lexi blushed, embarrassed that Emilio had seen her staring at him.

"So, your friend…Tony, how long have you known him?" Lexi asked as she opened a new toothbrush and removed it from the pack.

"Sounds like a good friend." She added as she reached for the toothpaste.

"About ten or eleven years now. When I was doing my thing, he worked for my cousin out in Brooklyn, a dude named Hector." Emilio stepped out of the shower and wrapped himself in a towel.

"My cousin got killed and he introduced me to Tony. Me and Tony did some business, he ran into some trouble a few years ago. Some kid got murdered in Flatbush and the police started asking questions. He didn't want to go back to the Dominican Republic and didn't want to be too far away from his money so I hid him out here in Jersey for a while. The smoke blew over, I think the case went cold, and we started focusing on legitimate stuff…real estate, construction, shit like that. That's what we're meeting for, we got a prospective buyer for some land we own in Dix Hills."

"Sure." Was all Lexi said.

"Sure what?" Emilio asked, kissing Lexi's shoulder as she mumbled I'll go. She jumped from the sensation and he attacked the nape of her neck. She hunched her shoulders to prevent being tickled then turned around to face Emilio.

"Sure, I would love to go anywhere with you." Lexi said staring into Emilio's eyes. The electricity in their stare blinded them to priorities. In sequence Emilio's towel dropped and Lexi's sheet followed. Emilio stepped into the warm puddle of white cotton and lifted Lexi onto the sink. She welcomed Emilio's manhood as well as his kiss and drifted into ecstasy.

10

CityofKings

The flight to France was breathtaking. Lexi and Emilio popped a bottle of Armand de Brignac Brut Gold to celebrate seeing the Eiffel Tower in person for the first time. Quise stayed home with Emilio's nanny - a first cousin he brought from the ghettos of the Dominican Republic to work for him. Quise had grown to like Giselle who at 23 was just thankful to be away from poverty.

Lexi was slowly becoming accustomed to Emilio's lavish lifestyle but still his taste in opulent things astonished her from time. The morning of their flight, a Bentley Brookland arrived at Emilio's home driven by a paid chauffer. Emilio had ordered the Bentley from a dealer in Stuttgart, Germany whom he had met at an auto show in Stockholm. The car was a mechanical masterpiece and Lexi enjoyed its effortless glide to Teterboro Airport. As the Brookland's 530 horses galloped onto the tarmac Adak runway at Atlantic Aviation. Lexi gawked at the huge Boeing business jets that dwarfed every other jet in sight. Emilio pointed out the French Built Dassault Falcon 900C.

Emilio's pilot had greeted the two of them at the stair door. Emilio asked if they had enough fuel and the pilot assured him they were fueled for maximum range. As Lexi observed the amenities on board the jet's engines revved without her even noticing. They would eventually hit cruising speeds of over 500 miles per hour, without Lexi ever realizing it.

Emilio's pilot steered his Falcon 900 corporate jet to Versailles - a bourgeois town known as the City of Kings. The Trianon Palace hotel sat on the edge of Louis XIV's royal estate. Lexi could see a woman enjoying a horse ride through the royal domain. Acres of gorgeous green garden backdrops, and splendid gardens flowed like green rivers. Lexi admired the stunning views of the royal estate and the world-famous Chateau de Versailles. Statues and fountains reflected the old-world charm of the hotel and Lexi had to admit that France was as beautiful as she had envisioned.

"Why don't we get something to eat." Emilio said after he and Lexi had settled into the Versailles suite that had been reserved for them. The suite was extravagant and benefited from the hotel's newly enhanced décor.

"This place is beautiful." Lexi said. It was now clear to her that she had no idea how much money Emilio actually had.

"It is." Emilio said, pulling a flat stack of colorful papers from a plastic bag.

"What's that?" Lexi asked.

"Money!" Emilio said, waving the colorful Euros.

"Wanna go shopping? They have the best boutiques in the world. And I've seen em all, from Barbados to Africa."

"Actually, I am a little hungry." Lexi admitted.

Emilio and Lexi took a seat in the La Veranda and enjoyed French cuisine. They had been at the hotel for over an hour now and Lexi was wondering where the people were that Emilio was supposed to be meeting.

"So where's your friend?" She asked.

"Funny you should ask." Emilio said preparing to stand up.

"He's right behind you."

Lexi turns and stands at the same time and just as she reaches her hand out to be kissed she makes eye contact with the man and her heart drops. Lexi reaches for her glass immediately to wet her parched throat. Her smile has completely vanished and her complexion is beginning to fade. She pulls her hand away from the man just as his lips prepare to kiss her skin and she asks to be excused. A look of confusion is shared between the men and Emilio nods to Lexi, excusing her properly.

In the restroom Lexi stared at herself in the mirror. All of Emilio's words were now clear.

"…he worked for my cousin out in Brooklyn, a dude named Hector…"

Then came Marquise's voice.

"…this dude Hector, I gotta get him out the way…"

Once again she heard Julio's voice and the conversation they had just had this morning.

"My cousin got killed and he introduced me to Tony. Me and Tony did some business, he ran into some trouble a few years ago. Some kid got murdered and the police started asking questions."

"Marquise." Lexi said to herself.

"That's the kid that got killed. Marquise got Hector killed and Tony killed Marquise for killing Hector."

Saying this made Lexi feel nauseated. She grabbed her stomach as tears began to pour from her face. She couldn't control it, too many emotions were struggling for control of her confused mind. But as it always did, Marquise's voice calmed the storm. She thought of their night in Jamaica and how Mar had woken her from her sleep.

"Lexi." He whispered.

"Hmmm?"

"You up?"

"Umm-hmm"

"Lexi, would you kill somebody?"

"I don't know...I…don't think I could bring myself to do something like that."

"What about if it was for me, if somebody hurt me, or you knew somebody was trying to hurt me… would you kill somebody then?"

"For you Marquise…I think I would."

Lexi knew she was no killer, but that there were some things worth killing for.

11

PoisonAffair

Lexi knew she wouldn't be able to disguise the puffiness of her eyes or the running of her mascara. She would have to come up with an explanation for her behavior and crying eyes - fast.

She walked slowly back towards the table where Emilio now sat alongside a Hispanic woman whom she hadn't been introduced to yet and Marquise's killer. Tony was the first to stand up and usher Lexi to the table. She was repulsed by his touch and wanted to spit on his hands. Ignoring Tony and his date, Lexi looked at and spoke only to Emilio.

"I'm tired, I think I wanna go back to the room and lay down."

Tony cut in.

"You'll miss everything, this place is the epitome of impeccable service…and they've got a shimmering heated indoor pool. I'm sure you brought something…nice to wear"

The word nice dripped off of Tony's tongue laced in lust and flirtation. She looked at Emilio and wondered if he could see what Tony was insinuating.

"We were gonna go by the Gallery bar, get a few drinks, have a good time. Tomorrow we were gonna go to the capital to do some shopping, maybe Emilio could get you one of those designer purses at Galaries Lafayette Department store. You have a very beautiful figure, maybe you could talk him into a Yves Saint Laurent dress or a pair of stiletto Versace shoes. The fun was supposed to start tonight though."

Lexi endured Tony's irritating voice and overt flirting to conceal her thirst for revenge.

"Cramps." She said, glancing at Tony's date who cast an understanding nod in return.

"Okay baby, you sure that's it?" Emilio asked, sensing something else was wrong.

"I'm sure. I just need to lay down for a few."

"Alright well I'll walk you up."

"No, I'll be fine, you go'head and entertain your guest. I'll be fine."

Lexi accepted a peck on the cheek from Emilio and cut her eyes at Tony's obnoxious wink. She was dizzy as she made her way back to their suite. She couldn't believe what was happening. Her nerves were on edge as she tried to prepare herself to take a man's life. How would she do it? She didn't have a gun so she would have to get close to him. She didn't know the first thing about poisoning a person. She would have to use her beauty again.

Emilio walked into the bedroom to find Lexi dressed in a two-piece bathing suit, waist and leg swathed in a white net that offset her emerald green Vera Wang ensemble. Whatever sickness she had been feeling earlier was obviously gone.

Lexi was trying to be strong.

"That's him." She said.

"Him who?" Emilio asked. He was lost. Noticing Lexi's nervous shaking, Emilio grabbed Lexi's shoulders to still her.

"That's the guy who killed Marquise."

"Your son's father?" Emilio asked.

As soon as Lexi nodded yes tears began to well up in her eyes. She held her head back and fanned her hands in front of her eyes. She didn't want to ruin her makeup. If Tony wanted to see her half-naked in a pool than he would. She would show him as much as he wanted, so long as he was dead by the end of the night.

Emilio released Lexi's slender shoulders and backed up. It made sense. Lexi had spoken about Flatbush and her mother's house there. Tony had caught that murder beef and needed a place to lay low. Emilio could specifically remember Tony saying two other people had been on the scene wit Hector's killer got killed - a pregnant woman and another man.

"What…why are you dressed?" Emilio said once the clouds of his reverie evaporated and he realized that Lexi was fully dressed.

"I wanted to go down to the pool." Lexi said, lying by omission.

"For what?"

Before Lexi could answer, Emilio answered his own question.

"No…I won't let you do somethin so stupid."

"You could help me."

"Help you? He's a friend…"

Emilio paused.

"So you still love him…your son's father?"

Lexi paused. She never gave thought to how her thirst for revenge could spark jealousy in Emilio. She was still ready to kill for a man who had been dead for years now.

"Don't do that." Lexi said.

"Do what?" Emilio asked.

"Feel like you have to compete. He's gone and you're here. Yes I loved him and probably always will but I'm in love with you and the way you make me feel. But seeing this man has made me think about my son's father and made me realize that I can't close that chapter on my life until I know this man is dead. Marquise would have done it for me. I think you would too."

Emilio walked towards the window and stared at the remains of Louis XIV's wealth. A well-kept domain that resembled the type of palaces Emilio had dreamt about for himself night after night as a young boy. He could see that he and the Sun King must have had the same passion for wealth. He wondered however if he and King Louis shared the same passion for any one woman. Emilio wondered how many times in the King's seventy-two year reign he sacrificed or would have sacrificed his kingdom for a woman. The tour guide had spoken of Louis XIV's mother molding him into an Apollo adored by the court. He had had his fair share of wives and mistresses but had indeed loved one woman more than any other, his first wife, the Spanish princess Marie Theresa. Marie he claimed caused him no other pain but dying. That must have been a woman he would have killed for Emilio reasoned as he stared at the palace that once housed ten-thousand people, including France's greatest monarch.

Emilio's mind drifted to his own dilemma. He was contemplating jeopardizing his own kingdom for a woman he knew only a short amount of time but was sure he loved. Tony was a friend and someone he had known long before meeting Lexi. Someone he had made hundreds of thousands of dollars with. He still had integrity, he still lived by a code of honor. Who did Lexi think she was even suggesting he murder his comrade.

"I can't let you do it and I definitely won't help you." Emilio said walking away from the window.

"Take your clothes off." He wasn't willing to negotiate. He began removing his watch and bracelet.

"Slip into something comfortable and relax, we're leaving first thing in the morning and you'll never have to worry about seeing him again."

"What do you mean? He hurt someone close to me."

"And what are you going to do, kill him in the fuckin Trianon Palace. Think about what you're saying. I understand you lost someone dear to you, I understand you want to get your revenge, but you have to be smart Alexis. And you also have to understand my position. You're my lady and I can see you're hurt, but this man is a friend of mine, he felt he was doing the right thing by killing your boyfriend."

"What? So you're saying he was right, that Marquise deserved to die?"

"No! I'm sayin his motives…"

"It's alright, I understand. Don't worry, I'll go to sleep and forget all about this."

Lexi changed into a nightgown and laid down in the bed - her back to Emilio. Emilio just shook his head and prayed the morning get here fast.

12

Stronger than Pride

After making sure Emilio was asleep, Lexi gently lifted his arm and slid out of his embrace. She knew she had to act quickly. She had to get back to the room before Julio woke up. Her body draped in satin, hand wrapped in the leather purse strap she would use to strangle Tony, Lexi lurked down the hall like a cat. She walked carefully on her tip-toes towards the Terrace Suite where Tony was staying. His door was open and she walked in as smoothly as the night breeze blowing through the terrace doors. The blue moon gave glow to Lexi's robe so she removed it. Naked, she made her way into Tony's bed.

"Where is she?" She whispered.

Tony's voice was hot in her ear.

"Home." He said.

"She doesn't ask many questions." Tony added smugly.

Lexi rolled over and on top of Tony, straddling his naked body. She could feel his erection and it made her more furious.

"Are you sure he's sleep?" Tony asked.

"I'm sure."

Tony reached back and palmed Lexi's back side. Lexi brought her right hand up as fast as possible and tried to wrap the strap around Tony's neck. Tony reacted quickly, flinging Lexi from on top of him then kicking her hard in her back. The impact of the kick sent Lexi flying to the floor. He reached behind his pillow and pulled out a midnight black .45 ACP Taurus that froze Lexi in her knee-scrambling tracks. She backed up slowly, retracting her steps towards the door. Feeling her robe with her feet, she gathered it up and wrapped it around her trembling body. She had miscalculated and now she was shaken with fright as she stared down the dark barrel of Tony's Brazilian handgun. Tony had no idea why Lexi was trying to kill him, he had an even harder time understanding why Emilio would bring a woman like this with him. Were they enemies now? None of this mattered at the moment. Reality was, the woman was trying to kill him and now she had to go.

Tony lined the barrel up with Lexi's torso and squeezed the trigger. Lexi closed her eyes as the bullet hit her chest and the echo of the blast rang loudly in her ear. The world began to slow down and a heroin-like euphoria knocked off her equilibrium and slowed down her senses. Slowly her mind caught up to real time and she began to lift her head slowly. The shot had indeed erupted but the echo was much more than an echo, it was a second shot and the bullet that had hit her heart was nothing more than fear. She opened her eyes slowly. There was no blood on her robe. She looked up and saw Tony laying beside the bed. He wasn't moving.

Lexi jumped when Emilio touched her from behind and told her to stand up. She was still stricken with paralysis shock. Even more so, she was still surprised to be alive. Lexi looked up at Emilio with eyes that expressed eternal appreciation for his timing. Emilio on the other hand couldn't believe what he had just done. Lexi's voice was in his ears.

"Marquise would have done it for me. I think you would too."

Emilio glanced over at Lexi. She was still startled but reality was setting in. Tony was dead, she was still very much alive, and now they had to get out of this hotel quickly.

"We have to go." Lexi said, breaking free of the inhibiting shackles of shock.

"Go where?" Emilio asked.

"Even if we did make it out of this hotel we would never make it out of this country." Emilio said.

"Why did you do it?" Lexi asked. Though she had suggested it, Lexi never actually believed Emilio would murder his friend for her.

"Love is stronger than pride." Emilio said. It was a reality his heart had finally accepted after years of rejection. He said it as if he had known it all his life.

"Get in the corner." Emilio ordered. His command startled Lexi who's mind had drifted as Emilio devised his next plan.

"What…what are you gonna do?" Lexi asked curiously.

"Just get in the corner." This time as Emilio said this he walked towards Lexi, guided her towards the corner furthest from door, then walked towards Tony. Emilio seemed to have to conquer some nerves because he hesitated as he reached down to grab Tony's gun out of his hand. Before taking the blood-spattered pistol, Emilio pulled the sheet from the bed and wrapped the end around his hand. Lexi watched closely. Her nerves were completely rattled by this time. Emilio's behavior was scaring and puzzling her even more. His next move would completely mitigate her confusion however.

Emilio sat with his back against the door. With his right hand he pointed Tony's gun at his left shoulder. Lexi took a deep breath and covered her mouth with her hands as her eyes grew wide.

Just as Emilio squeezed the trigger, Lexi covered her eyes.

The blast made Lexi jump and Emilio's ears went deaf to every sound besides the high-pitched ringing permeating his skull. Emilio had let out a guttural groan but was now calming himself by breathing slow and deep breaths. The burning sensation in his shoulder had him doubled over in pain. Lexi went to run to his side but he waved her off and before she could protest, Emilio grazed his left bicep.

"What are you doing?" Lexi asked hysterically. Seeing Emilio shoot himself once was enough for her.

"This has to look like self-defense. Now get the phone and push seventeen." Managed before his mouth clenched too tight for him to speak.

As Emilio placed Tony's gun back in his dead palm, Lexi told the dispatcher that she wanted to report a murder and needed medical assistance for her boyfriend who had been shot twice. The authorities finally arrived and Emilio and Lexi were taken into custody. The entire trip to Saint Pierre prison Lexi felt a pang in her stomach. She wanted her son by her side. She missed Quise and dreaded knowing she may be missing Emilio very shortly as well.

13

A Murder in France

Lexi was released from the police station house the next morning but was forbidden from leaving the country. Her passport was confiscated immediately. She would have to wait until Emilio's trial considering she was the only other eyewitness and technically still a suspect. Lexi was to reside in Paris and report to the police once a week. She was forced to obtain a long-stay Visa considering her stay in Paris was indefinite. Arrangements were made to have Quise flown over. He would be accompanied by agents the entire time. Emilio was driven to the local Palais de Justice two days after being released from the hospital to see a Jude d'instruction.

The investigating magistrate placed Emilio under provisional incarceration and under France's 1958 Code of Criminal Procedure classified his case as a judicial investigation and not a police investigation. He was booked into Versailles prison. Emilio had arranged to meet with a few reputable lawyers, and after weeding through the greedy and bias, Emilio comprised a very solid defense team.

Emilio would soon learn that France was very stiff on murder and citizens possessing firearms. He was told that should the judge find sufficient enough evidence to prosecute Emilio for voluntary premeditated homicide which is classified as an assassination in France - Emilio faced a life sentence. He would also have to be evaluated by court-appointed psychiatrists to determine if he was mentally fit to stand trial first. If found guilty of only voluntary but not premeditated murder he faced thirty years. However, if Emilio and his defense team could prove beyond a reasonable doubt that he killed Tony to protect himself against an unjustified attack and that his action was both necessary for legitimate defense and simultaneous with the attack against him, and there was no disproportion between his means of defense and the gravity of the attack against him, then he would not be held responsible for his deed.

Emilio was transferred from Versailles prison to France's second largest prison - Fresnes. Fresnes, a commune in Val-de-Marne, was just seven miles south of Paris. This closeness would prove to be a plus as Emilio's case would go on to take over four years.

Emilio's lawyers prepared his case from the outside while Emilio watched through tiny barred windows as months slowly turned to years. Lexi visited as much as possible. The short, uncongenial visits were tearing at the fibers of their relationship. They were not allowed to touch each other and the treatment they received was borderline rude.

Lexi constantly stressed how hard it was for her and Quise living in this foreign country where she knew no one. She rarely came outside to avoid the cruel stares of her neighbors. In a country where the homicide rate was less than 2 people per 100,000 Emilio and Lexi's case was very high profile.

Concealed carry is strictly forbidden in France unless you are a policeman on duty. Here was a case where two Americans had not only violated the law by carrying weapons but one had assassinated the other. As time went on, Emilio began to lose hope that he was going to make it out of France's penal system alive. This same doubt was beginning to loom over the heads of his lawyers.

The day of Emilio's trial, even the downpour was not enough to keep the press and public from showing up in throngs. Anti-American slurs were spewed at Emilio and Lexi as they entered the courtroom. Emilio feared those same prejudice would prevent him from receiving a fair trial.

The Prosecution tried to paint Emilio as a gun-toting thug who had knowingly, and willingly assassinated Tony Perez after catching him in the bed with his woman. The defense countered that Lexi's promiscuity was not on trial but rather or not Emilio had acted in self-defense. It was Tony who had perpetrated the law on several levels. You are not required to have a permit to purchase .22lr's or black powder pistols like the stainless 1858 Remington - Canon Court Emilio had used to protect himself from the military caliber .45ACP Tony had used to try to kill him. Handguns of that caliber were completely forbidden to civilians in France. Also, Emilio had only shot once with a legal small caliber weapon while his attacker had shot him twice with a weapon of war.

Still, the question of what Lexi was doing in Tony's room at that hour was what the jurors deliberated the next fifteen days. The case had taken over four years to go trial. Trial had taken two weeks and now the jurors were going into their third week of deliberation. All of this had exhausted Lexi, and strained Emilio. Quise had now spent four years in a foreign country and still had no idea of what his mother and her boyfriend had gotten into. All he knew was that it was serious.

As the French press continued to highlight Emilio's case, the length of deliberation, and what the outcome would be, Emilio just prayed the jurors would come back with a verdict soon. The amount of time the jurors needed to decide wasn't surprising considering the extraordinary set of circumstances. Finally, after 15 days of anticipation and anxiety. The jurors came back with a decision. Though they would never be able to explain Lexi's reason for being in Mr. Perez's room at that time of night, the evidence indeed suggested that Emilio de la Cruz had acted in self-defense. And the level of his defense didn't supersede the level of Mr. Perez's attack.

After the verdict was read, the courtroom and the streets outside of the courthouse erupted into a frenzy. Emilio began to search for Lexi in the midst of the ruckus and once their hands embraced they held each other until they were on the plane back to America…never once letting each other go.

14

Epilogue

Emilio and Lexi stared at the majestic path of the setting sun as it prepared to kiss the horizon. The soft colors filled them both with a serene sense of bliss. The clouds were puffs of violet cotton. The sky was a scorching pink fire and the sun - a flaming pink sphere. Lexi was happy to have Emilio by her side. After he killed Tony, she thought she would be forced to be alone once again. Instead, after receiving a suspended sentence, accepting his persona non grata status, and paying reparations to Tony's children, Emilio was free.

Emilio's lawyers explained that the essence of the suspended sentence is simply that a sentence is imposed but its execution is suspended on condition that the offender does not commit a further offence. It had all sounded unbelievable to Lexi but it was real. Emilio was set free and now here they were, back at Emilio's lake house gazing at the sunset. Lexi's mind drifted to Marquise, as it always did and probably always would. Her thoughts of him were peaceful this time, not confusing, saddening, or angering as they had sometimes been in the past. That chapter in her life dedicated to mourning her losses was done. She would now be more thankful for her gains. Lexi was now just thankful to be in a triumphant position. She had been tested by both love and the game and she had survived.

"Now I sit here in a corner of my being,
A memory of you came
Like the thick and bitter smoke
That rises from damp wood.

With it came so many thoughts -
The way parched wood breathes out
its crimson sighs of flame

I have put out both those fires.
The years of my life are like scattered coals.
Some have gone out, some smolder still.
The hands of time began to sweep them aside
and he blistered his fingertips.

From the hands of your love
I this earthen vessel fell, and was broken.
History came to my kitchen today,
but went away hungry."

-Amrita Pritam

INTERVIEW WITH SALEEM LITTLE

Published 2014-05-27

What is your writing process?

I believe my writing process is, no process. I'm a very firm believer that the more thought you give to something the more your own thoughts may get in the way. I try to leave myself open and receptive to inspirations of all sorts and allow what inspires me to manifest itself in my writing. I guess if there was any structured process to my writing it would be the process of eliminating any prejudices or other mental contaminations that may block me from receiving inspiration.

Do you remember the first story you ever read, and the impact it had on you?

I can't remember the first story I read, but the first story I remember reading was "The Outsiders". I think one of the biggest impressions it left on me was that heroes are flawed too. They're regular people who just so happen to do irregular things at irregular times; like Pony running back into the burning church to save the children. Right after saving the children it was back to hanging with the gang and getting into trouble. I could relate to the main character's plight; that battle against peer pressure and temptation, trying to overcome some pretty rough surroundings; being surrounded by so much ugliness but still seeing the beauty in life. This book was also the first book to show me that movies just can't rival the novels they're based on. The movie was great, but I still saw Pony as I imagined him in my mind.

What do you read for pleasure?
Anything dealing with the metaphysical, intangible world; those types of book usually bring pleasure and calm to the soul.

What is your e-reading device of choice?
I'm a little organic when it comes to books... I think they're all very conducive to the times we're living in however.

Describe your desk.
My sanctuary…

What is the greatest joy of writing for you?
A few people have told me they've cried, or have been very upset, or so happy and so engaged they couldn't stop reading. I'm a very humble person so that's incredible to me. I know it's a gift and I'm grateful but to know that characters, no more than figments of my imagination become so real to strangers that they can be driven to tears. That's my greatest joy, connecting with the rest of humanity mentally and reconnecting those common threads of joy and pain.

What do your fans mean to you?
They mean I'm an author. They mean I don't write in vain. The fact that I mean anything to them means everything to me.

Who are your favorite authors?
Kahlil Gibran, Mario Puzo, Donald Goines, Gabriel Garcia Marquez and quite a few others.

What inspires you to get out of bed each day?
Hope. Hope and goals. I think we all get out of bed because we have a little hope that we'll get a goal accomplished or at least a little closer to doing so. If not we'd all probably sleep all day.

How do you discover the ebooks you read?
Goodreads.com; that's where I get most of my notifications on new books.

When you're not writing, how do you spend your time?
Thinking about what I'm going to write. *Writing's my life.*

BOOKS BY SALEEM LITTLE

Apocrypha
Don't Judge Me
Love and War
Revolutionized
Kissed by a Dragon
G.O.D.:
Gold, Oil & Drugs
Writer's Block - Collaboration
Sincerely Yours 1
Sincerely Yours 2
Crying for Tears:
The Sasha Pierce Story
Enseunos
(*"Daydreams" Spanish Version*)
Daydreams
Especial
("Special" Spanish Version)
Special
Share
Get In, Get Out
Love and the Game
Cocaine
Invisible Chains
Muses of a Modern Mystic
U-N-I-VERSE VI:
Jesus The Man, The Myth, The Legend
U-N-I-VERSE VII:
Know Yourself

The Long Way Home
Featuring George Hopkins
Naked

A Preview of

REVOLUTIONIZED

A MEMOIR BY SALEEM LITTLE

CHAPTER 1

"This is blatant racism!" my Public Defender blurted out. I was amazed at how defensive she had become of and for me.

"What did you say?!" the judge shot back. He had dropped his glasses and cast a cold stare at my Defense Attorney. It was a stare that made even me shutter. Ms. Berry hadn't backed down, though her voice did crack subtly from nervousness as she responded.

"My client, a black man, is being sentenced to 5-10 years while his co-defendants, two white women, are guilty of the same crime, yet you sentenced them to four years of probation..."

"Well, Ms. Berry, your client also has a prior record..."

"Yes, for a simple possession of a small amount of marijuana... When he was a juvenile. He was sixteen years old..."

"Well, Ms. Berry, this sentence is well within the guidelines, and if your client can maintain good behavior, he should have no problem making it out on his minimum..."

My attorney wanted to speak but was silenced by another stern glare. No matter how much of her heart was wrapped up in my case, she still had a family she was helping to provide for. The jurors seemed pleased with the verdict and the prosecution smirked malevolently at me. I looked back to see my mother, who was in tears. Then at my attorney as the weight of my sentence began to set in.

"Sorry," she whispered to me before dropping her head and then... I was alone. I realized there was nothing I could do and no one that would be able to help me. My sentence was in and I would be going to a state penitentiary for the next five years, at the least. I, too, said,

"Sorry," to my mother and she asked, "Can I please hug him?" as I was being escorted out of the court room. I had done a good job of fighting back tears. Since a child of four, I had always had to be strong for my mother, and this situation was no different. I've always been like that, no matter how heavy my load, I tried to carry the burden for others. I hate to

see people hurting. So, although I was the one going away, I didn't want her to hurt any more than she had to.

In the back of the patty wagon, as I was being transported back to Cumberland County Prison, I cursed God vehemently. It was only then that I realized, I had been having one-way conversations with God my entire life - speaking to "something" that never responded - at least not audibly. My sentence was in so there was no reason to ask for help now. So, I didn't. Instead, I retreated into the dark recesses of my mind.

CHAPTER 2

It was the second marijuana stick and I was tired. It was a little after 11 p.m. and we still had a way to go to get to Jill's house on the outskirts of Carlisle, Pennsylvania.

"I'm good," I said as my girlfriend tried to pass the marijuana to me. At that point, I drifted off. Beneath my seat was a .45 caliber Ruger I had run from my county probation and was "living on the lamb" as they say. My source of income? A few pounds and a very loyal friend. Two weeks prior, I had walked into a pretty deadly situation. A group of guys from New York had positioned themselves on the same corner where my friends sold drugs - mainly cocaine, crack cocaine, and marijuana. This led to friction quickly and the friction inevitably boiled over to a full-fledged beef. I hadn't been a part of it because I was always out of town with my lady at the time between Duncannon and Carlisle. However, you're often held accountable for the actions of those you associate with, so as soon as I was spotted with my friends, I was a target.

I had no idea shootouts had taken place as I had yet to be briefed on the war, but they had. So now, the turf battle was deadly. One day I was spotted by one of the Hispanic guys and in noticing I was affiliated with his enemy he pulled a tech-nine out on me. I was unarmed so I nodded my head to signal he had the power. I was at his mercy, but by the age of nineteen, I was already ready to die. He didn't shoot, but the threat was enough.

After he pulled off, I ran to my friend's house and told them what happened.

"Yo! What's goin' on over on thirteenth street? This Spanish kid just pulled out on me," I said slightly out of breath.

"What?! Man, we got beef with them niggas..." said one of my comrades. Another friend, Ronald, said nothing. He simply loaded a few slugs in his shotgun and had another comrade drive him over to Thirteenth and Chestnut Street. Ten minutes later, he returned and smiled at me.

"I got him, Leem." A few hours later, I learned he had shot the guy who pulled the tech-nine out on me, leaving the guy's arm slightly paralyzed. Because of this, I wanted to keep him beside me. I wasn't a robber, I was a hustler, so I wanted to help him out. I brought him out of town with me and introduced him to my girl's friend. They hit it off, and now he was my muscle - although, I've never needed it - while I made my moves to keep myself alive while unable to get a job.

When I finally woke up - Ronald was asking us to stop the car. I didn't know exactly why and was too tired to find out. My girl asked me if it was ok and I said, "yes," not conscious enough to assess what he was doing.

We were in Downtown Carlisle, ironically enough right behind the courthouse. After a few minutes, I started to wonder what was taking him so long. After coming to, I had assumed he had only stepped out to urinate. But ten minutes was a long time so...

"I'll be right back," I said. The irritation clear in my tone and expression.

As always, I reached beneath the seat for my protection... It was gone. Immediately my awareness

"He took the gun." I thought. Fear emerged as I realized he had run off to commit a robbery, a burglary, or both. My girlfriend shook her head at the same time I had. Ronald was loyal as a dog, but when it came to com-mitting crimes or doing anything that took calculation, he was about as smart as one as well.

I shut the door and quickly walked off to find him. He was only a few feet away. Right beneath the streetlight, in the middle of a down-town side street, he had four men at gun point. I quickly surveyed the scene. The guys looked young, very young – like teenagers. And they had no money.

"What the hell are you doing?" I asked. The boys looked scared, but for some reason relieved as they could see my appearance would mean the end of this terrifying event.

"Man, let's go!" I ordered and made my way back to the car. Just for the fun of it, he hit one of the kids in the head with the gun. Once I got back to the car, I was fully awake... and pissed!

"You ok?" my lady asked.

"Yeah, this dude is fuckin' robbing somebody," I said.

"What?!"

Before I could respond, Ronald jumped into the back seat

"Let's go! Let's go!" he said.

I turned around as he went through his looted goods. A half-empty pack of cigarettes, two fugazy chains, and about two dollars and seventy-five cents. I just shook my head in disappointment as he discarded every-thing but the cigarettes.

CHAPTER 3

"Baby, baby, wake up! We're being pulled over."

For the second night in a row I had fallen asleep on our way home. And for the second night in a row I was being awaken to a situation I had to take immediate control of.

"For what? What happened? Were you speeding?" My first thought was she must've made a driving error. If so, we didn't have much to worry about. With panic in her tone, she exclaimed

"No, nothing I swear to God." I believed her. She never lied to me. It was the one thing I loved and respected about her. I glanced up in the rearview. Ronald was even more paranoid than she. His darker skin made the whites of his eyes that much more visible. They were lit up like miniature full moons.

"Yo... What are we going to do?!" He asked frantically. His eyes dart-ed in every direction and he fidgeted like a terrified rodent. He kept looking back and his trepidation would prove to be calamitous. The first thing I thought was: How could he expect our women to be calm if he was so irate?

"Nothing," I said. We're going to pull over and see exactly why we're being pulled over.

The lights. There's something about the ominous nature of police sirens and lights. I always charged it to the fact that those lights meant your freedom could be taken at any moment.

Ronald was way too jittery, and his actions were making me nervous. I knew immediately that something was wrong. This was no routine traffic stop. They had come with guns drawn. Jane rolled her window down and began to answer questions. By this time there was a police officer at my window as well. I kept my eyes forward and my hands visible.

"Why are you driving through here so late?" the officer asked. He was speaking to Jane, but his eyes were on everything but her - the make, model and color of the car, the interior of the car - the two passengers in the back seat. His partner's eyes were burning a hole in the side of my head.

"We were headed home," she answered honestly. From the corner of my eye, I could see Ronald making a move. He had noticed that his gun was slightly visible, so, foolhardily he reached down to shove it under Jane's seat.

"Put your fucking hands up!!!"

The officer who had been doing the questioning drew his weapon and pointed directly at Ronald.

This guy is going to get us all killed, I thought. And I quickly spat. "Listen, my name is Saleem... Saleem Little. I do have a warrant out of Dauphin County. It's only probation. You can take me now!" Luckily, he opened my door and began his pat down. Eventually, we were all out of the car. Jane looked terrified and every time she was asked a question, she looked at me to see if she should respond, and if so, what she should say.

Eventually, we were taken downtown for more questioning. It seemed like it took them forever to get to me. I would eventually discover why. I had fallen asleep on the metal slab that served as a bed. Wrapped in my t-shirt, I laid in a fetal position to try to generate some heat. The lighting was dim and the walls cold and imposing. I quickly rehearsed my story, concocted my make-shift alibi, then drifted to sleep.

I'm not sure how long I was asleep, but the loud clanking of my steel door being opened awoke me and in a split second I recollected exactly where I was at.

"Little, let's go."

I followed the officer to another room for interrogation and to be honest, I was just happy to be out of that cold cell. The light in the room was brighter and it was a lot warmer.

"Where were you at last night?" the officer asked, after informing me the session would be recorded.

"With the mother of my daughter," I said quickly. The officers looked at each other with a glance that let me know - they knew I was lying.

"Are you sure?"

"Yeah," I shot back, less convincingly this time. I had even given them an address and phone number.

"Listen, your buddy already gave you up."

I paused. I figured this was a ploy to get me to tell on myself. How-ever, recalling how afraid he had been, it wasn't inconceivable and some-thing in my subconscious said They're telling the truth.

"I don't know what he told you, but..." They cut me off.

"Look."

They dropped his statement in front of me. It dropped like a feather; my heart dropped like a brick. Still skeptical, I searched for a sign the statement was forged. Maybe they were trying to trick me into confessing or informing. As I studied the handwriting, I knew it was his.

"We didn't mean to hurt anybody. We just wanted some money. We're sorry. We... We... We..."

I didn't say another word the entire time. This guy decided to do a crime and incriminated us all after being pressured. There was nothing else I could say. By the morning, we were being transported to the Cumberland County Prison.

CHAPTER 4

"I sure wish I could just use some southern law enforcement..." the arresting officer said as he led us to his car. I caught it, of course. I can't remember a time in my life when I wasn't conscious. I read "The Destruction of The Black Civilization" by Chancellor Williams by the age of 18, so I knew some Europeans simply have an innate hatred, disdain, and envy of the original man. His comment hadn't gone over my head. Like most things in life, it did fly completely over my co-defendant's'. What puzzled me, was why his Hispanic partner ignored or pretended not to hear it. This man had basically said:

"I wish I could just lynch and hang you two niggers," and the Spanish officer didn't even as much as cast a side-eye. I guess being the only melanated officer on the force, in a predominantly "white" town, left him feeling powerless. It's amazing how the fear of losing job security made slaves out of many men.

I looked the officer dead in his eyes, to let him know his remark hadn't gone unnoticed and that I completely comprehended the innuendo. In this instant however, I really had to "pick my battle". My hands were cuffed behind my back and it appeared his Hispanic partner would have overlooked any abuse I would have suffered at the hands of this man.

Once we were in our cells in the Cumberland County Prison, I un-leased my venom on my co-defendant.

"If you were going to admit and plead guilty – why would you say 'we'? I could've beaten this fuckin' case. You did that shit on your own!" "I'm sorry..." Ronald said and tears began to pour down his face profusely. He tried to hug me, and I pushed him far away from me.

"Sorry won't get me out of here!" I snapped.

"I'm sorry I was scared. I didn't know... I didn't mean... I wasn't trying to get you into trouble... I don't know why I wrote 'we'; I was... I was nervous.

At that point, I realized I wasn't dealing with a rat, I was dealing with a terrified guy who thought "admission of guilt" would lessen the severity of his sentence... Now our sentence.

Finally, I gave him a hug and told him, "It's cool. We'll get through this..."

He was relieved. Inside I was still pissed. However, I did have the pre-liminary hearing to look forward to. I hadn't robbed anyone. I appeared on the scene late and only stayed for a minute, maybe less.

"As long as the witness didn't I.D. me, I should be able to walk..." I reasoned.

CHAPTER 5

Two months prior I would discover just how prevalent racism still was in America. Up until Jane, I had never officially dated a Caucasian woman. I had been intimate with one but was never bold enough to parade her as my woman. I still had a lot of spiritual growing to do. My life was spent - for the most part - in the slums of Harrisburg, PA where Europeans in impoverished neighborhoods was an oddity and interracial relationships were even more odd. Jane, however, had won my heart - not to mention - her home was far away from where I lived, which allowed me to sleep peacefully without the fear of being incarcerated by my probation officer, who had put out a warrant for my arrest.

Jane was from Perry County. The daughter of a well-to-do family. Her father drove trucks for a living and made enough to afford his wife the opportunity to be a "stay-at-home" wife. She had only chosen to continue working part time out of boredom - not necessity. They had a large house not too far from Musa Smith - a member of the only black family in Duncannon that I was aware of. According to Jane, Musa was a stand-out for Perry County Highschool who went on to play for the Georgia Bulldogs and then the Baltimore Ravens. I knew his story only because Jane told me - I think she had done so to make me comfortable.

Jane's father had the house built from the ground up and of all the things that amazed me - were the horses in the stable.

"You own horses?" I had asked in amazement. She didn't understand my shock. She also had never experienced poverty. They had a ton of land and a man-made path leading into the woods for dirt-bike and 4-wheeler riding. Equally impressive, was her father's rifle and shotgun collection he had decorated the ceiling with.

"You know if my dad were ever to catch you in here, he would try to kill you. He doesn't like black people." She had admitted. I pulled out my .45 and replied,

"Well, I would have to kill him if he didn't kill me first." I responded in all honesty and seriousness.

"What?! You're not going to kill my dad!" she had shot back angrily. It was a dose of reality and after we argued there was a slight disconnect. In silence, I pondered how I would have to then kill the entire family be-cause if anyone lived to tell, the judges would not accept my self-defense pleas – I'd be going to prison forever. She must've come to her senses and understood that of course, in a life-or-death situation, I would have to protect myself. She nestled close to me to indicate she was sorry. I held her to show her it was okay.

"Don't worry, it'll never come to that." I said. We made love and all was forgotten.

I would soon discover that her mother smoked marijuana as well. She showed me the bowls her mother smoked.

"I'm going to get your mom high... forreal," I said one day as I finished rewrapping a Dutch Master cigar after filling it with Hydro.

"No," she said, but she too was smiling.

"Mrs. Suzy, You want to smoke with us?" I asked as Jane led me to her room. At first, she looked nervous, as if she had wanted to keep her marijuana use a secret. However, as I lit the tip of the Dutch Master, her curiosity got the best of her.

"What's that?" she asked.

"It's called a blunt. Here, take a pull..." I said, extending the cigar to her. She took a pull and before I could say "not too hard", she was coughing and choking. I was laughing, but Jane looked a little concerned.

"Take it easy, Mrs. Suzy, this ain't your bowl," I said smiling. After she recovered, she took a nice steady pull, and this time, her exhale was smooth.

"I like it," she said before passing it to Jane. We finished the stick and at first, I couldn't tell how she felt. She hopped up and began cleaning in a fast pace - a little too fast. Five minutes later, we looked into her room and she was out cold. Her head was hanging slightly off the bed and her feet dangled from the other end. Her glasses were crooked, and she was snoring. It was hilarious.

The next morning, we went outside to Jane's car. We were going to a tattoo shop in center-city; Jane planned to tattoo my initials on the arch of her foot. First, she stopped to check the mail. My face grew stern as I read the words "Nigger Lover" on her mailbox. Someone had vandalized her mailbox overnight. She was obviously upset, but more so concerned with how I was taking it. I had learned stoicism at a young age so, besides a look of anger, just how agitated I was would remain a mystery to her.

"Are you ok?" she asked.

"Absolutely." I responded. And we pulled off.

The ride was spent in silence. We shared a marijuana stick and al-lowed the music to dictate the tone. I was quiet because of anger mixed with a slight amount of confusion. Jane's silence was predicated on feelings of guilt, empathy, and fear. Guilt: unfortunately, some people of European descent are forced to feel remorse for the near-sighted prejudices and racism of their people. Empathy: she could see that I was more hurt than anything. You don't know me personally, but you've lumped me into the "Nigger" box I had felt. And fear: she was fearful racism was going to jeopardize our relationship.

"You know you my baby..." I said, reassuring her after feeling the energy of her thoughts. She looked so relieved and gave me a huge hug.

Once downtown, Jane headed to the tattoo shop and I headed to a corner store for a box of cigars. The sun was at its zenith at this time; however, the heat was moderate. It was fall, so we weren't close enough to feel the intense heat. I glanced around at what was "Downtown Duncan-non". It was more a retail corridor than a corporate district. There weren't many tall buildings, but the arrangement was nice and quaint.

After surveying the area, I reached down to tie my sneaker. Once I lifted my head and prepared to take a step, a muddy blue pickup truck roared past me.

"Haaaaaa! Get the fuck out of here!" the two men in the back shout-ed along with other profanities I couldn't make out. They flew past so quickly I had no time to react or respond. I just sat there looking dumb-founded. The only coherent thought was:

Those must be the guys who spray painted the derogatory epithet on Jane's mailbox.

Shaking off the shock, I continued on my mission, even quicker now, as the episode amplified my urge to smoke. I really needed to calm my nerves at this point.

As soon as I entered the store, I knew I shouldn't have. There were no signs saying, "Whites Only" or "No Coloreds Allowed", but there was definitely a pair of eyes saying it. The small mom and pop shop was rather bare so I had no intentions of venturing too far into the store. I did no-tice a cooler full of sodas, Gatorade, water and other liquid refreshments, which brought my forgotten thirst back to the forefront of my mind.

Through the reflection in the glass I could see the clerks and their eyes were burning holes in my back. The husband sat tensely in a chair beside the counter and his wife waited impatiently for me to make a selection and quickly exit. Finally, I settled on a bottled water and brought it to the counter.

"Can I have a pack of Dutch Masters please?" I asked. I hadn't looked at the scarce tobacco shelf behind the woman – I had barely even looked at her. As I counted what I figured would be enough to cover the purchase, the round, brunette-haired woman said,

"We don't have none." At that point I looked up and realized they had nothing but one pack of White Owls and two packs of Phillies.

"Ok, I'll take the Phillies." I said. I was slightly disappointed. Phillies had no natural leaf, just a paper wrapping that led to a harsh and distasteful smoking experience that would more than likely lead to lung problems in the future.

"We don't have none." She repeated, as if these were the only four words in her vocabulary. I looked at the woman questioningly and then at her husband who had inched up to the edge of his seat. I then looked at the packs of Phillies to ensure I was seeing correctly.

"The ones right behind you." I said looking puzzled. Maybe she wasn't sure exactly what I said.

"The Phillies..."

"I said we don't have none!" she reiterated. By this time, she had fold-ed her arms against her breast and her husband was now so close to the edge of his seat that one move would have landed him on the floor. I was sure he had a pistol on him. Mine was in the car which did me no good. Not only was its location a problem, the fact that it wasn't registered was equally problematic

I nodded my head and gave them both a side-eye before returning my water. There was no way I was going to buy anything from this store. Outside, I grabbed a bottle from the vending machine and before I could take a sip the blue pick-up returned. This time my anger was at its boiling point. I ran to the car as they laughed and screamed. As trash was thrown at me, I reached beneath the passenger seat. The truck was a little past me by this point, but I still aimed. I wanted so badly to fire but the realization of where I was kicked in immediately. The guys saw the gun and ducked. They sped off quickly and I ran into the tattoo shop.

"We gotta go!" I said anxiously.

"What's wrong? I'm not done yet," Jane responded. However, she could see the gumbo of emotions in my eyes. Luckily the tattoo shop owner did as well.

"This truck keeps riding by, I think it's the people that spray painted your mailbox. They're screaming 'Nigger' and tried to run me over. I just pulled out on 'em but I don't know who all saw."

Jane's eyes widened in fear. The tattoo artist's eyes reddened from anger.

"Fucking assholes! Here give me the gun!"

I was skeptical and reluctant to give him my weapon. What if he wanted to kill me, too? He sensed my apprehension and said,

"Listen, bro, not everybody thinks like those assholes. If someone did see, I don't want them to find your piece on you. I'm licensed and if anybody comes in here, I got the right to shoot 'em dead!" He was sin-cere - genuine - I could feel it. And I liked him. I also learned a valuable lesson. You can't judge an entire race for the ignorance of a few. This guy was willing to hide me, cover for me, and kill for me if need be. I liked him.

"I'm just about done but that gives you guys enough time to let things cool down in case someone did see you... You won't look like you're running from the scene of a crime."

He was right. I gave him my firearm and took a seat - flipping through a tattoo magazine as he finished Jane's tattoo. Fifteen to twenty minutes later, she came back into the waiting area.

"You like?" she asked with a bright

smile. It read "Baby SL." and had a detailed heart encompassing it. "I love it," I said, sure that my ego had added to my approval. She had just tattooed my name on herself to prove her love to me.

Made in the USA
Middletown, DE
22 October 2021